CW00420164

ANSON

J. B. DEREK

Copyright © 2020
All rights reserved

'Please understand, Miss Anson. I am not trying to humiliate you. All I want to do is show you the truth.'

Tempany Bellman – 'Anson' – is an operative of Venezuela's counterintelligence service, OCC. She has been dispatched to Texas to deal with one of the financiers of the insurgency wrecking the country. If she succeeds, she has been told, she could help save the socialist revolution.

But before she can reach her target she is abducted by the CIA and forced to confront the possibility that everything she has ever believed is a lie. How she faces this version of reality will determine the fate of the revolution.

The main characters and events portrayed in this book are fictitious. Any similarities between the protagonists and any real persons are entirely coincidental.

No part of this book may be reproduced, or stored in a retrieval system, or transmitted in any form or by any means, electronic, mechanical, photocopying, recording, or otherwise, without express written permission of the publisher.

Contents

PART I

1. The Heist 1
2. Artemis 14
3. The Assassin 19
4. River City 36
5. The Bagman..44
6. The Red Pill..58
7. The Black Pill..70

PART II

8. High Stakes...78
9. The Raid 91
10. Absolution 103
11. Guilt..123
12. Breakfast For Two 127
13. The Knot..140
14. Playing The Field 151
15. Spinning The Web..164
16. The Ringer 172

PART III

17. Rio Grande / Rio Bravo 200
18. Raphael..206
19. The Raid II..228
20. Treason / Patriotism...238
21. Who Am I? 256

PART I

1. The Heist

The setting sun hung like a blister in the blood red horizon. It looked set to burst. To explode. To destroy.

Despite the heat, Larry shivered. *A portent?* he pondered. He didn't usually believe in fate or any of that crap. His end would come when he alone chose. But tonight he was spooked: surely no job which promised to be so easy could pass off without a hitch?

The apparent ease of the job was, indeed, the superficial reason for his nervousness. But as he delved beneath the surface he realised that, just as before each of the previous nine jobs, he was merely fishing for an excuse, *any* excuse, not to do it. Whatever it was that stirred inside him at such moments – fear? conscience? – it had never won out. But would it tonight? He felt queasy with indecision. He mopped his face and palms with his handkerchief, wrung the steering wheel, and bent his eyes back down to the cluster of buildings a quarter of a mile away, the lights of which were blazing in the gathering darkness. There was a motel, its sign luring motorists off the road with a garish red and yellow flashing neon arrow. Anyone so coaxed would have been sorely disappointed: the accommodation was a rickety, bug-ridden single-storey shack with a tin roof. Next to it was a small Chevron gas station; to the right a 24-hour diner; next to the diner a store. Only three cars and a pickup were in the courtyard, making it the quietest it had been all week. The sight galvanised him. 'Come on!' he shouted to Frank, who was relieving himself beside a bush in the dirt verge. Larry started up the engine and revved it hard.

'Cool, man,' drawled Frank over his shoulder, his voice barely audible above the roar from the old Mustang's exhausts. He took one last lungful of his blunt, pinged it into the scrub, then shambled back to the car while attending to his zipper.

'For God's sake!' seethed Larry as Frank flopped down beside him. 'I told you not to smoke that shit!' He hit the throttle, screeching the rear tyres and throwing up a cloud of dust into the gloom. It took all his willpower to check his agitation, wrench his foot off the gas, and set the car into a gentle trundle down towards the buildings.

'Have I ever let you down, bro?' grinned Frank dopily.

'Frequently.' He glanced at his brother's silhouette from the corner of his eye. He had to admit that if it wasn't for Frank's coolness there would be no way that he could possibly be involved in this line of work. He would probably be a rancher, or work in an office, or something equally as soul-destroying. He had Frank to thank for that.

As they passed the motel he swung left and rumbled into the concrete courtyard. There were a few customers in the diner, including a fat white guy in dungarees and a red peaked cap, who was sitting by the window reading a newspaper. Probably the driver of the bright red pickup, Larry guessed. 'Bill's Mart', meanwhile, with its big glazed frontage, appeared empty, save for the teenage girl behind the counter. Larry performed a lazy U, bringing the car to rest facing the road. 'Door and crowd control only. Any trouble, give the whistle. Five minutes max. Gorrit?'

'Yeah, bro,' nodded Frank, blinking hard.

Larry took his Glock from the side compartment, pulled the slide back to chamber a round, and slid the gun into the holster beneath his left armpit. 'Ready?'

Frank peeled open the left breast of his black Armani jacket, took out the stubby Colt revolver from his shoulder holster, pulled back the catch, flicked out the cylinder, and checked each chamber methodically. 'Ready,' he nodded decisively as he snapped it shut.

'Let's go.' They climbed out and walked smartly up to the store's tinted glass door. Larry pushed in first...and froze: partially hidden by a stack of shelves on the far side was a young blonde woman flicking through a copy of *Cosmopolitan*. The cowardly part of him, the part he had just managed to stamp down, told him to do a volte-face and flee. But before he could obey, Frank placed a comforting hand on his shoulder, whispered in his ear, 'Leave it to me,' and drifted off to the right. Larry swallowed hard. He felt like screaming. But then, almost as if he was sleepwalking, he found his legs moving him towards the counter, his destination the grey door behind the girl. She was perched on a high stool and reading *Twilight*, Taylor Swift playing from somewhere beneath the counter. She glanced up with a perfunctory smile. Larry ground to a halt and pretended to inspect packets of candy on the shelves backing the store-high window. In its reflection he could see Frank sneaking up on the woman. She didn't seem to notice him. Larry took a deep breath, grabbed a handful of Twinkies in his shaking hand, and slammed them on the counter.

'Okay, Miss...'

A clear, authoritative voice rang through the store. 'Hold on, sir. Don't do it.' *Shit! The cops!* Larry whipped the Glock from under his jacket and spun. The girl jumped off the stool, sending it to the ground with a crash, making his hand twitch so violently that he almost shot. He gasped. It wasn't the cops at all. It had been the customer. She was facing Frank with her hands in the air. She had taken some steps away from him, and was now in full view of Larry, as well as anyone who might be passing through the car park. Frank was pointing the revolver at her stomach. He looked amused. 'On the floor please, ma'am,' he said politely.

The woman did not look in the least bit frightened. She said coolly, 'Whatever you say, sir,' and began to lower herself. But then Frank leapt forward and smashed the gun into her face. The woman yelped, her legs buckled, and she fell onto her side, her head smacking off the white tiled floor. Her unseeing eyes were pointing straight at Larry. There was no expression in them, or on her pale face. She looked dead. But no: as blood began to spurt from her nose, she raised her hands to her face and cupped them over it to staunch the flow. Almost immediately blood seeped between the cracks in her fingers and spilled onto the floor. She made no sound, but her eyes scrunched in pain.

'*Jesus Christ!*' shrieked Larry.

'She's a Fed, bro,' Frank shrugged languidly. 'She was scoping me out.'

'Watch her!'

He turned back to the girl, who was pressed hard against the door. She was snarling at him. Remembering himself, he lowered his gun and quickly checked outside. It was still clear. 'Right sweetheart,' he said shakily, 'the combination.'

'*No fuckin' way!*' she screamed. 'My pa's gonna be here in ten minutes, an' he's gonna blow your fuckin' heads off!'

Larry stumbled back as if he'd been hit.

'Come on, honey,' said Frank softly. He stepped over the woman and, from his hip, pointed the Colt at the girl. 'Let's have it. Your pa'll pick up the insurance and we'll all be happy. No one'll get hurt.'

She pointed a quivering finger at the prostrate woman. 'Tell that to *her!*'

Larry knew her father *would* be coming in soon to close up. If they were still there when he appeared, there would be a shoot-out, and, assuming that the folks in the diner joined in, he and Frank would be killed. He glanced out again – still clear – then stared into the girl's brown eyes. They were glowing hot with rage, her teeth bared like a wildcat ready to pounce. 'Shit,' he hissed resignedly. He trudged round the counter, grabbed her by the throat, and rammed the Glock into her mouth, breaking one of her front teeth with a sickening crunch. His finger tensed on the trigger. 'Give me the combination,' he said deliberately, 'or I shall blow a hole in this ugly face of yours.' He despised himself for saying it. But he had no choice. He pulled out the gun, and she spat the tooth onto the floor. Then she spat in his face. '*Fuck you, asshole!*' He wiped off the bloody spittle with his sleeve, then, almost of its own volition, his left arm cranked back and unleashed a vicious punch to her stomach. The air in her lungs rushed out in a loud wheeze and she dropped to the floor, cracking her head off of one of the legs of the upended stool. He kicked her writhing body out of the way and pulled open the door. Just ahead, bolted to the floor, was an old-fashioned combination safe, black with gold trim, the etched numbers on its dial worn from decades of use. On top sat an ancient Dell system unit and monitor controlling the three CCTV cameras around the store. The safe contained five days' takings, which were due to be taken by the security truck to the bank first thing in the morning. If it had been a good week – which he knew it had – there would be as much as 50 grand in it. Perhaps more. He rubbed his chin. It would be impossible to lift, even if they had had the tools to unbolt it. He considered shooting the dial off. But that wouldn't work either, he immediately concluded, because it would have absolutely no effect on the lock. Besides, there would be a high possibility of being injured by the ricochet, and of the noise alerting the diners. If he had had a couple of grenades he might, he speculated, have been able to blow the door off; but then the cash inside would probably be incinerated. Maybe if he had an hour with a blowtorch? He gave a groan of defeat and kicked the safe, almost breaking his foot. He howled in agony and hopped around, clutching at his crumpled shoe. But he had no time to deal with the pain. Gritting his teeth so hard that he thought they would snap, he thrust his gun back into its holster, ripped out the system unit, tucked it under his arm, then hit the buttons on the cash register until it pinged open. There were thick wads of bills from the day's take. 'The safe's a bust, bro,' he grimaced as he stuffed the notes into his pockets. 'Let's go.'

Frank's stubbly, tanned face seemed to turn white. 'How…much in the register?'

'Five…six grand. Maybe.'

Frank shook his head in dismay, then banged the Colt against the side of his head. '*Argh!*' he wailed. '*Goddammit!*'

'No use complaining,' said Larry, surprising himself by the calmness of his voice. 'It's bomb proof. Let's go before this lil' ol' lady's pop shows up. He's gonna be mighty pissed.'

'*Bitch!*' cried Frank, his face flushing a deep crimson. He kicked a rack of potato chips, sending it flying.

'Move!' barked Larry.

Frank looked back to the woman on the floor. Other than the blood pooling beneath her head, she had barely moved. He pointed his gun at her head as if to execute her.

'*No!*' Larry screamed.

'Shit,' Frank gasped. He turned and gawped at Larry in bewilderment. 'I…uh…' He didn't finish the sentence. He re-holstered the gun, buttoned up his jacket, and shuffled out under his brother's glare.

Larry looked down at the sobbing girl. 'I'm sorry, sweetheart. You were very brave. Your pa will be proud of you.' He limped out after Frank. No one in the diner gave them a second glance. He relaxed slightly, and hurried on towards the car.

But before he could get very far, there came a terrific explosion from the store and glass showered them. Frank fell to his knees. Larry stumbled and dropped the computer, but managed to remain upright. He reached for the Glock and spun on his heal, shooting wildly. The entire window nearest the cash desk had disintegrated. Standing just behind the empty steel frame was the girl, holding a pump-action shotgun. But her face was contorting. Blood was oozing out of two bullet holes in her chest that he had somehow, miraculously, managed to skewer her with. He threw himself to the ground just as she let loose her second shot. The cloud of pellets fizzed harmlessly into the still Texas night, and she fell backwards like a chopped tree, the life fleeing from her defiant eyes.

As he struggled to his feet he was aware that some of the diners had spilled out onto the car park. He did an aimless sweep with the Glock, causing them to shrink back to the doorway. He picked up the box, grabbed Frank, who had got to his feet and was staring open-mouthed at the store, and scrambled back to the car. He threw the box into the back then scrabbled with the key in the ignition. Just as the engine fired, the big man in the dungarees and hat appeared at the window. Bellowing that the cops had been called, he bashed the window with a pistol and made a grab for the handle. Before he could pull it open, Larry slammed off the handbrake, screeched the wheels, and flew off like a bat out of hell. The man got off two shots, one of which pinged off the rear window, but didn't penetrate, and within seconds he and the rest of the would-be vigilantes, now numbering half a dozen, were reduced to fist-shaking dark specks on the road.

'Holy shit!' panted Frank, twisting round to check for pursuers. Sweat was pouring off his face. When the cluster of lights was out of sight, he struggled out of his jacket, threw it in the back, and put his head between his knees. He had barely controlled his breathing when he straightened himself up, wiped his face with his shirt, and, started rummaging around the glove box for his pipe. 'Holy shit!' he repeated, more excited now than scared. 'Did you see that crazy bitch?!'

'Yeah, I saw her,' said Larry morosely.

'Ha, ha!'

'This ain't funny. That should never have happened.'

'Whoa! Don't blame me. All I did was hit the broad. It wasn't my fault the kid was loaded.'

'*Oh, God,*' he groaned, shaking his head. 'I know. It's…it's just that she didn't deserve it. She was just protecting her daddy's place. You or me would have done the same for pa. I feel fucking terrible. And all for a lousy few Gs. *Fuck!*' he bleated, and punched the steering wheel.

Frank said nothing. He stuffed the pipe's ceramic bowl with grass and lit it with a cheap plastic lighter. He inhaled deeply and passed it to Larry.

'No,' he said. 'Maybe later. Gimme the Scotch.'

Frank produced a half bottle of Jonnie Walker Black Label. Larry twisted the cap off with his teeth, spat it onto his lap, then took three large gulps, almost finishing it. He gave a moan of relief, and Frank patted him tenderly on the shoulder.

They drove for two hours, heading southwest towards the border on increasingly quiet and narrow roads, the only traffic to speak of being the odd set of headlights far off behind them. The slightly drunk Larry nursed them along at 50, until, at last, in the scrublands northeast of Del Rio, he cut the speed and swung right at the dilapidated wooden mailbox with 'Rancho La Habana' daubed on it in flaking red paint. He followed the track up the hillock and down the other side to the small wooden house which had been their bolthole for the last six months. It had been ideal: it was invisible from the road, day or night, and their nearest neighbour, a lonely old widow called Marjory, was more than a mile away on the other side of the road.

Larry drove into the lean-to barn on the right, shook Frank awake, and killed the engine. The interior light from the Mustang guided him to the switch on the wall, which turned on a bulb in the barn and a light above the front door. He trudged along the cinder path around the house, leaving his

8

brother to gather his drugs. Larry pushed his way wearily in and turned on the lights of the living room-cum-kitchen that occupied most of the ground floor. He laid his Glock and the wads of stolen banknotes on the kitchen's wooden worktop, pulled two bottles of Coors from the fridge, and flunked himself down on the leather chair in front of the small television in the living area. He flicked through the channels until he came to a re-run of the Royals-Red Sox game from earlier. He dropped the remote, promptly downed the first bottle of beer in one, then settled back with his feet up on the wooden coffee table. Presently Frank came in, banged around in the kitchen, then emerged with a fresh bottle of J&B and two tumblers full of ice. He filled both to the brim, nudged one towards Larry's feet, and sat down on the brown fabric sofa next to Larry's chair. He drained his own glass at once, pulled a credit card from his back pocket, and laid out two thick lines of cocaine. Larry downed half his whiskey, rolled a hundred dollar bill, and vacuumed his line up his nose. He handed the note to Frank, who greedily snorted his, and fell back onto the sofa with a sigh.

'Wanna count it?' said Larry over the din of the ball game.

'Doesn't seem much point,' said Frank glumly.

'Come on, bro,' he said brightly. 'It's better than nothing.' But he didn't sound very convincing, and he knew it. Perhaps it was because he was every bit as demoralized as his brother. Their week-and-a-half long stakeout had promised to yield perhaps their biggest ever haul. But neither of them had spotted the fatal flaw in their plan – which was, if the girl didn't talk, there *was* no plan. Perhaps if the shop had been more isolated they could have taken their time and tortured her, or broken in later on in the night. But it wasn't. So there was no point in dwelling on it, Larry thought resolutely.

'I really needed the money,' moped Frank.

'But you *always* need the money.'

'But I *really* needed it this time. I'm broke.' He took a deep breath. 'And I want out.'

9

Larry nearly dropped his glass. He took his feet off the table and shifted round to face him. 'What do you mean?' He was trying to be stern, but couldn't disguise the hurt in his voice.

Frank refilled his glass and took another long pull. 'I...' He lit a cigarette, his hands trembling. He took his brother in his watery brown eyes. 'This life. Always on the run. Always in danger. Having to hurt people. I can't do it no more.' He shook his head, frowning, then turned back to his drink.

'But...*I* only carried on because I thought *you* wanted to,' protested Larry.

'Just listen to yourself! When was the last time *I* proposed robbing anyone? In fact, when was it *ever* me?' Larry wracked his brain. 'Never!' shouted Frank. 'It was never me. Not once. And we've done ten. And how many people have *I* killed?'

'Um...six?'

'*Fuck you!*' he snarled, his eyes flashing. 'I've killed none of them. None! It's been you. Every single time.'

'But...you've *wounded* just as many people as me,' he retorted feebly. 'Like the girl tonight.'

'Yeah, I've hurt people. But only if they looked like they would hurt *us* first. I hate it. Why do you think I've got to get juiced before we do them? I can't live with it any longer. I'd rather die than do it again.' He took his gun and slammed it on the table as if tendering his resignation. Then he sunk his head into his hands and began to cry.

Larry sidled up to him and patted him on the back. 'Shhh. Let's get a few more drinks down us. You'll feel better soon.'

Frank stopped his snivelling and nodded uncertainly. 'Okay, Lar. But I want out. Honestly I do. I'm not going to do it again.'

'Of course.' His tone was comforting. But his gaze was steely. And Frank's resolve began to wilt. Larry had held Frank a virtual hostage since their parents had died in a car smash when Frank was 14. And Larry wasn't quite ready to release him. Not yet. Not until they'd taken down three or four more scores. And big ones. And only then if they could stop pissing their takings against the wall in Vegas, which is what they had done with almost every last stolen cent so far. Frank would remain his prisoner. He slapped him hard on the back to give him a little reminder of who was boss. A tear rolled down Frank's cheek. He gritted his teeth and poured some more cocaine on the table.

'HEY THERE!'

'Fucking hell!' they gasped in unison, Frank clapping his hand to his heart.

'HELLO! IS ANYONE HOME?' It was a woman's voice, but not Marjory's.

'It's the Feds!' rasped Frank.

Larry shovelled the coke back into the bag and stuffed it and Frank's Colt under the couch. 'Who is it?' he cried.

'Sorry to bother you, sir.' The accent had the trademark nasally drawl of the South. 'I've run out of gas just over the hill. I saw the sign to your house and hoped you might be able to help, sir. I can't get a reception on my cell. I was wonderin' if I could borrow your phone. Or maybe some gas, if you can spare?'

They looked at each other. 'Doesn't sound like the Feds?' Frank whispered uncertainly. 'If it was, they'd be in here by now, and we'd be dead.'

Larry nodded. 'Get it, bro. I'll cover.' He tiptoed through to the kitchen to get the Glock, shoved the wads of bills into the cutlery drawer, then took up position at the bottom of the stairs, directly across from the door. He held the gun under the left flap of his jacket and nodded. Frank unbolted the door and edged it open. The woman was standing right behind it. 'Evenin', ma'am,' he said. His eyes started at her feet. Grubby tan boots. Dusty faded jeans. Red jacket. Pressed lips. Dried blood on her top lip. A big cut on her broken nose.

'Evening, asshole.' Before his brain could process that the voice that spoke was not the same as the one that had just called out, nor the one that had remonstrated with him in the store, a hand flashed and a pistol slammed into his face. He fell back, poleaxed, his head whacking off the carpet with a thud.

'Frank!' cried Larry as he whipped out the Glock. But before he could do anything with it, the woman fired. The bullet hit him in the sternum, ripping through him and throwing him back onto the stairs. She was on him in a flash. She kicked his gun away, put the hot barrel of hers to his temple, and said, 'You shouldn't have killed the girl.'

Then he had something akin to an out-of-body experience. He heard a bang, but it seemed distant. Then it felt as if a red-hot poker had been thrust into his skull. He imagined his brains being splattered over the stairs. His thoughts suddenly became muddled, as the neurons left in his head reached out, and failed, to grasp the parts that had just been blown out. He was aware, just, that he was wheezing loudly. Then an image seared itself into his retinas. It was the safe. The old, black, elusive safe.

And he was dead.

The woman spun and skipped back to Frank, training her gun on him. He had rolled onto his side, his hands up to his face to try to stem the gush of blood. '*No!*' he groaned. He raised his right hand in surrender. 'Don't shoot!'

She put the sole of her boot onto his chest and pushed him onto his back. 'Can you hear me?' she said in a cut-glass English accent.

'*Larry!* Wharrave you done?'

'Larry is dead,' she said coldly. She stepped back and lowered her pistol.

Frank pushed himself up onto his elbows, then slowly turned, his face contorting as he took in the bloody scene. 'Oh, God, no!' he bawled. '*Bro!*'

The woman smirked. 'Don't sound so shocked. You know as well as I do, *Frank*,' she sneered, 'that the chances of the police catching you are nil. So, as I was already rather upset about you breaking my nose, I decided that the girl would not go unavenged. So here I am.'

His head snapped back to her. 'Oh, shit!' he sobbed. 'I...I thought you were a Fed. That's why I hit you. I'm sorry. Please don't kill me.' He rolled onto his side again and clawed at her boot. 'I don't want to die. Please! I'll give you anything you want!'

She kicked his hand away with disdain. 'I don't want anything from you, you piece of shit. But your apology is accepted.' She made to leave.

'You...' he spluttered, 'you ain't gonna kill me?'

She screwed her eyes up and shook her head as if the question was illogical. 'Of course not. You smashed my nose and I smashed yours. You and I are even. Just as your *bro* and the girl are.' She made to go once more; but hesitated, then, as if as an afterthought, bent down, grabbed his hair with an iron grip, and held his face up to hers. The blood trundled down his cheeks like tears. 'But let me make one thing very clear to you, just so that you and I are absolutely straight with one another: should you choose to come after me, I will shoot you down like the dog you are. And in the highly – and I mean *highly* – unlikely event that you somehow kill me first, my employers will cut your limbs off with a chainsaw and throw what's left of you into a bath of acid. Do I make myself clear?'

'Yes, ma'am,' he snivelled.

'Good.' She let go, her pale face suddenly soft and smiling pityingly on him. She stood up and her graceful frame slid noiselessly out the door.

'Who...who the hell are you?' he whimpered, his curiosity overcoming his terror.

'My name is Hanna Rosen,' she said as she shut the door on him. 'And I kill people for Israel.'

2. Artemis

'Artemis', the head of Venezuela's counterrevolutionary office, OCC, swallowed the last of her 18-year-old Laphroaig and cleared her throat. Despite it being only ten in the morning, Tempany Bellman, sitting on the opposite side of her boss's paper-strewn desk, was rather irked that she hadn't been offered a glass. Still, she sat forward and tried to look attentive. As usual, Artemis – unlike most everybody else in the building, who was looking frazzled, and had done so for months – was striking: dressed in an expensive-looking green silk blouse, her glowing olive face, sharp brown eyes and glossy black hair – pinned up, business-like, with a black hair clip – gave her a youthful, exotic beauty which belied her 50-odd years. It was an ensemble that exuded authority, and made Tempany, dressed relatively shabbily in a cheap floral blouse and blue leggings, feel intimidated.

Artemis scanned her face. 'Tell me, Edith – and please, be candid – what is your view of our current situation?'

By 'current situation' she could mean only one thing: the apparent impending doom of the Chavez/Maduro revolution. Tempany had to assume that, given the recent disasters that had befallen OCC, this question was a test of loyalty, and that her answer would be recorded and pored over by Artemis and any number of interrogators itching to give her a working over for the crime of being a white, middle-class English woman.

Picking her words carefully, she said, 'Ma'am, while I don't think the situation is unsalvageable – I mean, Caracas, at least, is still functioning reasonably well – I think we must acknowledge that we are in trouble, and if we don't deliver something for the people, and soon, we are going to find ourselves in…a…a rather delicate position.'

'I see the English capacity for understatement is alive and well,' she chuckled. 'But you're close to the truth. We are in a most serious situation, a situation which, as you well know, has been engineered by America and Saudi Arabia with the sole purpose of crushing the revolution. And if they succccd, everything we have worked for, everything we have sacrificed so much for, goes up in smoke.' She poured another finger of whisky, drank it, and reclined back in her high-backed leather chair, resting her clasped hands on her stomach. 'Of course we – and you in particular –' she flattered, 'have been reasonably successful in rooting out the fascist counterrevolutionaries. But, alas, it has been like cutting the head off the Hydra: take out one, and two more spring up in its place. It has been a losing battle.' She gave her a sly smile. 'But now we're onto something that might level the playing field. Last week we detected three men setting fire to a factory in Maturin. I had them put under surveillance and their hideout searched. Luckily for us, these men are idiots, and had left details of all their activities, which has led us to a further twelve cells operating around the country, as well as a man in Bogota who is handling them all. This man is known to us,' she said cagily. 'The bank account which he is using to pay the terrorists is being replenished by one in Grand Cayman, which is registered to an accountancy firm in San Antonio – a firm which, as far as we can gather, has no clients and makes no money.' She opened a manila folder stamped 'SECRETO' in red ink, and tossed over an A4 photograph. 'Have you seen this man before?'

Tempany was looking down at a dark-skinned man in his fifties or sixties, dressed in a brown leather jacket, red shirt, faded jeans, and aviator sunglasses. He had thinning black hair swept back over the crown of his head, a deeply lined face, and a drooping black moustache over an expressionless mouth. He was standing on a street corner, his finger on a yellow pedestrian crossing button. Two tanned men in short-sleeved shirts lurked a short distance behind. Slightly out of focus at their backs was a café. The photo was taken from height – probably the second storey of the building opposite. The setting looked to be the USA, judging by the pattern of the crossing and the electronic sign just above the man's head, which was currently lit with a red hand. She examined his face up close, but drew a blank. 'No,' she replied, shaking her head.

'This is the fake accountant in San Antonio. His name is Francisco Orto. Except, it isn't. The man's real name is Juan Carranza. He was a captain in the Salvadoran military during the civil war. He was responsible for the massacre in La Vilas in 1985. He vanished when the treaty was signed in '88. And here he is.'

Tempany gave a low whistle. When she had been inducted into OCC, she had been taught all about the atrocities committed by the American-backed fascists in South and Central America during the 70s and 80s. Of all the murderous gangs operating then, the Salvadoran military death squads were the cruellest of the lot.

'I cannot emphasise to you enough the importance of this lead, Edith. We have a very big opportunity to uncover the extent of the counterrevolution, and to take out a large number of fascist insurgents. But most importantly, we have an opportunity to prove foreign involvement in our current difficulties, and to agitate world opinion against our enemies.' She leaned forward, putting her folded arms on the desk, and said, 'Your instructions are these: I want you to pay this man a visit. I want you to find out who, exactly, is on his payroll. I want you to relieve him of any funds he has. Most importantly of all, I want you to establish who he is working for, and to obtain written evidence of this, if any such thing exists. If there is nothing in writing, both a signed and recorded confession from Señor Carranza will do, for now.'

'He's surely Agency,' she shrugged.

'He's not,' said Artemis.

As with the man in Bogota, Tempany knew better than to ask exactly how she knew this. She suspected that Artemis had CIA HQ in Virginia penetrated, but it wouldn't do for her to have her suspicions confirmed, lest she be caught and made to talk – the less she knew about things outwith her remit, the better. One thing was for sure, though: if the man was not on the CIA's payroll, it made him a more viable target – namely, a target whom the CIA, OCC's principal and most dangerous adversary, would not particularly seek to avenge if harmed.

'Is he to be eliminated, ma'am?' asked Tempany matter-of-factly.

Artemis stared her in the eye. 'That, Edith, will be left to your discretion. I would suggest first using his life, and then the lives of his family, as leverage to get the information we require. If he gives you what we need, I would suggest leaving him alive. We are, after all, people of our word. However, if he doesn't talk, it would perhaps be best to liquidate him, both to avenge the civilians he murdered in El Salvador, and to remove at least one of the counterrevolutionaries.'

Tempany was not happy with this fudging. Even though Artemis had used such evasiveness on non-assassination jobs before, it seemed like an abrogation of responsibility: either she wanted the man dead or she didn't.

But Tempany quickly checked her agitation, because, as much as she didn't like it, this vagueness was simply Artemis's management style – which was her way of either trusting her staff to get on with it; or giving herself just enough wiggle room to evade blame in the event of her operations being botched. Whatever the case, and despite Tempany's hatred of the South American fascists, she immediately resolved to show the man mercy if he talked; and kill the son of a bitch if he didn't. She nodded. 'Opposition?'

'His security detail: one Battalion 316; two Colombian NCOs.'

'Sounds tricky,' said Tempany. 'They might not get out unscathed.'

'You must consider each of them to be enemies of the revolution. You are authorised to use any force you deem necessary.'

'Yes, ma'am.'

'Anson,' she said sternly, 'Señor Carranza went to The School. So whatever happens, don't get cornered.'

This was not-so-subtle advice that she should kill herself if captured. It was probably good advice. 'The School' was the School of the Americas in Georgia, which, Tempany had been told, was a CIA training ground for fascists from the South. Students were taught the arts of terrorism, assassination, and torture, and had been responsible for the slaughter of tens of thousands of civilians over the years. Indeed, it had been from The School that the Salvadoran death squads had learned their craft. It therefore had to be assumed that Carranza would murder her, gruesomely, if given half a chance. She stared down him. He wouldn't even lay a finger on her, she thought. Amongst her kills to date had been three confirmed alumni of The School, each of whom she had sent to their graves without picking up so much as a scratch in return. They were maybe good, and maybe the best the fascists had to throw at her.

But she was better.

3. The Assassin

Or so she had arrogantly thought. Because here she was, two and a half days later, standing outside a shack in the middle of nowhere, more blood on her hands, her nose mangled, and the rendezvous having been missed. And all because of a run-in with a couple of bungling idiots whom she should have left to go on their merry way. Going after them had been insane. She could have quite easily been killed – indeed, had the older man been slightly quicker, he might well have shot her first. And for what? *Maybe I'm not the wunderkind I think I am*, she thought with a smirk.

She needed to get out of there, fast. But she was hesitating, as the cold, rational, professional part of her urged her to turn back and execute Frank also. After all, and despite what she had just told him, it was he whom she had wanted to kill in the first place, and from the very second he had pulled that scary-looking Colt on her. She had been planning his demise even as she lay on the floor nursing her snapped septum. As soon as she heard them leave she had leapt to her feet, intending to get her gun from the car and take them on. But before she could move, the shop assistant was on her feet – and packing a Heckler! Tempany screamed, 'NO!' But her voice was muffled by the blast of the gun. A second later, bullets from the older man zipped past her ears and shattered cans of spaghetti on the shelves behind her. She threw herself to the ground just as the girl jerked back as she was hit. There was another shot from her, and Tempany threw up a prayer that it would do her job for her. But then there came the screech of tyres. Tempany sprang to her feet again and rushed to the counter. The girl was gripping the shotgun across her bloodied chest, her knuckles white. She was quite dead, her big brown eyes staring sightlessly up at the ceiling. 'Jesus!' Tempany had wailed, before quickly pulling herself together and hurdling through the now glassless window frame. She ignored the stunned customers from the diner, jumped into her Dodge, and set off in pursuit, latching onto the bandits' taillights. Seething, she had reckoned, vaguely, that she would try to force them off the road. But it soon became clear that the driver, at least, was intoxicated, as he began veering onto the other side. So she calmed herself with a cigarette and elected to wait and see, keeping a good half-mile behind.

It had then been her intention to execute both of them, and had remained so even as she shot the man Larry. But as soon as she saw the fear in Frank's eyes, the arm raised pathetically in surrender, her resolve crumbled. Executing him would serve little purpose. Yes, she was aware that letting him live would leave another of those pesky loose ends. But she also knew he wouldn't come after her; and he certainly wouldn't go to the police, not least because they would pin the murder of the girl on him as a proxy for his dead brother.

However, she thought, throwing the killer in her a bone, if he *did* try to stop her, she would be ready: her index finger was stroking the trigger of her PX4 Storm, and she would gun him down with no mercy if he dared make a move. With that thought she went into the barn, took the shop's CCTV control unit from the back seat of the bandits' car, and threw it onto the concrete floor. It broke apart at the first try, and she ripped out the hard drive, put it into her jacket pocket, then set off back up the hill. When she reached its brow she glanced back to the house to find that nothing had changed: the lights still blazed, the front door was still closed, and there was no sign of the man coming to kill her. 'So long, Frank,' she said with a cruel grin. She opened her jacket, pushed the safety catch down, slid the warm Beretta back into the silky green holster under her left armpit, and quickly zipped up against the now cold night. (It was the first time she had used this model, she reflected. She liked it. It was light, easy to handle, and had precious little recoil. She made a note to get more practice with it when she got back to the range at Anare.) She trotted back down to the ghastly red Dodge parked 20 yards up from the road. There were no lights to be seen other than from the starry sky, and the only sign of life was the constant croak of unseen desert creatures. She took off her jacket and holster, putting the latter into her holdall in the boot, kicked off her boots, then stripped and changed into a fresh white t-shirt, black pullover, jeans, and pair of trainers. She inspected the jacket by the interior light. It was splattered with the man's blood. She cursed under her breath. She liked that jacket, but it would have to go. She stuffed it, along with the t-shirt and jeans she had just got out of – the t-shirt, which she had been wearing in the shop, covered with her own blood – into a carrier bag she had been using for empty bottles and sandwich boxes. She jumped behind the wheel, lit a Marlboro Gold, started the engine, and did a three-point turn back to the road. She gazed into the darkness to the right, yearning to go back to where she thought the Mexican border was. It would be so easy, she thought enticingly, to lob back over the fence, or even swim the Rio Grande if absolutely necessary, and report back to HQ that all bets were off. After all, she had been caught up in an armed robbery, been injured, and had killed one of the bandits. To make matters worse, the police would be hunting for her as a witness. She was thoroughly compromised. She therefore had no option but to abort! And if she did, she would probably be commended for exacting retribution upon the man who had murdered the girl; for striking a blow for the working man against thieving capitalist pigs. Besides, if she tried to go back the way she had just come, there was no guaranteeing she could even make it back to civilisation: the last ten miles of the pursuit had been a bamboozling series of twists and turns, and there had been no road signs or houses or lights on that final stretch. The chances of taking a wrong turn, or going round in circles and running out of petrol, seemed high – and the last thing she wanted was to end up near the scene of the crime when dawn broke. She sucked on her cigarette. Going back the way she had come seemed dicey, but at least it led somewhere. It was quite possible that the road to the right, given its narrowness and isolation, was a dead end. She checked her fuel. There was about a quarter of a tank left, which, she reckoned, would be enough for about fifty miles, given the gas-guzzler she'd been lumbered with.

She sighed. As much as she tried to kid herself, she knew that her sense of duty would never, ever, allow her to abandon a mission, no matter how screwed up things had become. Besides, she had a revolution to save. She put her foot on the accelerator and headed left.

Wherever she was, she thought as she settled into a careful pace to nurse her fuel, she knew she was at least 100 miles from San Antonio. Given all that she'd put herself through to get there, the thought angered her. She had started in darkness in Puerto Palomas at 6.00am, walked a couple of miles west, then skipped over the rickety corrugated iron border fence with a rope ladder with two hooks on the top and into New Mexico (all the while wondering how she would get into the US in future if and when Congress ever got round to funding Trump's wall; probably go in via Canada, which had literally thousands of miles of unprotected border with the US, she concluded, rather obviously). She had an ancient hunting rifle slung over her back as a prop, and in the unlikely event that she was stopped, either by the border police or the redneck vigilantes who patrolled the area, she intended to put on her phoney Texan accent and try to charm her way out of it, saying she was out getting some shooting practice. If that didn't work, she would shoot it out with them. And if *that* didn't work, she would slip back over and probe for another way across. As it happened, and as with her five previous incursions into the United States, she came across not another living soul. After a five-mile march into Columbus in the gathering heat, she picked up the ten-year-old Dodge that had been left in Lima Street, the key for which was perched on the right front tyre. It was about eight in the morning when she set off on the 500-mile trek to San Antonio. The drive had been hot and boring, but she had made decent progress and was going to make the rendezvous easily. 60 miles from town, she turned off to stock up on water, give her aching body a stretch, and powder her nose. It was then that the bandits struck.

She pinged the Marlboro out the window and lit another. What was done was done. Now she had to focus on the most serious problem: missing the rendezvous with the local bagman. He would certainly have reported her non-appearance to his handler, who would then have reported it to HQ. Even now, Artemis would be strumming her fingers on the desk of her palatial top floor office fretting over her prodigy.

Or not, thought Tempany with a smile. On virtually every one of her missions to date, she had missed rendezvous or pick-ups or drop-offs at least once. It would have been more unusual if she *had* turned up. No. Artemis would be tucked up in bed with her husband (who was, according to office gossip, a general in the army). Magellan, her recruiter and sometime handler, meanwhile, would be in a casino somewhere, or sitting in a smoky room with some other desperadoes plotting the next blow against fascism.

The fact that her no-show wouldn't be causing panic, however, was hardly comforting, because every minute wasted increased the chances of her failing: the police had undertaken to continue to watch the terrorist cells until Tempany had taken care of her end of business – but only on condition that they did not pose any threat to human life – in which case the men would be immediately run in, as would the middle man in Bogota. While this would assuage, temporarily, at least, some of the mayhem in Venezuela, it would result in Carranza either going to ground or being on his guard, meaning that the mission would probably fail and the mystery as to whom the ultimate puppet master was would remain unsolved. On the other hand, if the terrorists *didn't* threaten to kill anyone wasn't particularly reassuring either, because the longer she took, the longer they would be free to wreak havoc on her friends.

She did not like this level of responsibility; did not like being such a crucial link in this intricate chain. It made things muddier than usual, and she felt weighed down by it. *Damn you, boss,* she thought.

And damn Artemis for saddling her with a sidekick. She had ordered Tempany to work with the local bagman – the same man who had taken the photo of Carranza and had tracked him to his ranch. Artemis's reasoning was sound: given the importance of the assignment and the extent of the opposition, at least one assistant, if not more, was absolutely vital. But Tempany didn't want backup, and had proven time and again that she didn't need it, and certainly didn't now, she thought stubbornly: she had memorised the location of Carranza's ranch, the roads leading up to it, the images of it taken from the Brazilian satellite five days ago, and the file photographs and details of the target and his henchmen. To all intents and purposes the job was already done, and, aside from coming up with the equipment that she needed, there was nothing that the bagman could do to help.

'*Stop it!*' she scolded herself. She was being an idiot. It was not a one-man, or woman, job, and she knew it. In fact, as she thought about it in detail for the first time, she realised it was not even a two-man job. It was a two-*team* job, because, assuming that she would confront Carranza at his ranch at night, simultaneously a team would have to break into his office. That job alone would need two men, at least. And the raid on the ranch? Before even getting to grips with Carranza, she would have to neutralise not only his three babysitters, who lived on the site, but his wife and two 20-something sons, his three maids, housekeeper, and cook; and she would have to do all this without much fuss, so that Carranza would not be alerted and thus given time to raise the alarm, destroy any incriminating files, or even kill himself before she had a chance to interrogate him. This team alone would need five, maybe six men in addition to her. Her instincts had told her this during the interview with Artemis, but she had shut her mind off to it, moodily and foolishly crossing her arms tightly across her chest when Artemis had ordered her to take the man with her.

There was a reason why she had been so unprofessional; why she had acted like a spoiled brat. Perhaps not a good one, but a reason nonetheless. The last time she had been ordered to take someone with her had not ended well…

She gritted her teeth, trying desperately to stop the familiar, lucid thoughts that had been tormenting her for a year. But, like water breaching a damn, they came tumbling back into her head. The dreamy blue eyes. The high forehead and long, thin, bookish nose projecting her hard, practical intelligence. The side-parted auburn hair. The gentle, self-effacing laugh. The long, shapely legs. The slim, soft body. The ethereal, almost regal air.

And the smile. The shy, dimpled smile. No one had ever smiled at her like that before. Not Bex. Not Kyle, her hipster douchebag ex-boyfriend back in Oxford. Certainly not her parents. It had made her feel wanted. It had made her feel special. It had made her forget for a time the melancholia which had dogged her since childhood.

'Aargh!' she winced, hating herself all over again. She had these thoughts at least once a day; and had had them every day since she had left her lover, 'Stephanie Spendlove', bawling her eyes out on the beach in Zanzibar a year ago.

Until recently, every single time these thoughts came to her – overwhelmed her, sometimes – she had come to the same cold, logical conclusion she had reached the day she had abandoned her: it was better for both of them if they had nothing to do with each other. Spendlove, after all, was in the infinitely less dangerous intelligence gathering section, SdI, and had a chance of a life, a proper life, outside the constant danger Tempany was in. And Tempany could not lose her the same way she had lost Bex.

As good as this logic had seemed, over the past few weeks it had begun to exert less and less control over her. The absence of her friend was beginning to feel like a hole in her chest, a hole that could only be filled by hearing her voice or touching her hand. For she was now admitting to herself something she had not admitted since Rebecca died: she was lonely. She was as lonely as hell. And she was now convinced that what she had done was not honourable or anything like it. It was cowardly. And cruel, to both of them. So she had been thinking about trying to get Spendlove's email from one of the secretaries in HQ. To contact her. To say sorry. To beg forgiveness. To pick things up from where they had left off – even after the beastly way she had treated her. But she hadn't yet for an even more cowardly reason: what if she had found someone else? This seemed highly possible – nay, probable. She was, after all, a very attractive woman whom men would be falling over themselves to be with. What if any approach Tempany made to her was thrown back in her face with a snigger of triumph that she was now engaged...or married, even! That would be almost as bad as seeing her go the way of Rebecca.

'*God,*' she breathed. This was driving her nuts. 'You've really messed this one up, Bellman, you idiot, and no mistake.' She shook her head, chuckling morbidly at her own stupidity. Her one chance of happiness and she'd flushed it down the u-bend. Her life was a mess. And it was a mess of her own making. 'But there's still time, Bells!' she said brightly. 'Try to get her number as soon as you're out of here. If she's married, say, "congratulations". And mean it. Then forget about her and move on. But one thing's for sure: you can't go on like this. It's making you sloppy. It will get you killed. Besides,' she added with a giggle, 'you're not even gay! So if she tells you to take a hike, do what you were designed for: get a nice young man, settle down, and have children.'

She said it to herself as a joke, but the mere thought of children filled her with despondency, and not a little dread: she had watched *Alien* too many times. Although her fear of giving birth was a moot point: she had to find a mate first to impregnate her with her xenomorph, and she hadn't been touched by anyone but Spendlove for four years.

She laughed. But her mirth at this train of thought was shattered by a sudden, terrifying vision: doing this ultra-dangerous job, still alone, 15 years hence…and barren! Too late; then living out the rest of her days as a lonely, bitter spinster. That was not a future she wanted under any circumstances. She would die first.

But what, then, of her idea of rekindling her dalliance with the awesome Stephanie Spendlove? Wouldn't that be equally fatal to her chances of children? She pondered the dilemma for a moment, then quickly realised that it was not being childless that scared her; it was the threat of loneliness for the rest of her life. She'd already had enough of it, and couldn't take it much longer. Besides, there were ways and means.

She took a deep breath, her jaw clenched. Here was the plan: Spendlove first; hunt for a man second. But she sincerely hoped that she wouldn't have to go to stage two. She looked at herself in the rear-view mirror, her eyes glinting in the glow of the dashboard. She grinned, and nodded her agreement.

She felt better, liberated, even, now that she was resolved upon a course of action. As her mind cleared, somewhat freed from the guilt she felt for having behaved so abominably towards Spendlove, she began to see the job in hand more lucidly, more tactically, than she had up until now. She had to forget about the fascist cells in Venezuela and whether, or when, the police would move in on them. She had to take her time and do things properly, otherwise, if she went off half-cocked, as she was about to have done, she would either have to massacre everyone at the ranch and probably not get the intel she needed – and certainly not any of the intel in the office in San Antonio – or, more likely, get herself killed. No. She would speak to her man tomorrow and try to get together two teams. If he couldn't provide them, she would signal HQ to see if they could send more bodies north. Even if it meant having to wait around for a week while she got ready, so be it.

An unsettling thought flitted through her head: Artemis should have known all this; known that two teams would be needed. Why hadn't she ordered her to take them? Furthermore, she, Tempany, by showing such a lack of interest in the job, and displaying hostility to the order to take the man along with her, had behaved unprofessionally. Artemis should have known that something was amiss, and should have tried to get to the bottom of it, or sent someone else.

After a moment's reflection, she concluded that she was being paranoid. The CIA had blown three of their operations in the past year, resulting in one of their intelligence officers and three of their local bagmen being killed, while another five had been apprehended and packed off to Guantanamo Bay, where still they languished while Artemis and the Defence Minister tried in vain to barter for their release. As such, everyone at OCC was on edge, fearing that the whole organisation had been penetrated. But there was no evidence for this, with the word around the office being that the operations had been blown owing to the agents having made elementary errors, such as leaving their phones on and allowing themselves to be captured on CCTV at inopportune moments. Given the poor quality of some of the people she had been sent to work with previously, this seemed the most plausible explanation. It was inconceivable that Artemis was setting her up now, for whatever reason. It was more likely that Artemis herself was feeling the strain, and had simply not thought about Carranza's office and the fact that it would have to be taken care of at the same time, and was just too preoccupied (or drunk) to take much heed of Tempany's petulance. Besides, it was entirely Tempany's responsibility as the field agent (which is OCC's shorthand for its five euphemistically-named 'extrajudicial counterrevolutionary adjudicators') to assess the situation on the ground and request more resources if required. It was possible, for example, that an opportunity would present itself without her having to go to the extra expense, and risk to security, of calling in additional manpower. Moreover, if the local man was half the superstar Artemis had painted him, she was probably confident that they would be able to work it out together, without confusing the issue by suggesting tactics which might prove to be useless on the ground. Yes. That was the answer: as with the kill order, Tempany was being delegated the responsibility to figure things out for herself – or, at least, figure things out with the bagman. It was entirely in keeping with Artemis's laissez-faire style: they were being trusted to get the job done, one way or the other, and didn't need babysitting.

It was a notion that should have buoyed her. But it didn't, because she was now fully aware that she had been guilty of a gross dereliction of that responsibility, of the trust placed in her, as she had neglected to do what she ought to have, and normally would have: ensconced herself in her office for a few hours and sketched maps and flowcharts until she was crystal clear in her mind about how the mission should be approached, thus giving her at least some idea of the extent and nature of the resources she would require. Instead, with her thoughts consumed by the lover she had jilted, she had huffily told Ruthie, the field agents' secretary, that she was going out, and had sat in a bar for two hours drinking tequila. By the time she got back she only had time to read the case file before the taxi turned up to take her to the airport, via her flat for some clothes, for the plane to Mexico City. She had then got drunk in the airport and on the plane. (She hadn't touched a drop for 24 hours, and did not feel at all fuzzyheaded, but she couldn't help but wonder if that mini-bender had been responsible for her having chased the bandits. Would a completely dry Tempany – a rare event these days – have made the same mistake? She suspected not.)

Disgusted with herself for having been so incompetent, she turned on the radio, slumped back in her seat and tried to relax. But then another problem hit her. She stopped the car, turned on the interior light and inspected her wounds. There was a deep gash across the bridge of her nose, and, despite her efforts to clean herself up while she was in pursuit, her top lip was encrusted with blood. Worse still, dark blue bruising underscored each of her bloodshot eyes. They would be black as coals in the morning. She switched off the light and smoked thoughtfully. No amount of foundation or concealer would help. It would, she reckoned, be at least five days until her injuries – the external ones, at least – healed. Until then she would be conspicuous, the first and most crucial thing people in her line of work had to avoid. She groaned, then flicked off the handbrake and set off again.

The moon was now dead ahead. She had been bearing roughly southeast, she reckoned, which seemed good enough. But there was still no sign of life. She drove on and on. Still nothing. Not a thing. She was getting anxious and began chewing her nails. The needle on the petrol gauge was hovering just above the red. If there was no sign of life soon, she would have to park up for the night and hope the route would be clearer in the morning. If it wasn't, she would have little alternative but to switch on her phone and get a fix from the GPS. But that would only be as a last resort – even though the phone had yet to be used, and although it had the company's call and message encryption on it, using the GPS would pinpoint the phone's location, which was dangerous, as it would make it easier for the NSA or CIA to piece together her movements and figure out exactly what she had been up to in the event that they took an interest in her later on. Indeed, using the phone through the cell network with the encrypted calls and messages was dangerous in and of itself, as, although the content of the messages would be masked, her approximate location would not be. Stealth and secrecy were the key elements of her job, and the less she used the phone the better. She made a decision: if she had to use the GPS in the morning, as soon as she was back on the road to San Antonio she would destroy it.

She drove on for another five miles, and began slowing, both to conserve fuel and because she was getting drowsy. Then, just as she was close to stopping, a light sprung up ahead. A second later it turned into two blazing headlights. They were moving quickly, and very soon raced up, and a van flashed by. She gave a sigh of relief: she seemed to be heading somewhere. Five miles further on, she came to a junction with a wider road, the sign at which declared she had hit Highway 55, and that Uvalde was 25 miles to the right. 'Hallelujah!' she cried. The chances of her being abducted and eaten by a *Texas Chainsaw Massacre*-style family of cannibals, she thought with a laugh, seemed to be diminishing rapidly.

It was some distance before she came upon the next car, travelling in the same direction – a BMW X5 with a couple of passengers in the back. It was doing about 50, so she tucked in a safe distance behind and followed on. Outlights of a house crept up on the right of the perfectly straight road. Then there came another house, almost on the verge. Then one on the left. Then a car came up from the other direction. The road went over a small hill, and to her delight there was a red glow in the sky ahead marking the town of Uvalde. She glanced at the luminous hands of her Omega Speedmaster. It was half past eleven. There was no way she was going to even try San Antonio tonight, which she reckoned to be some way off to the north east. She pulled over, leaving the BMW to canter its way into town, got out, and took the half-empty bottle of water from the passenger seat. She poured some into the dirt on the side of the road and stirred the puddle with her finger into a small dollop of mud, which she smeared over the number plates. She then poured the rest over her face, wiped the caked blood from her nose with a handful of Kleenex, washed her hands, and threw the tissues into the ditch by the road.

She drove slowly into the outskirts of the town, dimly lit single-storey clapboard sheds and houses on either side. Highway 55 came to a junction with a gas station on the other side, which was closed. There were no signposts, but there was a greater trail of streetlights to her right, which she took. After a mile or so she came up to gas stations on either side, both of which were also shut. The place had the air of a ghost town. She drove on, growing increasingly anxious that nothing would be open, and resigning herself to sleeping in the car. Eventually, the widely dispersed buildings on either side began to bunch up into rows of shops. None of them was open, but if felt like a good sign. She carried on, and at last hit a junction proclaiming Main Street, with what looked like the town's courthouse on the corner. On a hunch she took a left. After various shops and another closed gas station, she finally came up to an Exxon station which was open. She cruised past a cluster of fast food outlets, all of which were shut save for McDonalds, then, on the right was an Americas Best Value Inn. 'Yes!' she cried with a fist pump. Immediately after the motel was a bus station. Guessing that the town was laid out in a checkerboard, she took a left, then a left again, and soon found herself behind the food joints and the gas station. She trundled down the road between them and parked in the darkest part of the street under a clump of trees.

She got out, looked around, then quickly unscrewed both number plates with her Swiss Army knife. She stuffed them into the carrier bag, and then put on her blue baseball cap, tugging it low over her forehead, and donned her Ray-Bans, which weren't nearly as conspicuous, even at this time of night, as her black eyes. Leaving the key in the ignition in the sincere hope that the car would be taken, she slung her holdall over her right shoulder, the rifle in its tattered leather case over the left, took the bag of rubbish with the soiled clothes and hard drive, and walked further along the road she had just been driving. After only a hundred yards or so, she came to a bridge over a small lake. With a quick sweep to make sure no one was watching, she casually dropped in the rifle, then threw in the number plates and hard drive. She doubled back, took a right down the street where the car was, got her boots out of it, then threw them and the carrier bag into a reeking dumpster in the car park of Pizza Hut. She then walked casually onto Main Street and into the gas station shop, which was deserted. The boy behind the counter grimaced when he saw her nose. 'You got a phone?' she asked in her own voice, too tired to try being smart.

'Sure ma'am,' he nodded, and pointed to the payphone fixed to the wall next to the toilets.

'How far to San Antonio?'

'About 70 miles, ma'am.'

'Thank you.' She stuck in two quarters and dialled the bagman's number. It was answered halfway through the first ring. 'Evenin',' came the unruffled reply.

'Hello,' said Tempany. 'Sorry to bother you so late, but could you please tell me the exchange rate today?'

'20 pesos to the dollar. But you'd be better off investing in sterling.'

'Or euros,' Tempany laughed. 'I was supposed to meet you earlier. I'm sorry to have missed our appointment. I'm afraid I got held up.'

'Not to worry, ma'am. I had to report, though. I hope you don't mind. I feel a bit of a sneak.'

'Don't be silly. I would have done the same. Anyway, it was my bad.'

'I'm sure it couldn't be helped,' he drawled magnanimously. 'So where are you now?'

'Ah, ah, ah! I'll maybe tell you when I get there.'

'Which will be?'

She thought for a moment. 'Same place tomorrow. But I should be in town earlier. Can we say around eight?'

'Absolutely, ma'am. I'm looking forward to meeting you. I might have some news.'

'Excellent!' she said, and hung up. She bought black hair dye, a pair of scissors, a couple of bags of crisps, forty Marlboro, a bottle of water, a tube of Neosporin, some cotton wool, a packet of sticking plasters, and a bottle of Jim Beam. Then she bought a Big Mac and fries from McDonald's, and half-staggered across to the motel. She checked in with the night watchman at the small gatehouse, who, apparently used to seeing all sorts of things at this time of night, did not make the slightest allusion to her damaged face. She took a bus timetable and map of Texas from the leaflet rack by the desk, then made her way to the third room on the right of the courtyard beyond. The room was bland but functional, with a double bed against the wall and a television on a chest of drawers opposite. She stashed the gun in its holster under the pillows, took a few bites of her supper, then brushed her teeth and cleaned up her hands and bruised face, and put a blob of Neosporin and a Band-Aid on her nose. Then she took a long swig of Jim Beam, undressed, and climbed into bed. She flicked through the local TV channels for any news of the robbery. There was nothing yet. Almost immediately her vision began to blur, and she pressed the standby button on the remote as the energy sapped from her arm.

Just as sleep was about to overwhelm her, a notion hit her. The woman she had been pining after for this past year, the woman she had been beating herself up over for having treated so shabbily: she didn't even know her name! She knew her only by the rather silly moniker of 'Stephanie Spendlove' – which was almost as ridiculous as 'Edith Anson'! She gave a drowsy smirk, and thought of the moment when, lying on sunloungers next to each other in the dark on the beach, barely lit by the glow from the raucous beachside bar, on an impulse – an impulse spawned of her loneliness, given form by alcohol – she had felt out Spendlove's hand and rolled over to kiss her. Spendlove had recoiled, gasping, 'I'm not...' leaving the word 'gay' hanging in the air. 'Edith...Anson,' she added stiffly, 'I...I can't give you what you want.' But she didn't let go of Tempany's hand. 'All I want is you...and your smoking hot body,' grinned Tempany. Spendlove laughed. 'Flattery will get you...' 'Everywhere,' said Tempany. She leaned forward to try again. This time Spendlove relented. It was the first time in her life that she had kissed another woman.

She slipped into a deep sleep, a contented smile on her face.

4. River City

By the time she woke her smile and the comforting thoughts of her erstwhile lover were gone. Instead, the horrific image of the man she had murdered the night before was swamping her brain. The slicked back hair, the round, rugged face. The white shirt with a smoking black hole in it. The terror in his eyes.

She ran her hands over her face and torso. Her skin and the thin burgundy sheet draped over her were drenched. She groaned. No matter how many people she killed, no matter how much they deserved it, she could never get used to it. All she could do to stop herself going mad was to try to blank it out of her mind. Deafen her senses. But every time she did so, she felt a little bit of her humanity seep away. She often wondered what would happen if the cork bottling up all her guilt suddenly popped out. Would she be able to live with herself? Or would the next victim of her blood-soaked hands be her? She gritted her teeth and punched herself on the leg as she stared up at the yellowing ceiling. *'Get a grip!'* she growled. Maybe she would go insane eventually, she thought. But not today.

It was 12.30. Yet still she was exhausted. She wiped the sleep from her eyes, rolled onto the floor, and embarked on her daily routine of 50 press-ups and sit-ups. She pulled on her underwear, put on a clean white t-shirt, then did 15 minutes' running on the spot. Once she caught her breath she had a bag of crisps and a large Jim Beam and water, then went to the bathroom to inspect her face. She gave a sigh of relief to see that she hadn't, in fact, turned into the Elephant Man. The eyes themselves were merely red, the bruising circling them not particularly dark, and her nose seemed straight. She tentatively pulled off the Band-Aid. The pad on the inside was sodden. The gash itself was still looking nasty and the entire bridge was swollen. She thought of Frank, and wondered what his nose was looking like today. Then her mind drifted back to the time, many years ago, when she had woken in hospital to find that her nose had been shattered after being on the wrong end of a fascist mob. Then she thought of Alicia Mackintosh, one of the girls she had assaulted on her first day at St Catherine's, to where Tempany had been exiled after having being expelled from her boarding school in Norwich. For the first time she felt a pang of guilt about it. Whatever had happened to her? she wondered. Had Tempany's beating of her affected her in the long run? Was she shyer, more withdrawn, more scared, less successful than she otherwise would have been? Tempany had barely spoken to her since that first day. But suddenly she was anxious to find out how she had fared; and to apologise profusely for smashing her nose with a hockey stick. Because Tempany now saw clearly that, despite the fact that it had happened in a split second, and that it was clearly self-defence, the level of violence she had employed had been way over the top. Even though Mackintosh was bigger than her, Tempany knew that a slap in the face would have more than sufficed.

But then, as if in protest at her remorse, her mind threw up the image of Rebecca on that first day. Poor, sweet, bruised, bullied Rebecca, standing freezing under the shower. All guilt evaporated. She snarled at herself in the mirror. 'She deserved it, Bells. She deserved worse.' But, as it always did, the thought of Rebecca grieved her. She hung her head. 'Oh,

God, Bex,' she whispered. 'I miss you so much.' She took a deep breath and gave herself a shake. 'Get on with it, Bells.'

She peeled back her lips, to find with relief that her gums and teeth appeared intact. She was about to try to blow the blockages out of each nostril when curiosity overtook her. She pinched her septum and gently pushed. Instantly there was a loud squelch as it came away from the bone it had been trying to set to. It jerked about a centimetre to the left. The movement caused blood to spurt into the sink and over her fresh t-shirt. 'Damn!' It wasn't sore, but she felt ready to cry at the damage that had been done to her. She nudged it back into place, put her head in the sink, and blew hard on each nostril, forcing large globules of blood and yellow mucus into the sink. She tilted her head back, forcing the blood down her throat, then grabbed a handful of the coarse toilet paper and held it to her nose until the flow became a trickle. If she had been back in London, or even Caracas, she would have gone to A&E. Here, it was out of the question. She would just have to hope that it set straight. If it didn't, she was in for a pretty painful operation when she got back home. She jammed two bits of cotton wool high up each nostril, then cleaned up her face and redressed her nose. She then got out the scissors, and with only a few cuts chopped her shoulder-length hair up to the neck. With her lean face, pronounced cheekbones, curving jaw, and (normally) brown hair, she had always been told that she looked like Diana Rigg in her heyday. It was a comparison she rather liked. But now she was looking less like a 60s glamour puss, and more like a twelve-year-old boy with a smashed nose and a bad haircut. She wondered if she would end up like Diana Rigg's most recent incarnation: an evil old witch in *Game of Thrones*. 'Well, I've already got the evil bit down to a T,' she said mirthlessly. She scooped up the tufts of hair from the sink – the golden colour of which had itself come from a bottle – dumped them in the toilet, then went to work with the dye. Within half an hour she was a raven-haired twelve-year-old boy with a bad haircut. But at least she looked nothing like the woman who had been in the shop the night before.

After a long, hot shower, she lay naked on the bed for an hour, staring at the television. There was still nothing from last night. Perhaps, she wondered gloomily, armed robberies and murders were simply too commonplace in this part of the world – where every Tom, Dick and Harry carried a gun – to warrant attention from the news. When she got up she stuck another plaster on her nose, put on fresh underwear, her jeans, last fresh t-shirt, pullover, baseball cap and sunglasses, and stuffed her used clothes and the gun into her holdall. She paid the girl at the desk in cash, then made her way to the bus station to buy her ticket.

To kill time before the bus arrived, she walked back into the centre of town and visited a couple of clothes shops to replenish her wardrobe, buying pairs of black and dark blue 715s, a pair of white Adidas trainers, a black v-neck top, a grey t-shirt, and a red nylon biker jacket. Both the cheerful shopkeepers asked where she was from, remarking on her accent, and both asked concernedly what had happened to her. She chirped to both, 'England!' and told them she had been beaten up by her boyfriend, with whom she had been backpacking across America. She had therefore stolen all his cash, and was spending it while travelling to Dallas to get a plane home. They both congratulated her for her bravery, and, despite her protestations, she got a 10% discount from the one selling her the jacket and trainers. She then found a small bar, had a couple of Jack and Cokes, then walked back along to the bus station to catch the Greyhound at 3.55. The bus was about three quarters full, with no pair of seats free. She made her way to the rear, to be close to the emergency exit in the unlikely event of having to made a quick getaway, and sat next to a big middle-aged man in a white shirt and loosened red tie. He looked pleased that this young woman (despite her injured face) sat next to him, and chatted easily to her. He was a likeable man called Paul, who, it turned out, was a representative of the ranchers around Del Rio, and was making his way to Austin to speak to the state government about the water supply, as irrigation, human consumption, and years of drought had sucked the Rio Grande dry. It was pleasant having her mind turned from her own dangerous business for the two-hour journey.

She got out at the Greyhound station in the city centre. The early evening was warm and sticky, the sun still hitting the street from the cloudless western sky. She bought a street map from the station shop and quickly marked the locations of Carranza's office, the rendezvous point, and the nearby Marriot. Laden with the two bags of new clothes and her holdall, she set off along East Pecan Street, walked through a public square and a hundred metres of the shops-lined East Travis Street, and turned right onto Broadway Street. She kept to the right-hand pavement, marking the grey six-storey office building opposite. Carranza's rooms were on the third floor, above and to the right of the entrance in the centre of the building. She glanced up. The three windows that were his had their blinds down. She felt something approaching despair. Although she could not spot any cameras, the office was on a busy road, with shops on either side and a bar which she had just walked past, so getting in through the front door without being seen, even at, say, four in the morning, would be down to luck more than anything else. And, given the location, there was simply no way that they could get a ladder and try to cut their way in through one of the windows. Perhaps a better idea would be for her men, if she could get any, to conceal themselves in the building somewhere – one of the toilets, perhaps – and break in to the office directly once the front door was shut at night. But that was assuming that there was not a nightwatchman or a janitor or motion-sensor alarms. Alternatively, she assumed there would be a car park and a back door for tenants, which could be more vulnerable than the front – although her men would still have to disable the alarm system, assuming there was one. The easiest way would be to bribe someone on the inside – a cleaner, perhaps. But that would take time. In any event, she did not like her chances, and was instantly thinking about leaving the office and doing Carranza's place alone, gambling that all the information they needed was either there, physically, or in Carranza's head.

She shook her head. That solution was too imprecise. In fact, so imprecise as to be thoroughly stupid. She would be as well not doing anything, rather than half doing it. Indeed, the more she thought about it, the more likely she thought that any incriminating materials would be in the office rather than at his home – at least then Carranza could claim some semblance of innocence, especially given that the office was in the name of his alias. She gave a dejected sigh and put the problem to the back of her head. There was no point in worrying about it now. She would hear what the bagman had to say.

Navigating with the map, she carried on south for a short while, then headed right until she hit a bridge, from which she took the steps down to the riverside path. Branded as the San Antonio River Walk, there are bars and restaurants on either side of the San Antonio River beneath road level, presumably to provide the locals and tourists some refuge from the mid-summer heat. Already, even though it was just after six, the eateries were doing good business, tables being occupied by couples and families on either side of the path. Everyone seemed happy. Tempany perked up somewhat. Despite the fact that she hated its ingrained credo of individualism and greed, she rather liked America and its people. In fact, she would have happily lived in New York or San Francisco, both of which she adored (although she had been reading some disturbing things about the latter recently – she hadn't visited for seven years, but it had apparently been overrun by junkies; probably Trump's fault, she thought thoughtlessly).

She made her way to the rendezvous point, quickly checked for escape routes, then walked back up on to Market

Street. From there she took a right, and headed for the imposing multi-storey Marriot a short distance away. Booking in using her MasterCard in the name of Alison Worthington, in something of a challenge to the receptionist, who was eyeing her suspiciously, she pigged out and got an 'executive larger' room on the 10th floor, taking it for a week.

The room was bright and spacious, with a bathroom to the left, a king-size bed against the left wall, a small sofa and a table, a balcony with two chairs and a table looking out over the city centre, a closet, then, against the right-hand wall, a long sideboard with a television, coffee maker and cups and glasses. She dropped her bags, turned the television onto CNN, and went out for a cigarette, leaning over the balcony and staring into the dulling horizon as the sun set behind the buildings ahead of her. Directly below, sandwiched between two roads, was part of the river, that section tree-lined, with lights from the path twinkling up through the branches. It was 6.45. She checked the room, and found a fridge in the cabinet beneath the television with four bottles of water, but no mini bar. She phoned room service and asked if they could bring her up a bottle of Grey Goose. The man put her on hold, and presently came back on apologising that they could only bring her Absolut. The cost would be, he said hesitantly, $65. She couldn't be bothered haggling, so asked him to bring it up, along with a burger and fries and a bottle of Coke. A Latino waiter arrived with the order 15 minutes later. She gave him a 20, then sat out on the balcony and ate, after which she showered and brushed her teeth, put on the new black 715s and grey t-shirt and trainers and slugged down a cupful of Absolut. She checked herself in the mirror. Her black eyes and the deep, black gash on her nose were now looking hideous. But there was nothing she could do about it now. With a pair of tweezers she gently fished the cotton wool out of her nose. The swabs were completely black, but crusted, indicating that the blood had clotted and that the internal wounds were healing. She hung over the sink and gently blew on each nostril, forcing out more dried blood. When she could breathe through her nose again and was sure there was no fresh flow, she cleaned herself up, stuck on another Band-Aid, and sprayed some Coco Chanel onto her wrist and rubbed it on her neck. She put on her new jacket – the cool silk lining thrilling against her bare arms – and loaded her pockets with a box of cigarettes, her Union Jack Zippo, Swiss Army knife, $300 in cash, and street map. She put on her baseball cap, but left the sunglasses in her bag, judging that wearing shades walking alongside a darkened river at this time of night would draw more attention than her battered face. Just as she was about to leave, she thought of her gun. She had reckoned there would be no danger tonight and had been minded to leave it. But her intuition was nagging her. *Better safe than sorry, no?* Besides, in the event that there was trouble and she ended up in the clutches of the opposition, she had to have a means of carrying out Artemis's orders of killing herself.

'No!' she said decisively. 'I'm not killing myself. Never!' She'd take her chances under the torturer's pliers. She left the gun.

5. The Bagman

The rendezvous point was the first tree to the south of the steps down from the bridge on Navaro Street, in front of the River Walk entrance to the Westin Hotel. Tempany, prowling the path on the opposite bank, marked 'Ray Walker' at precisely 7.50. Dressed in a cream linen suit and an open-necked white shirt, he made his way down the steps from the bridge and leaned delinquent-like against the tree, smoking while staring into the narrow, slow-moving river. Now and then he would look up at the darkening sky.

Tempany observed him casually over the top of the street map. He showed no signs of nervousness, never glancing at his watch, never making any effort to look out for or signal anyone else. Her eyes scanned the rest of the riverbank. It was well lit from the hotel's windows. There were a few couples walking in either direction, but none seemed suspicious or in any way in league with him. On her side there were a few people sitting on the low wall bounding the building behind her. Nothing seemed out of place. She checked her watch, pinged her cigarette into the river, and walked up the steps onto the bridge. When she was halfway across the man looked up at her. He made no acknowledgement, and looked back down to the river and kicked out his cigarette. By the time she had trotted down the stairs, he had lit another, and was whistling softly while staring up at the building opposite, his head cocked and eyes scrunched as if he were counting the windows.

'Lovely evenin', ma'am,' he said as she approached. He looked to be in his early forties, his hair cropped short, probably in effort to disguise a receding hairline. He was clean-shaven with rosy cheeks, and had a nose which was bony and squint, as if it, like hers, had been smashed at some point. It wasn't a particularly handsome face, but his friendly smile compensated somewhat. He was about the same height as her own 5'9, and although it was difficult to make out under his suit jacket, he looked lean, and she guessed he was in reasonable condition for his age. With one hand in his trouser pocket, the other holding the cigarette to his lips, and his brown eyes narrowed in enquiry, he was relaxed and confident.

She put her back against the tree, her arm touching his, and lit a Marlboro. From the corner of her mouth she asked him what the exchange rate was. He gave her the reply, and, flashing a decent set of teeth, thrust out his hand. As she shook it, hard, she couldn't help but notice the Rolex on his right wrist. She never trusted people, even southpaws, who wore their watches in such a fashion. And she didn't really trust anyone who wore Rolexes – perhaps because her father, the capitalist pigdog, had three of them, as well as a super-expensive Audemars Piguet Royal Oak, which he wheeled out on his birthdays. She bristled inwardly at the thought of him, but quickly brushed it aside and smiled at Ray in return.

'I was worried when you didn't appear last night, Miss Anson,' he said in a slightly high, nasally Texas accent, which reminded her of Bush 43. 'I was sure something had happened to you.'

'No,' she shook her head. 'Just a little local difficulty. I'll maybe tell you about it later, if you play your cards right. I normally wouldn't share, but the thought of you hanging around here all night has got me feeling rather guilty.'

He laughed. 'Don't worry about me. I had other things to keep me occupied. And my man told me to relax. Said you go AWOL all the time.'

'Did he now?' she chuckled. 'That makes it sound like I'm unreliable.'

'That's not *exactly* how he put it. Said you had a tendency to get dragged into other things, is all. And, um, it kinda looks like you might have, ma'am,' he nodded.

'This is nothing,' she smiled, pointing at her face. 'You should see the other guy.'

His brow creased in concern. 'You seen a doctor?'

'It isn't that bad, is it?'

He leaned forward, his eyes probing. She could just about smell a hint of musky aftershave. 'What's under the plaster?'

'A big cut,' she said sardonically, emphasising each word.

'Is it broken?'

'Yep.'

'You want me to set you up with someone?'

She thought for a second. 'Possibly. Let's give it a couple of days, or until our business is done. We can talk about it later. And, um, thank you for the offer.'

'Don't mention it. I just wouldn't want a pretty face like yours ending up like this,' he said, jabbing a finger at his own nose.

'I don't know,' she smiled. 'There's a certain something to it.'

'Ha!' He turned away bashfully. 'I can see what they told me about you was true.'

'I wouldn't believe anything *they* say.' She hitched her back again to the tree and blew smoke rings into the still air. 'So,' she said, 'you said you had good news.'

He moved round to face her. 'Is that it?' he said, arching an eyebrow.

'What?'

'The small talk? I was rather enjoying it.'

'I see you think yourself a bit of a charmer,' she said, squinting at him.

He shrugged. 'I wouldn't go that far. But I was going to ask you if you would like to come and discuss our business somewhere more comfortable?' he asked hopefully.

'Let me guess: your house?'

'Of course not, Miss Anson!' he shook his head with faux indignation. 'What sort of man do you think I am? I mean, we haven't even been on our first date yet. I've got my reputation to think of.'

Tempany giggled. 'Okay. I'm sorry. I would do nothing to sully your reputation, which I am sure is spotless. What did you have in mind?'

'Mexican?'

'Well, I've just eaten. But,' she patted her stomach, 'I don't suppose a plate of soup or something will do me much harm. And, as it seems to be the only thing you get around here, Mexican it is.'

'Come on then,' he said brightly. He led her back up onto the bridge and headed north, Tempany keeping a pace or two behind him, fingering the penknife in her pocket. It was now twilight, the sky a deep blue, but it was still stiflingly hot. She was now regretting taking her jacket as the sweat was building on her face. After a few hundred yards they took a right, then crossed a bridge and walked down the same steps she had taken when going down to the River Walk earlier. The restaurant was immediately to the left. Most of the tables were taken, but there was one free by the river's edge, to which a harassed waitress ushered them. Tempany wriggled out of her jacket, hung it on the back of her chair, and took her baseball cap off. She could see the amusement in Ray's eyes as he saw her hair. 'Not a word,' she warned, jovially.

He held up his hands, shaking his head. 'I think it's cute,' he said. 'It makes you look…um…chic.'

'Thanks, I guess,' she smiled.

Tempany ordered a large gin and tonic, Ray a bottle of Miller; then Ray ordered filete guajillo, Tempany a shrimp cocktail and a bottle of Pino Grigio. When the waitress left, Ray looked around, then leaned across the table and asked softly, 'So, Miss Anson, tell me about yourself?'

'Ah...no,' she said firmly.

'Come on. Humour me.'

'I'd rather not. In fact, I'd rather get down to business.'

'Understood. But I thought we might get to know each other a bit first. Help us build some team morale, you know?'

She pondered this for a second, then elected to play along. There would be no harm in it. 'Okay, Mr Walker. What would you like to know?'

'You got a guy?'

She laughed. 'Are you serious?'

'Would you like me to be?'

'Not particularly.'

'Well?'

'If I were a lady I would say that it was none of your business.'

'But?'

She took a long pull of her gin. 'But I'm not a lady,' she shrugged. 'So the answer is no.'

'Why not?'

She didn't like the way this was going. Indeed, she didn't like talking about herself, full stop, let alone talking about something so intimate, and with a complete stranger to boot. Her initial impulse was to tell him to back off. But she held her tongue, reckoning that being a cow about it and insulting him would, given that she was deep behind enemy lines, not be the wisest of moves. So she propped her chin up on her upturned hand, plastered the smile back on her face, and replied, fairly honestly, 'It's because of this work, I suppose. There's no time. I really am on the job 24/7. And forming attachments is...well, it's not particularly safe.'

'I know what you mean,' he nodded. 'Are you lonely?'

She took another drink. 'Not really,' she lied. 'Although...I think it comes with the territory. I work alone. Mostly. But why do you ask?' she said, trying to shift the conversation onto him. 'Does it bother you?'

He stared into his beer bottle, and said slowly, 'I...well, it's weird. All my friends and family are round about. But...what I do here, my job, if it can be called that...it *is* lonely, I guess. It's just the isolation of it. I'm working by myself as well, pretty much all the time. There's no office I go to. No colleagues to hang out with. And there's no prospect of me ever getting a real job again,' he moped.

'And why would that be?'

His head jerked back. 'You don't you know?'

She did know. Or at least as much as Artemis had been prepared to tell her. Ray had been the Bureau's deputy chief of station in Austin. And he was corrupt. Not only did he have his hand in the till, he had been taking bribes from the Mexican cartels. He ended up getting caught trying to steal 15 kilos of impounded cocaine. He was sacked, but, incredibly, wasn't jailed, merely having all his unaccounted-for assets confiscated. Shortly after, Artemis recruited him. That was three years ago, and Artemis had – to Tempany's annoyance – waxed lyrical about his contribution to date. He had brought with him a vast network of contacts, stretching from commerce to law enforcement to organised crime, most of whom cared nothing that he had been disgraced, and were prepared to cooperate with him if the price was right. Through Walker, Artemis had been led to a dozen of OCC's enemies, all of whom had been variously involved in gun running, drug trafficking, or otherwise trying to destabilise the South. Most of these individuals had been liquidated; two of them in Miami by Tempany herself. At the end of Artemis's enthusiastic briefing, Tempany, sulking at being ordered to take him with her, had insolently said, 'I don't doubt what this man has brought to us. But how can you trust him? Anyone as corrupt as this, who would betray his employer, then betray his country, would surely betray us in a millisecond.' Artemis shook her head, disappointment dripping from her wise brown eyes. 'I know you've got to be wary of people, Anson. But don't automatically think the worst of them. That's the way our enemies think. And that's why we fight them.' It was a devastating rebuke, making Tempany even tetchier, and it had ended the interview.

Despite Artemis's words, however, and despite feeling relaxed in his company, Tempany didn't trust him. So she told him only the bones of what she knew – that he had been fired for having his hands in the till – and concluded by saying, 'It seems as if you're a bit of a scoundrel, Mr Walker.'

He giggled bashfully, and said with a shrug, 'I was being blackmailed by the Cubans and ended up in over my head. It's not the first time this has happened to someone in my position, and won't be the last.'

This was news to her, and she was amazed that he would tell her. A loose mouth like that was a sure way of getting killed. What was more, it opened up a whole host of other questions. What did 'the Cubans' – presumably the Cuban exiles in Miami – have on him, for example? And did they still have him in their pocket? If they did, were they using him to infiltrate OCC? And did Artemis know about this? She surely must? Tempany glanced around. The tables closest were still all taken, but the voices of the diners were just a formless hubbub, drowned out by mariachi music coming from the sound system inside. She turned back to him and leaned across the table, her face stern. 'I must say, Mr Walker, I admire your chutzpah. Talking to a complete stranger about such personal things is rather bold.'

He thought for a second. 'I guess you're right. It's just…it's just good to have someone to talk to in the flesh. And I like you already. Plus I'm a pretty honest guy,' he said without a hint of irony. 'I think that's part of the reason I got busted in the first place. I'm too open and I've got a big mouth,' he shrugged helplessly.

'Those are not bad things,' she said, remembering Artemis's scolding of her. 'You just have to be cautious.'

'I know,' he nodded sadly.

As the food and wine arrived, Ray, said, 'So, quid pro quo: what's your first name? I mean, Anson's very pretty and all, but it's likely to draw attention to us if anyone asks me about you.'

What an odd question, she thought. Was this his opening gambit to try to lower her defences in order that he could seduce her? Regardless of his motives, she decided to bite. 'It's Edith,' she said.

'That's…um, a bit unusual. But it suits you.'

She laughed, and cast a furtive glance at his left hand. There were no rings on it.

As they ate they chatted, mostly at his instigation, about US politics. The way he spoke animatedly about how terrible the Democrat field for the next Presidential Election was, and how great a guy right-wing Texas Senator Ted Cruz was, gave Tempany the clear impression that he was a Trump man, which put her on edge – wasn't Trump, after all, the embodiment of everything they were fighting against? Even so, Ray's enthusiasm was somewhat infectious, so she let him talk.

When they had finished eating, Tempany leaned across the table, and asked softly, 'So, what have you got for me?'

He drew his napkin across his mouth, tossed it onto his empty plate, and grinned inanely. He surely wasn't drunk already, she thought. She was beginning to feel it, a bit, although she was still alert enough. Whatever the case, he didn't seem to be taking things very seriously. 'Where shall I start?' he asked himself huskily. 'Good news, I think.' He leaned over, bringing their faces close. 'I assume you know all about our man and his security detail.'

'Yes.'

'And his movements?'

'His office on Broadway. His ranch.'

'Ah, but where will he be right....' he looked at his watch for effect, '*now?*'

She sat back and tapped her lips with her index finger. 'I'm sure you're about to tell me.'

'He'll be in a bar in Seguin,' he said. 'Goes there every weeknight at about eight, after he's had dinner with his family. Usually stays a couple of hours – sometimes up to four if he plays cards, getting drunk with two of his babysitters and any of his other buddies who show up.'

A thrill ran through her. 'How do you know this?' she asked, struggling to keep her voice down.

'Contacts, Edith.' He paused, as if he was going to be coy about it, but carried on without prompting, 'His driver's an old buddy of mine. Used to be the janitor of the Fed building in Austin. Such people make great employees for people like our man, because they never talk.' He chuckled deeply at that and fell back in his chair, his arms folded, smiling smugly.

'Holy shit!' she gasped. A drunken target along with a couple of drunken gorillas would be far easier to subdue. Plus, if Carranza had had a few drinks, it would make his lips looser. She would strike as they were coming out of the bar – probably neutralise the babysitters then abduct him as they were going to his car. She motioned to Ray to come in close. 'Right,' she whispered. 'I'll need some men.'

'How many?'

'Six. Two to raid the office, two for the ranch, and two to come with me to take on our man and his goons.'

His eyes roved around as he thought. 'Yep,' he nodded slowly. 'That can be done.'

'This has nothing to do with me, of course. I'll provide the funds, you give the orders.'

'Understood.'

'Now, the office is going to be a bit of a challenge. Any ideas?'

'I assumed you might need access,' he smiled, 'so everything's fixed.'

'How?'

'I've spoken to one of the cleaners. She's prepared to cooperate for three thousand. She'll let us make copies of the key for the back door and the master key for the offices. She'll also provide us with the alarm code. Our men can be in and out in ten minutes.'

'Excellent! Do you have the money?'

'Yep.'

'Good. We'll need to take all hardware, and any paperwork relating to the account in Grand Cayman. Also, ask them to do some rummaging around for password lists – but don't get them to spend too much time on that – if there's nothing lying around we'll be able to hack everything easily enough. Just bag everything up and I'll take care of it.' Just *how* she would take care of it she had given precisely no thought to. Probably the best way would be to drop it off with a technician from the embassy, whom she could get to come down and meet her after the job. He or she could then either try to pull the goods apart and hack anything stored in the cloud there and then, or ship everything back to HQ in the diplomatic bag.

As she pondered this, her irritation with herself for not having thought all this through earlier bubbled up again. But there was relief, too: relief that Ray was there, otherwise the mission would almost certainly be careening to spectacular failure. She wondered briefly if this was the principal reason for the high mortality rate amongst those in her profession: they all reach a point where they simply get sloppy; through arrogance, perhaps, or fatigue, maybe, or for stupid personal reasons like Tempany. At any rate, she felt she had dodged a bullet, and vowed never to be so negligent again.

She swallowed the last of her wine. 'Obviously at the same time I'll need the other two...no, on second thoughts, scratch that – we'll need two to get the stuff, and two for crowd control and to take care of the other goon at the ranch. Can you get another two men?'

He nodded.

'Good. Same deal as the office. Obviously I don't want any of the folks there harmed, so don't use anyone who's liable to get jumpy. Okay?'

'Okay.'

'The last two come with me to…what was the place?'

'Seguin.'

'Seguin,' she repeated. 'What day is this?'

'Wednesday.'

'I would like to go and scope out this joint before the job. We'll target Friday as D-Day. Can you get your men together for then? And sort out our friend the cleaner?'

He nodded again, looking certain.

'Friday it is. I would like to meet the guys coming with me beforehand. Can that be arranged?'

'No problem. I'll sort out a meet for tomorrow night. Here?'

'Here.' She counted on her fingers. 'So, we've got two men for the office, four for the ranch, and two to come with me. That's eight. How much?'

'Going rate for an evening like this is 20 grand a man.'

It seemed a bit steep. Would Ray be taking a kickback? Regardless, it wasn't her decision, and she would have to get the money approved. She would buy a laptop and send an email from her Proton Mail account via Tor on a Wi-Fi hotspot somewhere. 'I'll have to clear it with the boss tomorrow. I'll call you if she agrees, and then you can get to it. I don't know what your financial arrangements are, but it might be easier if the cash is wired to you. I mean, I don't really want to go into a bank and try to withdraw the amount we're talking about.'

'Don't worry. Just tell them to wire it to me and I'll take care of it.'

'Good. Now, about your men: they must be reliable. And discrete. No drunks or junkies.'

'If the men I have in mind are available, they are all highly experienced. No rookies. They'll do the job.'

'I'm almost afraid to ask, but are they ex-Bureau or Agency?'

He smiled and shrugged. 'Don't worry about it. They're pros. They don't ask questions. The fact that they'll be working for me will be enough for them.'

'Where will you be when all this is going down?'

'I was going to suggest leading the team at the ranch. What do you think?'

'As long as you're not afraid to get your hands dirty.'

'Not in the slightest. I want to help. And my hands are dirty already.'

'Good. I'd rather one of our own people on the scene anyway. Just make sure you don't get caught – we don't want our fingerprints on this.'

'Hey, have a little faith!'

She laughed, then sat back and folded her arms. The details of the raid on the ranch and her ambush of Carranza had to be worked out, but, other than that, what they had now was better than she could have hoped for. Indeed, having thought, when she first saw Carranza's office, that her prospects of being fully successful were zero, she was now daring to hope that she could come out with everything. There was a bloodthirsty grin on her face when she nodded at Ray and said, 'Yes. This will do nicely.'

She ordered a bottle of Bollinger to celebrate, and they chatted, at Tempany's instigation, about Bond movies, Tempany hoping he would say, 'Hey, you look like the dame from *On Her Majesty's Secret Service!*' To her disappointment, he didn't. Probably because she looked like shit, she reflected.

Ray paid the bill, and they walked back up the steps to the bridge on East Crockett Street. It was still busy with cars and pedestrians, the night still warm. They stood looking at each other.

'I know we've got a lot to get through tomorrow,' said Ray, 'but would you do me the honour of allowing me to walk you home?'

Tempany was slightly drunk. And she wanted comfort. 'Well, how could I possibly refuse such a charming offer. This way,' she said. She linked arms with him and dragged him off towards the hotel.

'Where are we going?' asked Ray in her ear.

'Well, *I'm* going to the Marriot.'

'Ah,' was all he replied.

They walked on in silence down Losoya Street, Tempany leaning against him, trying to make sure he knew what she wanted. After a short distance he patted his jacket and said, 'Damn! Excuse me.' He let go of her and pulled out a phone. She hadn't heard anything, and guessed it was on vibrate. He looked keenly at the screen, typed something, then put it back in his pocket and joined arms with her again.

They turned onto East Commerce Street, and, when there were no cars or people in sight, Ray turned her round and kissed her gently on the mouth. Tempany pulled him tight and returned it with interest. She ran her fingers over his prickly, clipped hair, while his hands wandered down her spine to the small of her back. She pulled back, eventually, and panted, 'Oh, my, Mr Walker.'

'I...I'm sorry,' he said sheepishly. 'That wasn't very professional.'

'Sod professionalism!' she laughed. He was a good kisser; his body was strong and firm. She wondered briefly if this was the man to provide her with children. *No*, she concluded immediately; this was just going to be a bit of therapy after all this time without intimacy. She was going to take him back and use him, that was all. Just as he was probably going to use her. She kissed him again, long and hard, then whispered into his ear, 'You're invited back to mine, if you want.'

'I want,' he said gruffly. He looked at his watch, then looked up at the oncoming traffic. He locked eyes with her again, and kissed her some more. At last she wriggled free and took his hand, desperate to get him back. He was looking along the road, and didn't move. A van swung into the side and screeched to a halt next to them. The side door flew open, and before she knew what was happening Ray had her by the left wrist and was bundling her in. '*Shit!*' she cried as her legs hit the van floor. Instinctively, she twisted her body and threw her weight into a knee to Ray's crotch and a palm strike to his face. Both hit home, and he doubled up with a grunt. She wrenched her arm away and reached for her watch. But just as she was fumbling with the push buttons, two iron-like hands grabbed her under the armpits and hauled her in like a rag doll. She started to scream, but one of the hands clamped itself round her face, sending a bolt of pain from her broken nose down her spine. Then there was a sharp sting in her neck, and Ray was inside and had her by the wrists.

Then darkness.

6. The Red Pill

Her head jerked back as the reek of ammonium carbonate filled her mouth. Her head lolled and she heard herself gurgling. There was a blast of it again, and her body jolted. Her nose was in agony, and she could feel blood running onto her lips. She was tethered to something...a chair, her brain told her. Her hands were tied behind the upright...with handcuffs, her wrists reported as they felt the bite of steel. She tried to kick free, but found her feet shackled too. Her eyes opened a fraction, sending harsh, artificial light flooding into her retinas. 'Smile!' said someone gaily. There was a flash accompanied by the synthesised sound of a camera shutter. It blinded her, and she clamped her eyes shut as red blobs floated across them. 'The camera loves you!' said the voice. It was male. American. Northeast, she guessed, with its hint of Irish-American. Her eyes edged open once more, and the camera flashed again. 'One more for luck,' said the man. She scrunched her eyes, but could see the flash through her eyelids. She blinked hard to try to get rid of the blobs. As they slowly floated away, her eyes focussed on the man in front of her. He was looking at a phone, then looking at her to check his handiwork. He shrugged. 'They'll do,' he said, and lobbed the phone over her head. 'Good catch!' he enthused to someone behind her.

Tempany coughed, put her head to the side, and spat a throat-full of thick blood onto the concrete floor. Painfully, she raised her head and looked around. She was in a large metal shed lit by fluorescent strip lights high in the roof. Behind her, three burly men in black, Ray, and a woman stood chatting round a table. A black van, presumably the one in which she had been abducted, was parked behind them. Beyond that was a roller-shutter door. It was a warehouse unit, the type found on industrial estates the world over. Which meant they were probably in a town somewhere. She ran her tongue over her teeth. They didn't feel furry or even particularly unclean. It hadn't been long since she had been abducted. Which suggested they were still in Texas; quite possibly still in San Antonio. Unsure if she had managed to set off the homer, she pretended to struggle with the cuffs and reached for her watch. It took about a millisecond for her fingers to work out, to her horror, that it was gone. Had Ray known about it? Had he taken it and thrown it somewhere to put HQ off the scent? She had to assume that the answer to both was yes. She thought, with utter despair, that she was on her own.

'That'll be all, fellas,' said the man. 'Thanks.'

She heard the van's doors opening and closing, the electric motor of the roller door labouring, then the van driving out. She turned again, to find that the three big men were gone, and that Ray was working the controls for the door, which was now clattering shut. The man in front of her motioned to the woman, who took an orange plastic chair from under the table and set it a few feet in front of her. He took off his jacket – a black dinner jacket with a red carnation in the lapel – and hung it on the back of the chair. He sat down and looked Tempany over with his pale blue eyes. He was wearing black tuxedo trousers, a dazzling white shirt, silver cufflinks, and a silver tie slide on a thin black tie. What looked like an Omega Planet Ocean, the one with the orange leather strap, peaked out from beneath his left cuff. He had a tanned, slim face, black eyebrows, and a mop of black wavy hair shot with streaks of white. The woman, who had scraped-back black hair and a pale, round, freckled face, appeared next to her with a bottle of water and handful of tissues. She tenderly cleaned Tempany's face, then fed her a few mouthfuls of water. Tempany didn't thank her – she knew that this apparent act of kindness was a cynical device to try to soften her up. She therefore ignored her, and, engaging the man, said with as much poise as she could muster, 'I haven't interrupted dinner, have I?'

The man smiled warmly. 'Funnily enough, yes. It was a rather enjoyable evening as well. I must admit to being slightly inconvenienced. You were, after all, supposed to be here last night.'

'I'm sorry for being so tardy. Am I under arrest?'

He smirked. 'No,' he shook his head. 'There is no formal legal process for people in our line of work, as you well know, Miss Anson.'

The use of her work name shocked her. It shouldn't have. She had obviously been blown, by Ray. Still, hearing it from one of the Opposition's lips made her flinch. She instantly regretted it, and, setting her face hard, said, 'So what's the game, then? If you're going to torture me, I can tell you you'll be wasting your time: I know nothing more than Ray.'

The man linked his fingers and laid them on his lap. 'There's not going to be any torture. Who do you think we are? Barbarians?'

'Pretty much. Isn't it kind of barbaric chaining defenceless women to chairs?'

'You? Defenceless?' he laughed. 'I can see you're going to be a good sport about this.'

'Well, let me fucking go then!' she spat. She struggled with her bonds again, and winced as they bit into her skin.

He shook his head. 'Maybe later. You must understand my caution. You are, after all, a serial killer, and I want to be sure that you won't try to kill *us* if I let you go.'

'If. Not when,' Tempany grimaced.

'Don't worry about that,' he said with a dismissive wave. He checked his watch. 'But time's a wasting. What, Miss Anson, did you make of the Noam Chomsky book, *Hegemony or Survival?*'

'What?' replied Tempany dumbly. She knew all the tricks of the interrogation trade – intimidation, psychological contrast, humiliation, sleep deprivation, torture – inside and out. And she knew this one as well as any: confusion; the aim being to so bamboozle the captive with unexpected and inexplicable questions – questions other than the standard, 'Who do you work for?' 'Why are you here?' 'Where are your confederates?' – that he or she, already under the duress of being captured, would become so disorientated as to crack. But even though Tempany knew all this, this question was so unexpected – and so unnerving because he obviously knew she had read it – that it hit the bullseye. Her breathing quickened and her jaw began to tremble.

'Doesn't ring a bell? Then how about,' he tapped his lips thoughtfully, 'how about *Dark Alliance?*'

'I...I don't know what you're talking about,' she floundered. She could tell by his squint smile that he knew she was lying.

'I'm sure you've come across it, Miss Anson. It's the frankly preposterous tale of how the CIA introduced crack cocaine to LA. No? Then how about *Rogue State?*'

She inhaled sharply. This was her bible, a compendium of all of America's crimes since the Second World War. She swallowed hard. 'Where's this going?' she croaked.

He held his hands up. 'Don't worry, Miss Anson. This is not some sort of trick, and I'm not trying to confuse you,' he said soothingly. 'I'm just wanting to understand why you see yourselves as the good guys, and you see us as the Devil incarnate.'

'And who, exactly, is "us"?'

'You already know the answer, Miss Anson.'

'Agency,' she said flatly.

The man said nothing, but tilted his head to the side as if in acknowledgement.

'So which faction are you? Trump or Deep State?'

He threw his head back and let loose a high, good-natured chuckle. *'Please,'* he scoffed, shaking his head. 'Suffice it to say, and despite the nonsense you've been filling your head with, there are no factions...save the usual office politics you get in any organisation,' he conceded with a shrug. 'But come, tell me, I'm genuinely interested. Why do you think we're so evil?' He leaned forward, rubbing his hands eagerly.

'Because of all the atrocities you've committed in the South,' she said robotically.

'Atrocities?' he smirked. 'Like what?'

His dismissiveness set off the blue touch paper. Her face flushed and she screamed, *'Are you fucking kidding me?! Guatemala, El Salvador, Nicaragua, Chile, Venezuela. I could go on all night!'*

He shook his head and sighed. 'I know all about you, Miss Anson. You're a smart woman. But this? This is just as I feared. You. You and your people. You're living in the realm of the paranoid. Please tell me, Miss Anson, what you think happened in... say... Chile?'

'What I *think* happened? What I *think* happened *did* happen: you overthrew a democratically elected president and installed a fascist dictatorship!'

The man laughed. 'That's certainly one way of putting it – a way of putting it without any context whatsoever – which I suppose is how you and your commie buddies roll. Another way to put it, in its full context, is to say that Salvador Allende was a Marxist who was elected with only 37% of the vote, and he and his controllers in Moscow used that to start setting up a communist dictatorship and enslaving everyone.'

'And Pinochet *didn't* enslave them?'

'No,' he shook his head. 'No he didn't. Apart from the fact that he suspended democracy for a few years while stabilising the country after it nearly fell to socialist tyranny, the people of Chile were free to go about their business.'

'Apart from free to pick the people who governed them.'

He tutted. 'Miss Anson, you're making the mistake of overvaluing democracy. Democracy is, simply put, sometimes not suitable for certain countries in certain situations – situations such as when a critical mass of the voters are of such low education and awareness that they can be tricked by Marxist propaganda into voting for their own enslavement. Pinochet knew that this is what had happened in Chile, and saw it as his job – with the full backing of parliament, I might add – to take control of the country and be steward of it until such time as his people could exercise democracy responsibly again. And then, when he was satisfied that the danger had passed, he freely relinquished control and let democracy be restored. I don't know about you, but I think that sounds like a pretty sensible way to run a country. In fact, your own country – and I'm talking about Britain here – could use a dose of Pinochet itself, as the utter mess your establishment made of Brexit proves that your democracy – indeed, your entire society – is rotten to the core.'

'What…what the hell are you talking about?' she shook her head in bewilderment. 'I couldn't give a shit about Brexit! We're talking about Pinochet. The man *you* sponsored. That *you* invented. The man that murdered thousands of his own people!'

'Two and a half thousand, to be slightly more accurate. But let's not split hairs. Those people – well, most of them, anyway – were the very people who had been trying to put him and his countrymen into chains. Obviously, if you don't think that killing your would-be slavers is justified, you'd think Pinochet was a monster. On the other hand, if you believe in freedom, if you believe that a government which steals the land and property of its people should be stood up to, you might think that what Pinochet did was entirely warranted. You might even think it was a moral imperative. As for me, Miss Anson, I tend to take the latter view, because if anyone tried to steal *my* stuff and enslave *me*, I would kill the son of a bitch.'

This defence of Pinochet – a defence she had never heard before – was like a punch in the face. With her eyes smarting, she blurted, 'You...you're trying to excuse this man?! Are you insane? He was a fascist!'

'Was he, Miss Anson?' he said softly. 'He was certainly an autocrat. But autocracy and fascism ain't the same thing.'

She was about to shout, 'Yes they fucking well are!' But she knew they weren't, and knew that the man would call her out on it. She groped for some other riposte, but found, to her horror, that she knew practically nothing about Pinochet or his ideology; she knew him only as a mythical figure hate. The best she could do was, 'He was still a murderer, and you still funded him. Just as you funded the fascist death squads.'

'Ha! *Death squads*,' he mocked. 'The people we supported were not the jackbooted Gestapo types of your imagination. They were not evil, and they certainly were not fascists. They were simply anti-communists, and mostly peasants, who didn't much care for the idea of having their land stolen and being murdered by Moscow-backed hoods. They were determined to fight to maintain their liberty and their way of life. In short, they were fighting for fundamental American values. Which is why we helped them.'

'But...they were butchers! They murdered millions!'

'No, Miss Anson. They were exactly what they claimed to be: freedom fighters. And most of the atrocities you think they committed? Works of fiction concocted in Moscow.'

'You're lying! You lying piece of shit! I've seen pictures, news reports of what they did! I've seen hundreds of people burning in ditches. Women and children hacked to pieces. That wasn't propaganda!'

'Are you sure about that? Are you *sure* the bodies you saw were killed by the freedom fighters, and not the communists?'

'I…' She had assumed that what she had seen and read was true – that the American-backed 'fascist death squads' had been responsible for countless hideous atrocities throughout South and Central America. But she now realised that there was no way she could be 100% certain that this was the truth. What if the man was right? What if they had been hoaxes designed by the Marxists to garner international sympathy, and get groups like the Contras defunded by Congress – which they eventually were? In fact, if the atrocities were indeed false flags, it was exactly the sort of thing she would have done herself.

But…surely he was lying? Wasn't he? Surely this was just smoke and mirrors as part of the interrogation? She took a deep breath. 'You're just trying to confuse me,' she said. 'It won't work. I *know* the gangs you controlled committed atrocities.'

He nodded. 'They did. I'm not denying that. But the *scale* of what you think they did, simply never happened. And don't think it was all one-sided either: the people we were helping were locked in bitter civil wars with the communists, and there were atrocities on both sides. But, regardless of what they did to each other, the crucial thing you must understand is this: the US government was never, *ever*, the one on the ground pulling the trigger. Not in Nicaragua. Not in El Salvador. Not in Chile. Not now in Venezuela. So those atrocities you've been blaming *us* for – most of which never even happened as you think they did?' He shook his head. 'Not guilty, ma'am.'

'But you armed them!' she whined. 'And you trained them in that dipshit school of yours in Georgia.'

He groaned and rolled his eyes. 'Do you honestly believe that Congress would fund the teaching of terrorism and torture, which is what you conspiracy nuts think goes on there? It's ludicrous. The School does, and has always done, exactly what it purports to: it teaches leaders from the South civics and good governance. We're actually trying to do them a favour, to give them a chance, and what thanks do we get?!' he said exasperatedly. 'Now, it is possible that some of your enemies have been there, and that some of them have been responsible for some unsavoury activities. But I can assure you that we did not teach them their techniques. Think about it: if we were the teachers this stuff, why were our people in Afghanistan and Iraq getting their methods from that TV show *24?* Your belief is just false. Completely and utterly. *Sheesh!* I used to work there, and about the most extreme thing they make the students do is get up at 8 in the morning. I kid you not.'

She felt like she was being whipped. 'So you didn't carry out any atrocities in Vietnam?' she challenged weakly.

'No. Not intentionally, at least. You must understand that, just like the people we helped in South America, we were in a desperate struggle with a bunch of fanatics, who would routinely slaughter whole villages in retaliation for any kindness any of the villagers had shown us. They were savages, and in order to try to beat them – in order to save the locals from them – we had to resort to some pretty extreme measures, like deforestation to strip them of their hiding places. Granted, the chemicals we used look pretty messed up from this vantage point – chemicals which, incidentally, we banned as soon as it became known they harmed humans – but it was absolutely necessary in the context of what was happening at the time: the context of trying to save the South Vietnamese we were pledged to defend; and to ultimately hold back an evil ideology which had already enslaved hundreds of millions of people from the South China Sea to the Baltic, and was intent on enslaving everybody else. Make no mistake, Miss Anson: unlike the people of Chile under Pinochet, the people living under communism had no freedom at all. No freedom of speech, freedom of assembly, freedom to watch the TV shows or listen to the music they wanted, or freedom to even leave their countries. They weren't even able to buy food that their overlords hadn't chosen for them beforehand.

They were slaves, period, and we were trying to stop the spread of that slavery. And if you think that that ideal was nonsense or somehow evil, you need only look at what happened when Congress voted to defund our involvement in Vietnam: the South went to the wall almost immediately, and tens of thousands of its civilians were put to death. And by pulling out of Vietnam we opened the door for the communists to take over Cambodia – who then slaughtered everyone they believed to be anti-communist – which, in their view, was anyone who could count to ten. That is what happened when we pulled out of an area, and that is what would have happened everywhere else had we and the people we supported not been actively fighting against it. I know this is an inconvenient truth for people like you, who have this romanticised view of communism and don't care for history. But I can assure you,' he said earnestly, 'that that is what happened. That *that* is the reality.'

'But…Iraq had nothing to do with communism, and you trashed the place!'

'Yes, Iraq turned out to be a blunder of almost biblical proportions. It should never have happened. But I don't think you quite appreciate the climate in America at the time. People were scared. People were angry. And that fear and anger infected, almost inevitably, the decision-makers. They were only human, after all. Yes, it should have been a time for cooler heads to have prevailed, but we were gripped by a kind of collective insanity. And who can blame us? We had been subjected to the biggest terrorist attack in history, and we were out for blood. When looked at in that context, Iraq, and, indeed, the whole of the Middle East, got off easy.'

'3,000 deaths on 9/11 next to the hundreds of thousands who died in Iraq? You call that "easy"?'

'False equivalency, Miss Anson! How many civilians did we actually kill?'

'Um…200,000?' she guessed – low, she thought.

He gave a snort of derision. 'Try a thousandth of that. And, unlike the terrorists, we did not kill *any* of them intentionally.

'But…'

'But nothing!' he said testily, his friendly demeanour slipping. 'The hundreds of thousands you think we killed? Pure fantasy. They were killed by each other.'

'But it was *your* fault!'

'No!' he cried, shaking his head. 'We got rid of Saddam. But you cannot blame us for the fact that people up and down Iraq hated each other. In fact, the people to blame for that were your lot. If *you* hadn't botched the carve up of the Ottoman Empire, if *you* hadn't gifted the Wahabbists the Arabian Peninsula, none of this would ever have happened!' His face was red and his nostrils flared. He took a deep breath and settled back in his chair and said softly, 'You see, Miss Anson, two can play at that game: Britain is every bit as bad as Al Qaeda and ISIS, because it was your botched imperialism that led to 9/11. It is my view, therefore, that your goddamned sewer of a country, which has been rotted by decades of the most insane cultural Marxism and is led by a bunch of snivelling cowards and traitors, deserves to be wiped off the face of the earth.'

'No. No it doesn't,' she bleated childishly, suddenly thinking about her green and pleasant homeland, and loving it, and feeling deeply protective of it, for the first time. 'We were a force for good! We improved the lives of everyone. Everywhere we got out of got worse. Including here.'

'Ah!' he exclaimed, holding up a finger. 'From *your* point of view, perhaps. But perhaps not from the point of view of, say, the descendants of the American colonists you were trying to screw, or of the Indians and Irish who starved in the famines you presided over.'

'But they weren't our fault!' she protested feebly. 'They were acts of God. Whoever had been in charge wouldn't have been able to do anything about them. I mean, it wasn't as if there was UNICEF or anything back then.'

He nodded vigorously. 'Precisely! Just as most of the things you are accusing *us* of weren't our fault. But can you see your hypocrisy here? You are prepared to look at the British Empire in some context, but not *our* activities. I wonder why that is?'

'Uh…I…I don't know,' she stammered.

'I've got a theory. Want to hear it?'

'No.'

'Well, here goes anyway: it is because, like most extremists, you see evil in everything your supposed enemies do, and therefore refuse to consider for a single second that their motives could be anything other than malign. This allows you to blind yourself to context, and, indeed, reality. It also allows you to excuse or turn a blind eye to any wrongdoing by your own side, thinking it all for the greater good of defeating the primary evil – ie, us.' His eyes narrowed. 'Although I am quite surprised to hear you defending the British Empire? I thought you Marxists hated it?'

'I…' She couldn't think.

'Regardless, it's fairly obvious what has been the cause of this cognitive dissonance of yours. You know all that sensationalist bullshit by Chomsky and those other guys OCC forced you to read, and all that fake news they pumped you with? It was designed for one purpose and one purpose only: to make you hate us; to make you hate us so blindly that you would do anything OCC told you without question and without hesitation. Simply put, Miss Anson, they've brainwashed you.'

'No!' she mewled. 'They're my friends!'

He smiled sadly and shook his head. 'No, Miss Anson. They're not your friends. In fact, they're very much the opposite.'

7. The Black Pill

He gave a nod, and the woman appeared and handed him an A5 notebook. 'Please understand, Miss Anson. I am not trying to humiliate you. All I want to do is show you the truth. There are some things about your activities that you must know.' He produced a silver pen from the inside pocket of his jacket and flipped the cover. The first page was covered in handwriting. He ran the pen over the first few lines.

'Hit number one,' he declared. 'A year after you were hired. Señor Gallego in Nicaragua. A freedom fighter. Or Contra, as they were defamed. He had been carrying out operations against his government, apparently. Two shots. One to the back of the head; one to the heart, just to be sure. Although it might have been the other way around?' He arced an eyebrow at her. Gallego and his small band of thugs had been blowing up bridges and railway lines in order to try to destabilise the Ortega government. She and Pascal, her babysitter from HQ, had infiltrated the group's camp in the dead of night and taken him out. They were a ragbag malnourished bunch, who were trying to relive the glory days of the 80s, and she rather regretted killing him – and certainly in the cowardly manner in which she had done it: while he was sleeping. But at least he had died in his sleep, which was more than could be said for the people he had (at least according to OCC) massacred when he ran with the Contras. So he deserved it. Possibly. She said none of this to the man, and just stared blankly at him.

'Hit number two. Señor Tarantini. One-time Salvadoran military.' Tarantini had, from his home in Belize, been whipping up via social media a sizeable following of dispossessed fascists, and had been conducting them, from the comfort and apparent safety of his home, in a never-ending stream of protest against the socialist government back home. These protests had been turning increasingly ugly, culminating in a car bombing in Izalco, killing 20. Until now, she had felt less guilty about him: the car bombing aside, he had been a major in the Salvadoran army during the civil war, and had, like Carranza, been leader of one of the death squads...although what the truth of this was, she now wasn't sure. 'Double tap to the back of the head in his bedroom in Belmopan,' reported the man.

'Then,' he continued, 'Señors Aquino and Ozorto in Miami.' He tutted and shook his head. 'These two fine upstanding members of their local community were American citizens.' They were also, or so she had been told, members of the anti-Castro Commandos F4 who had been running sabotage raids along the Cuban coast for years. 'Interestingly, you were slightly more inventive here. Señor Aquino met his end stabbed through the chest three times while lying in his bathtub. Señor Ozorto took a crossbow bolt to the throat while walking home with his wife from the cinema. Charming.' He looked up from the notepad, his face set hard. 'Notwithstanding what I said earlier, if we were so minded to prosecute you, for these crimes alone you would certainly be convicted. And, without wishing to pre-empt the justice system, I think it would be a nailed-on certainty that you would be executed.' He looked over her head and said, 'Florida still has the electric chair, doesn't it?'

'Sure does,' said Ray.

The man looked back to her. 'It would be a shame seeing a good-looking lady such as yourself having a date with Old Sparky,' he said, trying not to laugh, 'but justice might have to be served, if only for the families.' Tempany felt ill. He flipped the page and sat back in his chair, casually crossing his legs. 'All that being said, from a certain vantage point – well, certainly from the vantage point of the fantasy world which you and your Marxist buddies inhabit – it could be construed that these people somehow deserved it; that you, Miss Anson, are some sort of Leninist angel of vengeance.' He smirked at the phrase, evidently pleased with himself. His head bobbed to the side and he looked up to the roof. 'Yes,' he said distantly. 'If I were on your team, I suppose I could buy that. In fact, you might even be something of a hero to me.' There was a 'but' coming. Her stomach clenched, and the feeling radiated into her spine and bowels. She felt as if she was about to lose control of her functions. She put her head to the side and retched, but nothing came out but a long streak of saliva, which dribbled onto her t-shirt and down onto the floor.

'Poor Mr Han,' said the man theatrically, shaking his head. 'Shot through the forehead in his hotel room in Seoul. His "crime" was that he had been an agent of yours, but had been doubled. Your job was to take him out before he could blow your networks in East Asia – ha! such as they are!' he sneered. 'The problem is, that simply wasn't true.' He gave her a second for a rejoinder, then continued, 'In reality, Mr Han was not an agent of yours, nor affiliated to you in any way. He was, in actual fact, an executive for SinoComm, and was about to break free of the hive and defect to Uncle Sam. That would have been reason enough for your masters in China to want him dead. But it was what was in here,' he tapped his skull, 'that is, evidence of all of China's intellectual property theft from the US, which made the Chinese want to murder him before we could pick him up. And this is where OCC came in. You see, your Chinese overlords are rather sensitive about bad publicity, and did not want their fingerprints on the murder of Mr Han while he was abroad. So Señora Artemis was contacted by her opposite number, and you were dispatched to murder Mr Han under the auspices of the story you were spun. Alas, Miss Anson, on this occasion you were not so much a Leninist angel of vengeance, more a Leninist patent enforcer.' He laughed, and she could hear the woman and Ray titter behind her.

Her mouth dangled open. Somewhere in the maelstrom that was buffeting her brain, she realised that he had stitched her up like a kipper: he had undermined her core beliefs, then led her to this point, this sucker punch to the guts. Almost as if she physically felt it, her body flopped forward as far as it would go and she wheezed loudly. The pain in her shoulders and wrists was excruciating, and she slowly, reluctantly, sat back up to face the onslaught.

He turned the page. 'And then, Señor Raoul,' he said. His eyes, now cold, were fixed on her and not the notebook. 'You were told that he was a drug kingpin who was using his profits to fund fascist activity to undermine the government of Venezuela. The first part was true. But the *real* reason you killed him was because he was running the drugs ring on behalf of *your own people*, and had been skimming from the millions of dollars of profits he was supposed to be handing over. This was a big issue for your government, which, as you know, is desperate for foreign currency. So he had to be made an example of. Señor Raoul was therefore taken out, by you, and another man put in his place – a man who is, for the time being, completely loyal to Caracas, and is handing over all the money he is supposed to. So you see, Miss Anson, you have actually been a facilitator in the trade of hard narcotics into the United States. I don't need to tell you how seriously my government takes such matters.'

'This…this can't be true,' she whispered.

'Oh, it's true all right,' he nodded. 'And then,' he said, 'the *pièce de résistance* of your life of crime. Last year you killed a man in Dodoma...well, "killed" is perhaps too kind a way of putting it: garrotted with a length of piano wire would be more accurate. And "boy" would be more accurate than "man". You were told that this boy was an ISIS terrorist who was planning an assault on Caracas in retaliation for your government's proposed banning of Islamic dress. You and your bloodhound, Miss Spendlove – you and your whacky names! – had tracked him from Paris through Africa and finally to Dodoma. Where you murdered him. Then you had yourself a nice holiday on the beach. Good for you. You deserved it given the amount of blood that was drenching your hands.

'However, there was a slight problem with the story you were told. It turns out that Mr Jebreen wasn't an ISIS terrorist at all. He was, in fact, just a normal kid who had been to university in Paris to try to become a doctor so that he could help his people back home. His "crime"? He had slept with the daughter of Señor Busquez of your foreign ministry, who, it rather goes without saying, doesn't like Muslims much. The job, Miss Anson, was nothing more than an honour killing.' He closed the notebook, handed it back to the woman, and folded his arms.

Tempany stared at him open-mouthed. Then she hung her head and started to weep.

'Miss Anson, these "friends" of yours are no such thing. They've used you for their own evil ends, and in so doing they've turned you from being a noble crusader for the people of the South, into a common thug who has murdered at least two innocent people.' He took a handkerchief from his breast pocket and gently dabbed her eyes. The gesture made her feel, probably as calculated, even worse. 'Don't blame yourself, Miss Anson. Please, don't. The people to blame here are your bosses. The sheer immorality of Marxism has turned them into monsters who think nothing of making you commit appalling crimes on their behalf. Mr Han and the boy? They're irrelevant to them; collateral damage which they couldn't give a shit about. Just as they couldn't give a shit about *you*.' He sighed. 'Miss Anson, please forgive me, but I'm angry. I'm angry on your behalf. I can't believe what they've done to you. At how they've brainwashed you and used you. *Jesus!'* he barked, his face reddening beneath his tan. 'If I were your father and saw you right now, saw what they'd done to my little girl, I'd be fucking homicidal. I would be on the first plane to Caracas and I would kill as many of the bastards as I could lay my fucking hands on.'

A grey haze seemed to descend upon her eyes, and she felt her body go limp. She felt she was about to pass out...she *wanted* to pass out...

Whether she did or not she wasn't entirely sure, but some time later she felt again the sting of smelling salts in her nose and eyes. She spluttered and groaned, and when her eyes cleared they found that the man was still sitting in front of her. His face was lined with concern, and he said, 'I'm sorry. I didn't mean to hurt you. I...maybe I shouldn't have messed around with you first.' His voice was low and halting. 'It was cruel. Would you like a drink, or a cigarette?'

'Yes, please,' she sniffled.

The woman appeared with the bottle and fed her some more water. Then Ray slipped a lit Lucky Strike between her lips. She took three long lungfuls, spat it out on the floor, and said, 'You're a dead man,' without much conviction.

'I'm sorry, Edith. I didn't want any part of this. But I had no choice.'

'There's always a choice, Ray.'

He opened his mouth to say something else, but just shook his head and withdrew.

'Better?' asked the man.

Tempany nodded. 'Could you...please, could you get me out of this chair, sir? I'm hurt. And I...I want to go home,' she whimpered. By 'home' she didn't mean her hotel, or her flat in Caracas. Or even her flat in Soho. She wanted to go home to her parents. She wanted to see them again. She wanted to love them. She wanted to *be* loved by them. She wanted everything to be over. She wanted a bullet from the gun she had left in the hotel. She wanted the cyanide capsule she had left in Caracas.

'Soon. I promise,' he said soothingly. 'And we'll get that nose of yours looked at. You'll be fine. But we must get our business done first. It won't take long.'

He sat forward and said earnestly, 'What I need, Miss Anson, is your help. We want to bring down the fiends who made you do these hideous things. We want to take down Señora Artemis. But most of all, we want what you want: we want to free the people of the South from poverty. If you provide us with intelligence for six months – six months' maximum – we will give you $10 million. After that, we will get you out, and we will give you a guarantee that your former employer will never harm you. Please,' he beseeched. 'Please help us, Tempany.'

Something snapped. Her name. It was impossible. She screamed and thrashed at her bonds. Before the man could lay hands on her, she threw her weight to the side, sending the chair tumbling. Her head smashed off the concrete.

She prayed the blow would kill her.

PART II

8. High Stakes

The dealer turned the final card – 'the river', in poker lingo.

It was the four of diamonds.

It was all she could do to stop herself jumping on the table and screaming. Instead, with a huge effort, Katie Kirkwood managed to maintain the troubled, slightly agitated look she had been deploying ever since she had been dealt her cards.

It looked like being the perfect culmination to a marathon four-hour session – a session which had already seen two big-mouthed Texans wiped out to the tune of around $200,000 each, and two of the remaining six players reduced to pittances. Her target, Esteban Gutiérrez, had amassed the biggest pile of chips; but Katie wasn't far behind, with almost $550,000. About $200,000 behind her was a girl called Felicia, who was to the left of the dealer, and a black guy next to her, Gomez. The game was shaping up to be a showdown between the four of them, and a small crowd had gathered round the table to watch the action.

The game was no-limit Texas hold 'em, with each player being dealt an initial two cards, face down, then having to make the best five-card hand possible in combination with five community cards dealt, incrementally, face up into the middle, with betting after each round of cards dealt. The 'blinds' – the mandatory bets for the first two players to the left of the player with the dealer button – were $1,000 and $2,000, with no limits on bets thereafter.

In this particular hand, Katie, sitting to the right of the dealer at the lozenge-shaped green baize table, was on the button. Once everyone had been dealt their two 'hole' cards, Gutiérrez, after Felicia and Gomez on the blinds, was first up. She bit her fingernails as she watched him. He showed no emotion as he robotically glanced at his cards and called and raised $8,000. There was simply no telling what he had – it could have been a pair of aces or a three high.

Next up was a thin, white guy called Jeff, who was friendly and had chatted easily to her during lulls in play. But now he was down to his last 20,000 and looking glum. He tossed his two cards into the middle in disgust, then said, 'Thanks for the game, folks. But my luck ain't gonna change. I'm done.' He gathered up his remaining chips and slouched off.

Then came Franco, a Latino, who wasn't quite as low as Jeff. He, too, burned his cards, and everyone looked to see if he would follow Jeff's lead. But Franco just smiled and stayed put.

Then it was Katie. If Gutiérrez thought he was good at masking his hand, Katie was fairly adept at it too. But she was far more theatrical about it. She would sometimes appear euphoric and chatty with bad hands, and downcast with good ones. And sometimes she would do the reverse. There was neither rhyme nor reason to it; her mood and betting patterns simply vacillated between hands. It was infantile, to be sure, but it had wrong-footed her opponents all night.

This hand, though, called for a little more thought. According to convention, the cards she was sitting on warranted a re-raise. But she wasn't wanting to frighten the horses. She stared at Gutiérrez, whose jet black eyes stared unblinkingly back. He was a fairly handsome, hard-looking man with dusky skin and a five o'clock shadow. His head was tilted to the side as he weighed her up, a slight smile on his thin lips. She wilted intentionally under his glare, hanging her head and chewing her lip. She lifted her cards under her cupped hand and stared at them for several seconds. Then she pretended to count her stack. At last, she nodded and croaked, 'Call.' As she hesitantly pushed two $5,000 chips into the middle she raised her chin slightly, inviting Gutiérrez to observe as she swallowed.

Both Felicia on the small blind and Gomez called quickly. But neither worried her, yet – calling on the blinds is usually automatic with only a semi-decent hand.

'The flop' – the first three community cards dealt into the middle – produced:

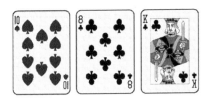

Felicia checked.

Gomez checked.

They obviously had nothing.

Gutiérrez bet $20,000.

The best he could possibly have was three tens. Other than that, if he had a king and a ten or an eight in hand, he would now be sitting on two pair. Or he might have two clubs and be holding out for a flush draw. Or two aces. Or, perhaps, a combination of cards – jack/queen for instance – and be looking for a straight. Or else he was bluffing. She considered the latter unlikely: if he had nothing and was trying to bully the pot and force her out, the bet would have been bigger. Much bigger. He definitely had something, she concluded.

As with the first round she procrastinated, biting her nails, checking her cards, counting her chips, staring at the flop. Then she called.

Both Felicia and Gomez folded.

Then came the penultimate card – 'the turn'. It was the eight of diamonds.

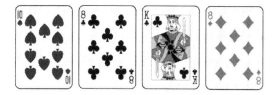

If Gutiérrez was holding a pair of tens, he would now have a full house of three tens with two eights. All well and good, she thought.

His next bet of $50,000 – big, but hardly a confidence wager – seemed to confirm her theory, though there was a slight possibility that he was sitting on four eights, and was not betting bigger in order to try to reel her in. But she considered this highly unlikely: not only were the odds against four of a kind a little under 600:1, there had been absolutely no reaction from him, not even a blink or a widening of his eyes. No. No matter how skilled he was, four of a kind would elicit some sort of response. She was confident he had a full house, at best.

This time, while Katie hesitated, Gutiérrez lifted his wrist to his face and stared at his watch, then tapped it. But impatient he most certainly wasn't: he was smiling and looked confident. He snapped his fingers above his head and ordered bourbon on the rocks. It was only as the drink arrived that, with a nervous smile, Katie called.

The wait for the river was tense, as – if Katie's theory was correct – a ten would have given him four of a kind and spelt disaster. But the four of diamonds that landed was completely harmless, sealing her victory. All that remained was to take him to the cleaners.

He was eyeing her intently while sipping his whiskey. As she had betted conservatively by only calling and never raising, he was probably thinking that she had a pair of aces, at best, which was now backed up by a pair of eights – the Dead Man's Hand. And, in the absence of an ace on the river, he had won. The only consideration now, mirroring hers, was to wring as much money out of her as possible. Bet too much and she would probably fold. So he bet moderately. Or moderately, at least, in terms of the sums Katie was now contemplating. But she made sure to join the other players and now sizeable crowd when they gasped in unison at Gutiérrez's bet of $100,000.

Gotcha! she thought. He had reeled *himself* in, without her having to do anything: he had bet too much now, and would have to chase it to the end. Still, she continued her nervous act, blinking and swallowing hard, staring at her cards, and looking around at the other players as if she were a rabbit caught in headlights. Then, rather than raise, which might have made him smell a rat, and to make it appear that she was trying to buy her way out of the two pair that Colonel Gutiérrez probably thought she had, she mumbled with a breaking voice and with tears in the corners of her eyes, 'All in.'

There was another buzz of excitement as she pushed her stack to Cliff, the dealer. He had flushed a bright pink and sweat was spreading from the armpits of his silk shirt with playing card motifs. He looked anxiously into her eyes, as if to say, 'Don't do it!' But he quickly had his head down and started counting. Eventually, he pushed the pile into the middle and declared, 'Madame calls and raises $357,000.' There were some whistles and a few cries of '*Holy shit!*' Gutiérrez was sneering in triumph. She shrugged helplessly at him and glanced at his pile. Then she hung her head and stared at the back of her cards. The babble had hardly subsided when he declared, 'Call!' He quickly threw in the $357,000, leaving him only a few thousand. Without prompting from the panicked dealer he turned his cards. She felt a jolt of relief that she did not see two eights. 'Sir has a full house, tens full of eights,' the dealer declared as he pushed the two eights and the ten slightly up from the row of community cards.

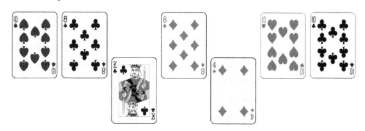

'Well, señorita, let's see 'em,' snarled Gutiérrez, his hands twitching as they readied to grab the mammoth prize.

Katie clapped her hand to her heart. With her mouth gaping she stared at Gutiérrez's ten of hearts and ten of clubs. She looked at Felicia, Gomez, and Franco. They all looked devastated. They had each been willing her to beat the arrogant Latino who had been bullying them all evening. Felicia, a pale, fragile-looking thirtysomething, couldn't return Katie's glance. Katie wanted to smile at her to let her know everything was all right. But that would spoil the main event.

'Madame?' prompted Cliff despondently.

She turned her frown onto Gutiérrez. Then turned the first card. She could almost see the cogs in his brain whirring behind the snake eyes as they scrambled to work out what was happening. Just as the answer hit him, causing his eyes to smart as if he'd been pepper sprayed, she turned the king of hearts, and chuckled softly.

There was a short, stunned silence; then applause. Felicia threw up her hands and squealed with delight. 'No fucking way, man!' laughed Gomez. Franco was shaking his head in disbelief. She felt hands slap her on the back while a dozen shouts of '*Well done!*' rang in her ears.

Gutiérrez fell back in his chair, wheezing loudly.

'Madame,' said Cliff faintly, 'has a full house, kings full of eights.'

Unable to contain herself, she said 'Boom!' smugly, and gave the shell-shocked Gutiérrez a flick of her eyebrows. Then, grinning like a Cheshire cat, she got to her feet and nodded her appreciation to the excited crowd. 'Thank you for the game, ladies and gentlemen,' she said suavely. She smiled at her opponents, save Gutiérrez. They all smiled back warmly, even Franco, whom she had helped almost wipe out. 'I'm afraid I'm going to have to leave you, though. That's about as much excitement as a girl can take for one evening.'

Cliff pushed over the huge pile of chips and plaques. She threw 10,000 back to him. 'Thank you for your service tonight, Cliff. Can you get someone to take this lot to the cage?'

Cliff thanked her breathlessly, then beckoned over two attendants. They scooped the chips into plastic buckets and ferried them to the cage by the entrance. Katie winked at Felicia, who blushed furiously, then followed the money.

The two cashiers counted then re-counted her winnings. It had been a good night. An amazing night, in fact: less the rake and the $10,000 she'd given Cliff, there was $1,029,000 – $829,000 more than she'd gone into battle with all those hours ago. It was about six times more than she had ever won at cards before. She was good, she knew; and Cortez, her controller, knew it, too, hence the reason he had wired her the $200,000 to play with. But Katie was also astute enough to know that to win that amount of money at poker was not a question of skill. It was down to luck: if she had been dealt rotten cards all night, like Jeff and Franco, no amount of bluffing would have got her out of it – she would have lost eventually, and lost the firm's shirt if she had decided to chase it. As it was, Lady Luck had definitely been with her – she couldn't have asked for better cards, and then it was just a question of optimising her bets – which was more, to her, down to common sense and a modicum of amateur dramatics than any particular skill or knowledge of the odds. As such, she was feeling no real euphoria at having won, but more exhaustion, and relief at not having blown the firm's money Le Chiffre-style, especially at a time when the people who were ultimately fronting the cash were, quite literally, starving. Not that losing would have resulted in her being physically harmed, she told herself; but her standing in the organisation would have been shattered, and she would have found herself frozen out...which, when she thought about it, might not have been such a bad thing, given the circumstances. Perhaps she should have let herself lose? She couldn't help but laugh out loud at her train of thought.

Smiling to the cashier, Katie scribbled down the firm's Credit Suisse account in New York and went up the small flight of stairs to the empty bar while they wired it through. She sat on a stool, ordered a Pepsi from the bored-looking barman, and absently stirred the ice and slice of lemon as she pondered her next move. She had succeeded spectacularly in the first stage of her plan (such as it was) for the evening: relieving Gutiérrez of some of the money he had stolen from Guatemala, and at the same time revealing herself to him. But now that she was in a position to tackle the second, worming her way into his confidence – which she reckoned she would now do by offering to buy him some drinks in consolation – she found that her heart wasn't in it. Just as she knew it never would be. She had tailed the man for two weeks now, including breaking in to his apartment and riffling through his stuff, and it was glaringly obvious that he was not planning a *coup d'état* in Guatemala, as OCC had told her. He was, in fact, a drunken, whoring layabout, for whom such a plot seemed to be the furthest thing from his mind – and beyond his means in any event. About the only thing he had going for him was that he was a bit of a card shark, who had been playing on the no-limit table every other night, coming out ahead on four of the five nights she had observed him (the night he lost he was down about 90 grand – a significant hit in itself, but, overall, he was up about 200 – a formidable performance). His poker skills aside, it hadn't taken Katie long to reach the conclusion that he had been denounced by someone with an axe to grind, with the intention of getting OCC to murder him on his or her behalf. This sort of treachery was by no means unusual, and Gutiérrez had many enemies: he had been in Guatemala's last right-wing government, fleeing to the United States when the socialists booted it out. It was money embezzled from Guatemala that Gutiérrez was gambling with and pissing against the wall – which is what had got Katie's goat and made her want to take him on. But the notion that he was hiring a private army of exiled South Americans to overthrow the government back home was ridiculous. She had emailed the gist of this to Cortez three days ago. But Caracas believed in their informant so blindly that her assessment was ignored, and she was ordered to proceed with the mission: infiltrate his inner circle (which essentially consisted of him, she had thought bitterly), and get the names and addresses of his confederates (of which he had none). The future of socialism in the hemisphere was too important to jeopardise for the sake of a hunch, she had been told. She had felt sick to the core when she read this. Not only was it insulting, in demanding that she raise her head above the parapet she would be putting herself in real danger. Not that she minded danger now and again – it was an occupational hazard, even in SdI. But this was pointless. Proving that this man was beaten? That he was killing himself with Scotch? That he was getting his kicks by gambling with the stolen money? Any idiot could have worked that out. She emailed something to this effect in reply, finishing with: 'I've worked for you for four years and have not failed once. And yet you still don't trust my judgement. Tell the boss I'm not happy. I want to come down and see her the moment I'm done here.'

She was now regretting her choice of words. For one, threatening to go over Cortez's head and complain to Artemis directly would turn Cortez against her. Although Cortez had been easy-going up until now and something of a friend and mentor, she knew instinctively that he would make a dangerous enemy. Secondly, Artemis would not be happy that one of her intelligence officers was trying to circumvent the chain of command by turning up at HQ and demanding to see her. She would reprimand either Katie or Cortez, or both. Thirdly, and this was the worst, her message would be interpreted exactly as it was intended when she wrote it: a threat that she would walk. And if she had learned anything about the South Americans, it was that they don't take kindly to threats.

'You idiot,' she grumbled. She shook her head at herself in the mirror behind the bottles of spirits.

Trying to look on the bright side, she thought it possible that Cortez would have just deleted the message, realising it had been sent in a fit of pique, and that he would have a calm chat with her about it the next time they met. Supporting this notion was the fact that, when she had received confirmation from him that the firm would front Katie the $200,000 – Katie's bait of the prospect of clawing back some of the stolen money proving, as she had suspected it would, too strong for them to resist – there was no hint of animosity or recrimination. Plus, the 800 grand profit she'd just turned would surely put her stock back into the credit column. She made a decision: she would email Cortez when she got back to her room, tell him about the evening, and then apologise for the earlier message and ask him to forget about it; for although she was intent on leaving OCC, and had been building up to it for over a year, she would do so in a more friendly, graceful manner, in order that they would have no excuse to put a bullet in her head. That seemed like a good plan. She smiled at herself, then put her head down and took a long pull of Pepsi.

'*Señorita!*' She spluttered and glanced in the mirror. She half expected to see Gutiérrez coming to kill her. But it was Alfonso, her bag carrier from the consulate. He had obviously just got out of bed: his unironed cotton shirt was damp with sweat, and his usually slicked back black hair hung sloppily down his forehead. 'Thank God you're here!' he puffed in Spanish.

Katie quickly remembered herself and turned back to her drink. 'What are you doing here?' she whispered roughly from the corner of her mouth.

He sidled up to her. 'I have a message. Here.'

He slipped her his phone. She put it on her lap, cupped her hand over the screen, opened the solitary message in the open inbox, and typed in her password for the day. When she saw that it was from the boss herself she thought her heart was going to fail – she had seen Katie's message, and was demanding to see her! But no. It was worse. Much worse. She read it three times, then groaned as she looked at herself in the mirror. Her blue eyes were wide and scared and her mouth agape. She seemed to have turned white.

'Are you okay, ma'am?' he whispered.

She shook her head listlessly. What a mess. But she had to move. Even if it meant she was going to her death, she had to move. She narrowed her eyes, nodded at herself, then turned to Alfonso.

'What are your orders?'

'To go with you. On an extraction job.'

'Have you got the car?'

'Yes.'

'How long to get to San Antonio?'

'An hour and a half, maybe.'

It was 30 minutes since the message had been sent; 45 since the beacon had been triggered. It would take half an hour to get her gear. Would she even be alive by the time they got there? Or would they be going to pick up a corpse? She shivered at the thought. 'Are you armed?'

He nodded. 'In the car.'

'How many rounds?'

He shrugged. '20?'

'That'll do. You got a silencer?'

He shook his head.

'We might need to be stealthy about this. Can you lay your hands on one?'

He shrugged. 'I don't know, ma'am. It's late.'

'Try.' She thought for a second. 'And we'll need some things for crowd control. See if you can get some...em...some tear gas. Some pepper spray. And a couple of stun grenades. That kind of thing. I've got to pick up my weapon and the rest of my stuff from the hotel. I'll drive while you make the calls.' She sent a one word message in reply, then deleted both from the phone. 'I'll navigate once we're on our way.' He nodded as she handed the phone back. He was stony-faced as if he, too, realised that they might be going on a suicide mission. She felt sorry for him. He was, after all – on paper, at least – only a cultural attaché, and not really cut out for this sort of thing. Moreover, he had a wife and three children, who, she knew, would be destitute without him. But as much as she wanted to, she couldn't relieve him of his duties. He had signed up for this as much as she had, and if he got killed...well, that would be the luck of the draw. Besides, she was going to need him.

She put her hand on his forearm and smiled sweetly. 'Thank you, Serge. I'll meet you outside in a moment.'

He nodded again and walked out smartly, punching numbers into the phone.

She finished her Pepsi and left a ten on the bar. As she walked back to the cage she could pick out a red-faced Gutiérrez arguing with the dealer at one of the blackjack tables. Two stewards were looming up behind him. This would have been the ideal opportunity to step in and bail him out. And she was now actually wanting to do it, because, as unappealing as her original assignment was, it was infinitely less dangerous than the one she had just been handed. She shook her head grimly, blew him a kiss, and turned to the cage.

9. The Raid

Anson's beacon was triggered 15 minutes ago. It is in San Antonio. Currently moving. Please attempt extraction. If you are in a position to go, text back YES and get moving immediately. Alfonso will go with you. Switch your phone on and we will direct you. This is an emergency. We will fix it.

You are authorised to use any force necessary.

We have sent a local man, Zulu. He is driving a brown Ford Ka, reg. WNZ - 739.

If you cannot go reply NO – we will find another way.

A

Just over two hours later they were touring through an industrial estate on the edge of San Antonio, Alfonso having put the foot down in the big Chevrolet, hardly ever dropping below 100 as they hammered their way up Highway 57 then Interstate 35. Part of her – a base, cowardly part which, mercifully, didn't exert any particular hold over her, otherwise she would have been a blubbering wreck – had hoped that they would be stopped for speeding…although it was probably just as well they weren't, she reflected, as she would have had a difficult time explaining the arsenal they had assembled: the two Berettas with silencers, two M84 stun grenades, a Stun Master stun gun, five rolls of gaffer tape they had picked up from a gas station, and the hunting knife sheathed to her right ankle. They would probably have been shipped straight off to Gitmo, even Alfonso, with any claims of diplomatic immunity thrown back in his face.

As it was, they made it without incident. Indeed, there had been hardly any traffic on the road at all, and the industrial area they were now passing through was quite dead, with no traffic in sight, and all of the shabby warehouses on either side looking abandoned. Despite all of Trump's bombast, Katie thought, this was the reality of 21st Century America: where once there had been life, enterprise, hope, now there was decay and defeat, with all the good, dignified manufacturing jobs having been shipped off to China, and the working classes reduced to service sector serfs. She felt no sense of triumph at this turn of events. In fact, she was somewhat maudlin that Roosevelt's Arsenal of Democracy, which had saved her homeland from the Nazis, had come to this.

The GPS on her phone was reporting that the beacon was in the last building in a row of three industrial units down a cul-de-sac to their right. She told Alfonso to slow down and drive past the junction. The side road was unlit, and she couldn't see as far as the target building. She switched off the phone and told Alfonso to take the next right, which led into another cul-de-sac with three similar units on their right, backing on to the units they had just passed. About half way down, level with the second shed, was the local man's Ford Ka. Alfonso pulled up behind it and killed the engine and headlights. They were still, just, within the light of the street lamps on the main road, and almost immediately they saw a man with a torch emerge from the gap between the second and third units. She snatched her gun from the glove box and jumped out.

The man threw his arms in the air. *'Don't shoot!'* he cried in a strangled whisper.

'Who are you?'

'I'm...em...Mr Zulu.' He was white, short and round, with tousled sandy hair. He was wearing dark overalls, which were unbuttoned down to his chest, with a checked shirt underneath. His face was drenched with sweat. They went through the day's recognition code, then Katie approached and asked quietly, 'What are your orders?'

'To wait for you, unless a realistic opportunity arose to attempt extraction myself.'

'I take it it hasn't?'

He shook his head. 'Not really.'

'Opposition?'

'I'm not sure. A black SUV turned up an hour ago. A man came out of the building and climbed in. Then they all got out and went inside. There were three of them. Then 20 minutes later a black GM van came out with two men in the front. I couldn't tell if our target was in the back. I ran back here to pursue, but the signal stayed put.'

'Any guards outside?'

'No.'

'Wow,' she breathed in amazement. 'The people who went in: all men?'

'I'm not sure,' he shrugged. 'It's dark down there. And I...well, I was trying not to be seen,' he added sheepishly.

Katie thought. There seemed to be no question that Edith had been abducted and that her beacon hadn't gone off accidentally, and that she was still in the building. Who were these new people? Her inquisitors, probably. They would be going to work on her right now, she thought with a shiver.

'Access points?'

'There are two doors at the front – a metal roller-shutter, and a wooden staff door. The roller door can only be opened from the inside. And the wooden one is locked.'

'How do you know?'

'I tried it.'

'What sort of lock is it?'

'Mortice.'

'Is the key in the lock?'

'Yes.'

'Hmm.' She had a picking kit in her bag. But the problem with picking a lock is that it is noisy and time-consuming – it seemed impossible that she would be able to do it without drawing the attention of the people inside. Moreover, she would have to push the key out, which would clang when it hit the floor. She would have to shoot the lock...or, better still, perhaps, simply knock on the door and rush whoever answered it. But either way, the commotion would give the abductors the time to not only kill Edith, if she was still alive, but to ready themselves to kill Katie and her men too.

'Don't worry, ma'am,' grinned Zulu, reading her mind. 'These units,' he said, nodding to the building beside them, 'back on to the one the beacon's in. And at the back of each unit is a toilet window.'

'Is ours open?' she asked hopefully.

'No. But the frame's rotten. It doesn't look like it would be much of a challenge to someone with a knife.'

'Well, that's handy,' she smirked. 'Are you armed?'

He smiled and patted the left side of his overalls. Zulu was acting fearlessly. Alfonso, on the other hand, was clearly scared: he had hardly said a word since they'd left, and had chewed his nails as he drove. He was now breathing loudly close behind her. She decided. 'You got a silencer?' she asked Zulu.

'No.'

'What are you carrying?'

'M&P.'

'Right, swap weapons with Alfonso and take his silencer.'

They obeyed without question, and Katie and Zulu screwed the silencers onto their Berettas. 'Okay gentlemen, here's the plan: Zulu and I will go in through the toilet window. We'll take the grenades. Alfonso, you go round the front with the tape. Zulu, you let Alfonso in once the opposition's been neutralised, then the two of you tie them up. I'll take care of our friend. If she's still alive.'

'Uh...ma'am,' stammered Alfonso, 'what happens if you *don't* neutralise them?'

'Simple: shoot the lock off and rescue us. Or go home. The choice will be yours. Give us five minutes from the time we get into the toilet. If Zulu doesn't come to the door you'll know we've failed. Okay?'

'Yes, ma'am,' he nodded.

'Okay, Zulu?'

'Yes, ma'am.'

'One last thing – we don't want to kill these guys unless we have to. We must assume that they are Agency or Bureau. If we kill them we'd be signing a suicide note – not just for us, but for our entire organisation. Understood?'

They both nodded.

'Let's do this.' She got her backpack from the boot and gave Alfonso the carrier bag with the tape. She had changed into a t-shirt and jeans in the car, and over the t-shirt she now put on a black nylon jacket, which she zipped up to the neck. Then she tied her hair up with a rubber band and pulled on a pair of black leather gloves. Finally she put on her blue baseball cap, and slid her Ray-Bans into the jacket's breast pocket. Zulu buttoned up his overalls and wrapped a scarf over the bottom of his face. She nodded at him to lead the way. 'Quickly now, lads,' she said. Zulu switched on the torch and scampered off through the gap, quickly followed by Katie then Alfonso. They followed the passage for 30 metres until it met a narrow cinder path at the back of the two rows. The building holding Edith was on their left.

'Come down with us,' she whispered to Alonso, 'and give us a hand through. Then get round to the front.'

'Okay,' ma'am,' he whispered.

They hurried on down the gap, until, almost at the end of the building, they came to the toilet window. It was at head height, about three feet square. She would make it through easily enough, but she wasn't sure about Zulu, so she decided to go first. She took her hunting knife from her ankle and went to work on the wood. It was, indeed, rotten from years of neglect. She easily cut a big dent out of the frame just below the latch, then slipped the blade up and pushed up the metal arm. She sheathed the knife, gave the backpack and her gun to Alfonso, and whispered, 'Pass them through once I'm in.' Zulu put the torch between his teeth, linked his hands and offered her a boost. She put her left foot into the cradle, pulled the widow open, and began to wriggle through. The toilet was directly underneath. She put her right hand onto the cistern lid while gripping the disintegrating window frame with her left, and awkwardly manoeuvred her legs through the frame and down onto the toilet seat. As soon as her feet were on it she pulled the backpack and gun through and whispered, 'Take the torch from Zulu and kill it once he's in.' No sooner had she said this than Zulu was handing his gun to her and squeezing through, panting loudly. 'Shh,' she murmured. She guided his hand onto the cistern, got down to the floor, then put her arms up to help take his weight lest he fall. But he managed it, and was soon on the concrete floor beside her. The torch went off, and she heard Alfonso trudging away. She handed Zulu his gun and one of the grenades from the backpack, from which she also took the stun gun, which she put in her back pocket. Taking the other grenade and leaving the backpack on the floor, she whispered in his ear, 'We'll throw them together. I'll count to four. At two, pull the pin, but keep your hand on the safety lever. At four I'll open the door and we'll throw 'em. I'll crouch and throw mine underarm.   You stand and throw yours in over me. Understood?'

'Yes, ma'am.'

'I'll have a look first. If they spot us, leave the grenades, we'll just charge in.'

''Kay.'

She put on her sunglasses, flicked up the safety on the pistol, squatted, and put her left index finger to the door handle...and froze. From the room beyond came a blood-curdling scream, quickly followed by a crash and shouts. With her heart hammering her ribcage, she turned the handle, praying that the door wouldn't creek as she nudged it open. It didn't, and she opened it just wide enough to see two men bent over something, and a woman standing a short distance behind them. Katie shut the door softly, took a deep breath, and started the count. 'One...two...' they pulled the pins out with their teeth in unison 'three...four.' She opened the door halfway, and lobbed hers towards middle of the shed. As the grenade left her hand, the safety lever pinged back, hit her chest, and fell onto the toilet floor with what seemed like an almighty clatter. Zulu threw his at the same time, and she saw it sailing into the air. As she pulled the door shut there were two clangs as the grenades landed. There was a shout from the woman then, BOOM...BOOM.

The air shook, and Katie and Zulu burst in, training their guns through the dense smoke on the three shapes that were swaying around. The woman fell to the ground, clawing at her ears. Katie took off her sunglasses to see through the smoke. It was then that she saw the body shackled to an upended chair. 'On the ground *NOW!*' she screamed at the two men. The one nearest her, wearing an open-necked white shirt, had his hands over his ears and had tears coming from his sightless eyes. She took the butt of her pistol over the crown of his balding head. Blood spurted and he crumpled to the floor. The other man, in a white shirt and black tie, looked equally as shell-shocked, but somehow processed the order.

He staggered forward as if drunk, then collapsed onto his belly, his arms reaching behind his head. 'Go!' she shouted to Zulu. He ran to the door, let in Alfonso, and in a flash they were on the man she had hit, trussing him up and covering his mouth and eyes with the gaffer tape. It was only as they moved on to the second man that Katie lowered her gun and looked slowly, reluctantly, down to the body in the chair, praying it wasn't Anson's. At first she wasn't sure: the hair of the woman on the chair was chopped short and dyed jet black; Edith's had been long and brown and silky. But it was wishful thinking: it was her all right. She looked like she had been in a car crash. Her deathly pale face was clamped to the concrete floor, drool dripping from her mouth. Under her cheek was a pool of blood, which was coming from her nose. Across its bridge was a sodden plaster. Black bruising enveloped her eyes, both of which were shut tight. Blood was splattered over her grey t-shirt. Not a single muscle in her body moved.

She put the gun in her jacket pocket, took off her gloves, and dropped to her knees. She put her hand – which, she noted with amazement, was rock-steady – on Edith's cheek. It was ice cold. A shiver coursed through her body. Edith was dead. Her hand began to tremble, and her fingers could merely fumble at her neck as they tried to find a pulse. Then they moved shakily over her mouth for signs of breath, then down to her cuffed wrists. There was nothing.

She got woozily to her feet. She was vaguely aware that she was sobbing. She took out her gun again and stumbled over to the man she had hit. She put her foot on his spine, and, through swamped eyes, aimed at the back of his head. He started to thrash violently, squeals issuing from his nose.

She pulled the trigger and blew his brains out all over the floor. Almost immediately she felt the body go limp through the sole of her trainer. It was the first person she had ever killed.

'*Ma'am!*' shouted Alfonso.

She went over to the second man, putting her foot on his spine and gun to his head.

There was movement in the corner of her eye. She thought she heard coughing. Had she imagined it?

Then Zulu was next to her, his hand on her arm. 'No, ma'am,' he whispered in her ear.

She turned, dazed, to find Alfonso stooping over Edith, a comforting hand on her shoulder. She was blinking hard and gulping for air. Katie rushed over and fell to her knees, her shaking hand pawing Edith's cheek. 'Oh, Edie, I thought I'd lost you,' she wept.

Edith's eyes met hers. '*You!*'

She took a long, ragged breath to steady herself. 'Me,' she said. She looked up at Zulu and barked, 'Keys!' Zulu rushed to a table by the door, frisked a cream suit jacket on the back of a chair underneath it, and found a bunch of keys. Katie and Alfonso pushed Edith and the chair back onto their feet, and Zulu bounded over and fumbled with the cuffs on her ankles. He quickly found the right key, and the locks clicked open and her feet were free; then her hands, and Edith slumped forward, wheezing like a burst football. She took five rasping breaths, then fell back, her head lolling and eyes smarting. They eventually settled on Katie, and she gasped, 'Jesus, Spendlove. Where the *fuck* did you come from?'

'Oh, I was around,' she giggled. 'Can you walk?'

'I...I'm not sure,' she grimaced. 'Could you give me a hand, darling?'

She let the 'd' word bounce off her and took Edith by the forearms and pulled her up. She tottered momentarily, but Katie held her upright. Gaining her senses, Edith gritted her teeth and pulled her arms away, saying unconvincingly, 'It's all right, Spen. I'm okay.' She rubbed her eyes, exhibiting deep cuts that the cuffs had gouged into her wrists, then surveyed the scene: the bound man and woman, the woman's body shaking as she sobbed; the dead man, his blood and brains splashed on the floor. She slowly moved her head from side to side, then doubled up with her hands on her knees, exhaling loudly as she breathed. 'I can hardly hear a thing,' she mumbled to herself. Then she straightened up and ran her fingers over the side of her head. 'Thank God,' she sighed. 'I haven't split my skull open.' She gave herself a shake, then went to the table, patted down the cream jacket, and pulled out a watch. 'What a cheapskate!' she laughed. 'That bastard' – she pointed at the dead man – 'not only tries to rat me out, but steals my watch as well!' She pressed the two plungers, de-activating the homer, and strapped it on. Then she poured water over her face from a bottle on the table and wiped off the blood and dirt with the jacket, which she tossed disdainfully on the floor. On the back of the chair where the jacket had hung was a red biker jacket. She put it on, pulled out a packet of cigarettes and the Union Jack Zippo Katie had bought her a year ago, and lit up, taking a long first draw, and moaning as she blew out the smoke. She turned to her rescuers, smiling.

It was incredible. Even with the battered face (or maybe because of it) she was still the most beautiful, graceful woman Katie had ever met. She had spent the last year both hating her and trying to forget her. Indeed, if she could have hired a surgeon to have removed the part of her brain which Edith Anson inhabited she would have done so in a heartbeat. But now, the mischievous smile she had hoped she would never see again made the memories of all the pain, all the suffering, vanish. She was back to the moment they first met – Edith Anson, gaily attired in a white summer dress and a straw hat with a red band, a ray of sunshine amid the grime of the Gare du Nord and the gloom of the Parisian spring day. Katie was still, and always had been, always would be, completely and utterly in love with her. She was aware that tears were still spilling down her cheeks. Edith's smile turned tender. 'Thanks for saving me. And you guys.'

'Don't mention it,' said Katie, wiping her face.

The men muttered bashful thanks, and Edith clapped and declared, 'Chop, chop, people. Let's go.'

'Ma'am,' said Alfonso, 'what about...' He nodded down at her blood.

She shrugged. 'My DNA's all over the place. It would take us years to get rid of it. I'm just going to have to take my chances. Besides, they've got my mugshot, so I'm screwed anyway!' she chuckled.

Katie picked up the spent grenades and bullet casing, and the two pins and safety levers from the toilet floor, and put them and her gun and the stun gun into the backpack.

She came back out to find Edith squatting down beside the man with the tie. She ripped off his gag, to which he gave a yelp of pain.

'I'm sorry,' said Edith.

He took a few breaths, then said calmly, 'My colleague? Is she safe?'

The woman, lying close by, squealed. 'As houses,' said Edith. 'I'm afraid, however, that our friend Ray didn't make it.'

'Oh, Jesus,' he groaned.

'There's the matter of the photos you took. It's not good that I'm on your system. How long will they stay on it?'

'Forever.'

'Can they be deleted?'

'Not by us.'

'Then by whom?'

The man didn't reply.

Edith looked up to her rescuers and shrugged. 'Dammit,' she sighed. 'Oh, well, we're just going to have to make the best of this we can. Our business here is done,' she said to the man. 'However, you must understand that we have to be long gone before you report back. So I'm afraid we'll have to relieve you of your phones.' She checked his trouser pockets, then patted down a black dinner jacket on a nearby chair, drawing a blank in both. At the same time, Zulu pulled iPhones from the woman's jacket and the jacket Edith had thrown on the floor, and stamped on them until they were smashed. 'That's all, ma'am,' said Zulu.

'Good,' said Edith. 'I'm going to leave you ungagged, so it shouldn't take you too long to chew your friend out of her restraints. But you're going to have to give us until,' she looked at her watch, 'at least eleven in the morning to get out of here. I'm going to leave a couple of men outside, and if you attempt to leave before then they will be most unhappy. Do I make myself clear?'

'Crystal.'

'Good. There're only nine hours to go. Get some sleep once you've freed yourselves. Then it'll almost be time to go home. It's a small price to pay for staying alive.'

'That's fair,' said the man gratefully. 'Thank you.'

She whispered something in his ear, got to her feet, put on a blue baseball cap that was on the table, and nodded to her team, who filed out ahead of her. She switched off the lights and closed the door behind her.

'What did you say to him?' whispered Katie.

'I told him I was Mossad,' she laughed.

10. Absolution

It didn't take long for Edith to wilt as the adrenalin sapped from her body. By the time they got back to the cars she was leaning heavily on Katie, whose arm was round her shoulder.

Not daring to tempt fate, Katie had given only a fleeting thought as to what they should do if they got her out. She had vaguely figured that they could make a beeline for the border and slip over in the morning. But that was now out of the question: Edith was in no shape to attempt it, either swimming across at Eagle Pass – as Katie herself had done two weeks before – or jumping the fence in New Mexico. They would have to wait two or three days, at least. Or maybe longer until the bruising around Edith's eyes and whatever damage was under the sticking plaster cleared up, as she would stick out like a sore thumb. Whatever the case, Katie was resolved to stay with her, regardless of the danger. 'Zulu,' she said, 'we're going to need a motel. Out of the way. Know anywhere?'

'We'll go to mine,' said Edith groggily.

Katie was sceptical. 'Won't the Feds know you're there?'

'No. And my phone and weapon are there. I have to go back for them.'

'Hmm. Where is it?'

'Marriot River Walk…em…San Antonio.'

'San Antonio? Are you kidding me?! That's miles away.'

'Um...where are we?'

'San Antonio, you idiot!' she laughed, frightening herself by how good it felt to mock and get some measure of retribution on the woman who had jilted her. She gave herself a silent rebuke, cleared her throat, and asked, 'What do you think, gentlemen?'

'It's risky,' said Zulu. 'If they put out an APB it'll be difficult for her to move around. It's probably best to make a run for it now.'

'Alfonso, could you get onto your man, please. Tell him we've achieved extraction, and ask him if he can get word back to HQ that the opposition has photos of the major, and to see if there's anything they can do about it.'

Alfonso took his phone out and retreated a short distance. He spoke quickly, and the call was over in a minute. 'He's on it,' he said.

'Ma'am, I think she needs a doctor,' said Zulu concernedly.

'Well, she's got the next best thing,' Katie smirked. But she immediately realised that her confidence in her own medical skills was entirely misplaced: her training, such as it had been, had completely deserted her ten minutes earlier. How on earth had she missed that Edith was alive, or not paused to give her CPR when she thought she wasn't? She had lost her mind, resulting in the murder of an unarmed prisoner. She could find a scrap of solace in the notion that this was further confirmation, if any more were needed, that she had made the right decision in flunking medicine and going to work for OCC. But that would not bring the dead man back to life. She was both horrified and disgusted with herself. But there was no time to wallow. She was in charge, and her team was waiting with bated breath on her lead. She would punish herself later; and her dubious medical skills would have to do. She turned to Alfonso. 'What do you think?'

'If she lies low for a few days until her wounds have cleared up she won't be so conspicuous. After that, it should be easy to slip out – provided we can get the database fixed. Just put a hat and sunglasses on her, and no one will give her a second glance.'

'Hey! *Her's* standing right here!' said Edith.

'Sorry, ma'am.'

Staying where they were was risky, as Zulu said. But they couldn't possibly leave Edith's phone: if the CIA got hold of it, it would have to be assumed that they would be able to crack its encryption – in which case OCC's entire communications apparatus would be compromised, meaning that their IT systems would have to be overhauled or even replaced, costing a fortune and paralysing their operations for weeks. They certainly had to go the hotel – in which case, she concluded, they would be as well staying there while Edith's wounds healed, rather than drawing attention to themselves by checking out in the middle of the night and checking in elsewhere.

'Okay, yours it is. Have you got a key?'

She patted her back pockets and produced a key card.

'Good,' said Katie. 'Do you know the way, Zulu?'

'Yes, ma'am.'

'Could you take us there, please? Alfonso, you can head back. Try not to get stopped.'

Alfonso said falteringly in Spanish, 'But…I don't want to go.'

Katie nudged Edith onto Zulu and hugged Alfonso. 'I know, Serge. And I don't want you to go either. You were, and I swear this, a hero for coming with me tonight. But, just as you've watched out for me, it's my duty to watch out for Anson.'

'I…'

'Shh. I know,' she whispered in his ear. 'Look, we've been lucky tonight. But hanging around the two of us right now is not safe. Get back to the consulate and report everything to your boss, and tell him to get it passed along the line to mine. I would also suggest throwing your phone into the nearest river, getting the plates on the car changed, and getting out of the country as soon as possible.'

'I...yes,' he said resolutely, pulling out of the clinch. 'Yes, Miss Spendlove. Thank you.' He retrieved Katie's holdall from the Chevrolet and put it into the boot of the Ka. Katie got her phone from the passenger seat, took out the battery and the SIM card, and put them all in the backpack. Alfonso shook hands with Zulu, wished the women good luck, and drove off.

Katie sighed. Alfonso was in love with her. She felt bad because she didn't reciprocate it in any way. He was good-looking enough, for sure. But he was married. And, besides, there was Edith.

'Take off your clothes,' she ordered her. Instead of the cheeky retort she expected, Edith complied meekly, shivering as she stripped down to her underwear. Katie took the cigarettes and lighter and a wad of notes from the jacket and put them in the pockets of another jacket in her holdall. She helped Edith into one of her blouses and a pair of black trousers and shoes, then put her sunglasses and jacket and her red baseball cap on her. 'Good girl,' she said once she was dressed. 'Now, let's get you in the back.' Zulu pulled forward the front seat and Edith clambered in. Katie stuffed Edith's clothes into the backpack, then the gloves, jacket, trousers and trainers she had been wearing, all of which had been sprayed with the man's blood, the jacket and trousers also reeking of cordite. She put on a fresh pair of jeans and her boots and a pullover.

It took just 20 minutes to get there, including a stop for supplies. Zulu dropped them off in a dark spot around the corner from the hotel, undertaking to incinerate the backpack. They said their goodbyes – Edith giving him a lingering hug – then made their way round to the entrance. There was only one receptionist at the desk, who was busying herself at a computer. She paid them no heed, neither did the two well-dressed drunk couples lounging around on the lobby's sofas, nor the security guard standing watching the news on one of the lobby's TVs. They shuffled towards the lift, Katie holding Edith up as if she was drunk, and both of them keeping their heads and their faces out of view of the smoked glass CCTV domes in the ceiling.

As soon as they were in the room, Edith dropped the bag of supplies on the floor and shuffled into the bathroom. She left the door ajar, letting Katie hear the shower being turned on, the toilet flushing, and the shower door opening and closing; then a short time later opening and closing again. Finally the bedraggled and thoroughly miserable-looking Edith shuffled out with a towel wrapped round her. The plaster was gone from her nose, revealing a deep gash. Katie, who had switched on the television and closed the curtains, sat Edith on the sofa. She made her swallow two Advils, then rubbed Neosporin into the weals and cuts on her wrists and ankles (she didn't say anything, but she knew Edith would be scarred for life). She bandaged the wounds, then tended to small cuts on the right-hand side of her face, covering them with strips of medical tape. Then she examined her nose, staring at it from different angles and prodding it. 'Your nose is broken, and it's squint,' she said bluntly.

Edith nodded. 'I tried resetting it this morning. Ray's man must have put it back out when he was tranking me.'

'This happened before tonight?'

'Yep. I, um, got caught up in an armed robbery,' she said with a nervy titter, which made Katie disbelieve her.

'Good grief, what are we going to do with you? Now, I'm going to try to reset it. Believe me, Edith, you want me to do this. Be brave.' Edith gripped the arm of the sofa as Katie gently held her septum between her thumb and forefinger. Then she jerked it to the left. There was a squelch and a crack and Edith gave a shriek of pain. Blood started to spew, and

Katie quickly stuffed cotton wool up each nostril and swabbed up the blood from her face. She then put some Neosporin and a Band-Aid over the cut on the bridge.

'There, there. You'll be as good as new.'

'It doesn't feel like it,' she sobbed nasally.

There was a bottle of Absolut on the counter beside the television. Katie half-filled a cup with it. 'Drink.'

'What have I done to deserve this?' she said. 'I thought you didn't like me drinking?'

'I don't,' she smiled. 'But you've earned it.'

Edith drained it, and sighed, 'Thank God.' Her face seemed to perk up and the light in her eyes switched back on.

'Bed,' ordered Katie. She helped her up and pulled back the sheets. Edith let the towel slip to the floor, and, with zero embarrassment, allowed Katie to take a long look at her body. Katie didn't feel any type of thrill, as she might have done in different circumstances – a thrill that Edith was clearly trying to elicit. All she could feel was grief. Her friend's body, although still limber and desirable, was peppered with bruises. Coupled to the bandages and the tape on her face, and the mystery surgical scars on her abdomen that Katie had quizzed her about last year (she had guessed that it was from keyhole surgery on her spleen, but had been met with silence), she looked broken. She *was* broken.

When there was no sign of her offer being taken up, Edith gave a snort of indignation, climbed into bed, and petulantly pulled the sheets up to her chin. Katie swallowed, kicked off her boots, and lay down facing her on top of the sheets. Propping up her head on her upturned hand, she stared into Edith's bloodshot eyes and said softly, 'Why did you do it, Edie?'

'What?' she asked dumbly.

'Don't,' said Katie sadly. 'I put my life on the line tonight. I murdered somebody. For you.'

Edith frowned, and said nothing.

'This is typical of you. Always thinking of yourself. Well, let me tell you something: you will never, *ever*, hurt me again. I won't allow it. Do you understand me? You're going to tell me, and you're going to tell me now, why you ran off.'

Her eyes began to water and she blinked hard. 'I…oh, Jesus.' She put her arm around Katie and buried her head into her chest. Sobs rippled through her body. 'Oh, Spen. I fucked up so badly. I'm sorry. I'm so sorry. I didn't mean to hurt you, I swear to God.' She looked up, doe-eyed, her lips quivering.

'But why? After you told me you *loved me!*' Her mind zeroed in on the most painful memory of all: on the beach in Zanzibar, Edith declaring that she wasn't going to pack it all in and run away with her after all; that she had been ordered back to HQ for some stupendously important job; that she had to be there by tomorrow. She said goodbye, and marched off. Katie stood there, alone, bawling her eyes out. 'I locked myself in the room for days. Crying whenever I wasn't sleeping. I wanted to kill myself. You owe me an explanation, at the very least.'

'I told you. I was needed.'

'Liar. You'd spent the entire month bitching about how much you hated it. How much you wanted out. And suddenly, when they said jump, you said, "how high".'

'I…I'm not a very safe person to be around. I didn't want you to get hurt.'

'*What?!*' She jumped off the bed, her fists clenching. 'And you think what you did *didn't* hurt? I would rather have been killed than have been treated like that.'

'I'm telling the truth! I couldn't bear the thought of losing you. I wouldn't have been able to live with myself if something happened.'

'So your insane solution was to turn your back on me? To have nothing to do with me?'

She nodded weakly.

'Don't give me that!' she seethed, jabbing a finger at her. 'I know *exactly* what happened. You were depressed when we met. You used me to feel better about yourself. And as soon as you did, you realised that your professed hatred of the job, of our organisation, had merely been a passing fancy, and that actually everything was all sunshine and daffodils. Plus, you were addicted to the thrill of it all. So what you've done, to rationalise this to yourself and justify your treatment of me, to help you sleep at night, is concoct this fable that somehow you were acting for *my* benefit. In *my* best interests. To protect *me!* Yeah, Anson, you're just like the Dalai Lama.'

Edith's sniffling stopped and her jaw tightened. *Uh, oh!* thought Katie. *I've overdone it.*

'You don't have a fucking clue!' she snarled, anger flashing in her eyes. She pushed herself up, and for a split second Katie thought she was going to have to defend herself. But, even though Edith Anson was one of the most dangerous people alive, she was not concerned: Edith was a wreck, and Katie was confident that she could throw her back on the bed and subdue her. As it was, force wasn't necessary: Edith's body froze, then she fell back onto her pillow and wept, 'I'm so sorry, Steph.'

'Oh, no, Edie,' she sighed. She got back on the bed, put her arm around her, and whispered, 'I...I was wanting to hurt you. But...I wasn't really. This has been so hard for me. I...I think I wanted revenge. But I didn't. I'm not making much sense. But believe me, I didn't mean to be so horrible. It was shameful of me.'

Edith stopped crying, dabbed her eyes with the pillow, and turned to face her. 'I deserve it,' she sniffed. 'If I'd realised for a single second that I'd hurt you so much I...I would have made things right, I swear I would.'

'I know,' nodded Katie. 'I know.' She ran her fingers through Edith's messy thatch of dyed black hair and kissed her brow. Her poor, battered, scarred lover. Tears welled in her eyes, and she struggled unsuccessfully to hold them in.

Edith looked her in the eye, took a deep breath, and said, 'Stephanie. Darling. I…I want to tell you…I want to tell you about the scars.'

'Shhh. It doesn't matter, Edie. I don't care.'

'But I do. You asked me where they came from. I wouldn't tell you then. I *couldn't*. But…I want to tell you the truth about why I left you. And the scars? The scars are part of it. Part of this whole mess. You deserve to know. You have a right to.'

Katie thought for a moment. She needed this explanation as much as Edith needed to get it off her chest. She nodded. 'Tell me,' she said softly.

Edith smiled. Katie smiled back. And they kissed. 'Tell me,' repeated Katie.

'This…um…this might take a bit of time.'

'We've got all the time in the world.' Edith, oddly, laughed uproariously at that. Katie smirked, and said, 'Well, at least until the Feds kick the door in.'

Edith smiled crookedly. 'That's about the size of it. Could you get me some water, please?' she croaked.

Katie got up and poured her a glass of water, and Edith put a t-shirt on, stacked two pillows against the headboard, sat herself up against them, and pulled the sheet up to her waist. She drank the water in three gulps. Katie sat down at her feet, cross-legged. Edith grinned, her big pearly teeth cutting through the mess of her face. 'This is just like a sleepover,' she said. Katie laughed, and gave her feet a gentle squeeze of encouragement. Edith's brow furrowed. 'Where do I even start with all this?' she asked helplessly.

'Just take your time, sweetie.'

'You're going to think I'm a total psycho.'

If that was some sort of sick joke, Katie didn't laugh. She just shook her head.

'When I was 14 I got expelled from school in Norwich and packed off by my parents to Scotland…'

'You got expelled?' she asked, more out of politeness than genuine curiosity – the fact that Edith Anson, one of life's rebels, had been expelled from school did not surprise her in the slightest. 'What on earth for?'

'Assaulting the headmaster,' she shrugged.

'Wow. Maybe you *are* a psycho.'

'Maybe. But it wasn't quite as it sounds. I...I was in a fight with some of the other girls, and I felt myself being pulled back. I turned and swung. Problem is, it was the head trying to break it up, and I punched her right in the eye. I was expelled pretty much instantly. My parents...' She sighed. 'My parents hated me, and used it as an excuse to send me to school in Scotland, presumably to get me as far away from them as possible.'

Katie rubbed her shins through the sheet. 'I'm sorry, darling.'

'Don't be,' she said stoutly. 'Anyhow, on my first day there I came across this girl, Rebecca, who was getting the shit bullied out of her in hockey. I got into a fight with the bullies in the changing room afterwards. I...I'm not particularly proud of it.' She cleared her throat and shook her head slightly, as if trying to blot out the memory. 'At any rate, that was me and Rebecca pretty much BFFs from then on. It was...it was rather cynical of me. I befriended her precisely because I knew that she, being the class outcast, would be an easy friend to make.'

'Don't be silly! Making friends with someone? Especially someone who is being bullied? That's not cynical in the slightest. It's actually rather sweet, if not downright heroic! And could you imagine being *her* for a second? She has this...well, *you* showing up and protecting her when no one else would. She probably thought she'd hit the jackpot.'

Edith chuckled morbidly. 'Well, it was a poisoned one. Because, halfway through our third year in uni, I dragged her to a protest against a bunch of Nazis in Hyde Park. There was a riot, and Rebecca was...' She paused and took a wheezing breath through her nose. 'She was murdered. Stabbed right in the heart. And I literally got my head kicked in.'

Katie's mouth opened and she shook her head. 'Oh, Edie. I...' Her voice trailed off.

Tempany's mind bent back to those few catastrophic moments. A Nazi tough masquerading as a steward getting hit on the head with a dart; pulling it out and releasing a jet of blood into the cold February air; ripping off his fluorescent jacket to reveal the traditional neo-Nazi uniform of white polo shirt, faded jeans held up by red braces, scuffed black boots; his gloved hand whipping a butterfly knife from his trousers; hopping over the crush barrier in front of them; lunging at Rebecca; Rebecca gasping and falling to the ground, her lifeless eyes pointing at Tempany; Tempany, standing gawping in terror, then taking a blow to the side of the head. Then falling to the ground; and trying to reach out to Rebecca to revive her, or something. Then the sole of a boot crashing into her face. And then darkness. Then coming round in hospital to the sound of her own screams.

'I woke up in hospital to find that my jaw, nose, and arm had been broken, and my spleen ruptured. That's the scars on my abdomen.'

'I guessed as much,' said Katie gloomily. 'About the scars, I mean.'

Edith nodded. 'Then, as if that wasn't bad enough, the doctor told me Rebecca was dead.' She looked Katie in the eye. 'Those were the worst moments of my life, Steph. I...I hate thinking about them. It's like the worst nightmare you've ever had.'

'Look, Edith, you really don't have to talk about it. It's fine. I don't need to know any more.'

'Well, I'm on a roll now, so what the hell! The police came to question me in hospital. They had rounded up about 20 of the Nazis and were holding them on public order offences, but couldn't charge any of them with the murder as there was no evidence on the knife, and, in amongst all the chaos, no one else had actually seen Rebecca being killed.'

'Had you?' asked Katie hopefully.

She nodded slowly. Her eyes narrowed and her jaw flexed. She no longer looked helpless. She looked mean. 'They had the man in custody. But when they showed me his mugshot something came over me. I decided not to tell them. I knew that if I did he would probably get away with a manslaughter rap and be out in five years. No way, I thought. So I decided to keep my mouth shut and kill the son of a bitch, or die in the attempt. I got his name and address from the court reports, and, long story short, I shot him in the shoulder as he was opening his front door one night. Then I set about him with steel toe-capped boots. I...' she frowned. 'I rather regret that as well. It was unnecessary, and cruel. I snapped most of his front teeth in half, and must have been pretty close to castrating him. I was just...I was scared shitless, and blinded by hate. Then I stabbed him through the heart with a hunting knife, just as he had done to Rebecca. He was dead in seconds.' She paused. There was nothing on her face now. No joy, no grief. Just emptiness. She looked at Katie and moped, 'I told you you'd think I'm a psycho.'

'No,' she shook her head. 'Absolutely not. Would I have done what you did? Probably not. But that's not because I'm morally superior to you or anything. It's because I simply wouldn't have had the courage. And besides, you don't appear to be particularly pleased about it. If you were truly psychopathic, you simply wouldn't care about causing him suffering, or would even be celebrating it.'

'Perhaps you're right. But there's a kicker. I decided to take out the Nazi mob's leader as well, a guy called John Barrett – ever hear of him?' Katie shook her head. 'He'd incited the riot. So I shot him through the head when he was getting out of his car in Manchester.'

Katie stared at her for a few beats. 'Honestly?' she asked, incredulously.

'Honestly.'

'How…how could you have done all this?'

She gave a dismissive shrug. 'It was easy enough. I bought the weapons off a guy in London for five grand. And I already had a fair idea how to use them: I got into shooting when I was in Scotland, and ended up getting quite decent. So decent, in fact – and one doesn't want to brag,' she grinned, 'I was asked to try out for Scotland's Commonwealth Games team.' She threw her head back and chortled.

'I take it from your hilarity that you didn't?'

'Of course not! I'm shy,' she said unconvincingly. 'Besides, I'm English! Why the hell would I want to shoot for Scotland?'

They both laughed, and Katie moved over to sit next to her. She kissed her on the cheek and said, 'Has anyone ever told you you're pretty funny?'

'Rebecca thought so. But my last dipshit boyfriend didn't. Kept telling me I was a manic depressive and should pull myself together.'

'That's horrid!' cried Katie, feeling a twinge of jealousy.

'I don't know. Maybe I was. Or maybe it was his way of trying to control me.'

'Sounds like a right piece of work. I hope you've got him out of the picture,' she said, her voice slightly thicker than intended.

She shook her head. 'Nothing to fear there, Steph. He was sleeping with sluts behind my back. Everyone knew about it and was telling me to ditch him, but I was in denial. *Idiot!*' she scolded herself. 'I turned up at a party one night, and here he was, sitting in the living room tonguing some skank's throat. I freaked out and started screaming at him in front of everyone, and threatened to cut his balls off. And that was the end of that.' Again they both laughed, Katie out of relief that the man had been binned.

'So,' continued Edith blithely, 'I killed the man Barrett. But the rifle did its job a little too well, and caused the other thing I feel guilty about: his girlfriend was getting out of the other side of the car when I hit him, and got splattered. You ever seen *Carrie?*'

'The original or the Julianne Moore remake?'

'Ha! The original. The girl was looking like Sissy Spacek at the end. It was horrific. You should have seen her, Spen. She was screaming her head off. Worst of all, I read later that the bullet went clean through Barrett's head, hit the top of the car, and lodged itself in the building behind her, missing her by inches. If it had hit her I would have been forced to turn the gun on myself. In fact, I would have done it right there and then. I...I've often wondered about sending her some money to help alleviate the trauma – as well as my guilt. But I've always come to the conclusion that that'd be crazy.'

'It certainly would be. I take it, since you're here, that the police never caught up with you?'

'They did, kind of. They came and questioned me about a month after all this went down, but I managed to put them off the scent by breaking down and crying about Rebecca. Not very noble, I know, but it did the trick. Besides, I was confident they had nothing on me other than motive, as I had gone north in a pretty decent disguise, paid everything in cash, and had burned all my clothes and dumped the weapons.' She shook her head. 'Alas, Steph, I wasn't quite as smart as I thought I'd been. About two weeks after that, I got a knock on the door from this guy calling himself Magellan – have you come across him?' Katie shook her head. 'He's one of the firm's talent spotters. It turned out that Barrett had beaten up a Brazilian guy in London a few months earlier and paralysed him. The police didn't do anything, and his family was out for blood. They went to their government, who in turn went to OCC, who sent a hit squad to take him out...which, luckily or unluckily for me, just happened to be on the scene when I pulled the trigger.'

'Wow,' breathed Katie.

'My thoughts exactly,' nodded Edith. 'Not that they saw me take the shot, but I'd made a couple of basic errors that made them latch onto me. Error number one was that I walked past the scene, took one glance at my handiwork, then walked straight back to my hotel. What was wrong with that?'

Katie thought. 'Um…it was such an unusual thing in Britain that any normal, curious person would have stopped to look and see the commotion. And phoned an ambulance, or something.'

'Bingo! By the time I got there – about five minutes after I took the shot – there were about a hundred people gathered round, filming with their mobiles. A few were comforting the girl. And the only person not to loiter or even appear particularly perturbed?'

'You.'

'*Moi.* What an idiot! Then, as if that hadn't put a big enough target on my back, as part of my disguise I had poured water over my hair and had the rifle folded up into a holdall to make it look like I'd been to the gym. But the bag was too weighed down to have been gym kit. In fact, it looked – and was – seriously heavy. So when they saw this woman take hardly any interest in the scene, and carrying a bag that looked like it had a few bricks in it, they suspected that I was the shooter, and put a tail on me to find out who the hell I was. They followed me all the way home, and saw me burning my clothes in a wood north of Rugby, throwing my guns into the Cherwell, and emerging from my flat in Oxford the next day with no glasses and short brown hair instead of long blonde, which I'd had the day before.'

'I'd quite like to see you as a blonde.'

'Well, it was certainly better than this,' she giggled, pointing at her hair. 'So, Magellan showed up once he knew I was off the police's radar, told me he knew what I'd done and that he was impressed, and asked me to join OCC as a field agent. As I had nothing better to do I agreed pretty much immediately. And so here I am, five years later, smashed to bits, again, and people trying to kill me, again. Doesn't seem like much has changed,' she laughed.

Katie was sceptical about all of this, reminding herself that a central part of their job was the spinning of falsehoods to cover their tracks; whilst at the same time assuming that anyone they came into contact with would be equally as mendacious. Moreover, Katie had heard nothing about the events Edith had spoken of, and she reckoned that, unless they had happened on particularly busy news days, they would have merited at least a passing mention in the papers. Most suspiciously of all, she had never even heard of 'John Barrett' or his group.

On the other hand, and notwithstanding the apparent lack of press coverage, the slaying of Edith's friend and the subsequent assassinations could be verified in seconds, making it unlikely that she was making it up.

Then there was the clincher: the details of the story were just too precise to be some sort of cover. Barrett's girlfriend covered in blood; Rebecca stabbed through the heart; Edith being asked to shoot for Scotland. There didn't seem any chance that she was lying – or, if she was, she was one of the greatest actresses to ever live...or a schizophrenic – which, although she was clearly disturbed and probably suffering from PTSD, Katie doubted.

Katie smiled tenderly and engaged her eyes. 'You do realise that I could find out everything about you in about ten seconds with all this?'

'I know,' she nodded. 'You're the first person I've ever told this to. The boss knows bits. Magellan knows bits. No one knows it all.'

Katie reached down for her hand and squeezed it. 'I'm honoured,' she whispered.

'There's one more thing, Steph. The whole reason I've told you this. And this is the truth. I...I was slightly liberal about why I took off. I *was* scared for you. I didn't, and don't, want to happen to you what happened to Bex. But...but I could have lived with that danger...not least because you're far tougher than she was,' she smiled weakly. 'But the night before I left you, I closed my eyes, and for the first time since she died, I couldn't see her. I couldn't even remember what she looked like. All I could see was you. It terrified me. I don't want to forget her. She was my everything. She was the only reason I carried on. The only reason I fought. I thought that, without the memory of her, I would be nothing. Nothing, Spendlove. So when...when I felt I was replacing her with you, it was as if I was betraying her. My dear dead friend. The friend I got murdered. I felt ashamed. And scared. So I ran.'

'You should have trusted me.'

'I know. In fact, I think I knew it the very second I turned my back on you. I was just so confused.'

'And you're not any longer?'

'I...I don't think so. I realise now that Bex is dead, and that no amount of hurt I inflict on myself, and others, including you, is going to atone for not being able to save her. Nor is it going to bring her back. I don't want to forget about her. God knows, I don't. But it's history now. Ancient history. And you're alive. She isn't.'

'You two, were you...?'

'What?'

'Um...you know.'

Edith's eyes narrowed; then her head snapped back, shock writ large on her gaping face. It was immediately apparent that the notion had never even occurred to her. 'No. No, of course not! She was my best friend. Just as you are. In fact,' she said glumly, 'you're my only friend. But...' She bit her lip. Katie knew what she was thinking, because it was exactly what she was thinking herself: that she wasn't really gay; that she wasn't attracted to women. Just *a* woman. Thus it was difficult to express exactly what she was. What *they* were.

'It's…it's different with you. You're…I don't know. You know the score.'

'I'll take that as a compliment, I think,' she giggled. 'And I'm sorry for asking. It was tactless and inappropriate. I'm just…well…this is rather a lot to take in.'

'You've got nothing to apologise for, Steph. Nothing. As for me, I deserve to be strung up for what I did to you.'

'No arguments here.'

Edith kissed her hand. 'Oh, Stephanie, can you ever forgive me?'

She breathed deeply. 'Honestly, I don't know. The way you treated me was despicable.'

'I know. And I'm sorry. But…' She pressed her lips together and stared into Katie's eyes. 'Steph, I've missed you every single day. It's made me miserable. And I'm so desperately lonely. And I'm…' She nodded down at her body. 'Look at the fucking state of me! I'm a wreck. I'm a borderline alcoholic, I smoke over 20 a day, and my body doesn't feel as if it's going to make it past the next 30 hours, let alone my 30th birthday. I don't want to die. I need you, Steph. I need you to take care of me,' she pleaded.

Katie recoiled. Being with her was one thing; having to nursemaid her, in her obviously parlous mental state, was something else entirely. For a start, there was the responsibility of it. Secondly, it would make it far more difficult to leave her in the event that things got too much, or, more mundanely, that they got on each other's nerves. She decided to throw down a marker. 'What if we don't get on?'

'I guess we'll just have to try it and see. If you'll have me, that is,' she added pathetically.

She smiled. 'You don't have any disgusting habits do you, like leaving your underwear lying around or stacking the sink full of dirty dishes?'

Edith laughed and shook her head. 'No on both counts. Although I do bite my toenails.'

'Eww, gross!'

'Only joking. Steph, I think you'll find I'm pretty well housetrained.'

'We'll see,' she snorted. She looked into the beseeching trauma of her eyes, and knew there could only ever be one answer. She decisively snuffed out the flicker of doubt and fear, leaned forward and kissed her gently on the lips. 'Okay, Edith: in the event that we get out of here in one piece, I'm in. If you'll have me,' she added magnanimously.

Edith grinned and hugged her tight. 'Of course I'll have you, darling. Of course I will.'

'But there are a few conditions.'

'Anything.'

'You never, ever pull a stunt like that again.'

She shook her head vigorously. 'I won't.'

'And you'll talk to me when things are troubling you. When *anything's* troubling you. We'll be honest with each other. We'll conduct ourselves like adults.'

'I promise.'

'Now, this is important, Edith: if you're intent on shaping up and are wanting my help, you will have to do what I say, when I say it.'

'Um…like what?'

'If you are struggling with anything – quitting drinking, smoking, depression, anything – if and when I say so, we will seek professional help.'

She looked aghast. 'I…I thought you could do it?'

'No, Anson,' she shook her head. 'I am not a professional, as I think I amply demonstrated tonight. You need to tell me that you will be prepared to do whatever it takes and whatever I tell you, otherwise you're on your own.'

She smiled salaciously. 'Oh, my, lieutenant. I had no idea you could be so domineering. I kind of like it.'

'You're not going to kid your way out of this. You need to swear, right now, that you'll do what I say.'

Her look turned serious and she nodded. 'Okay, Steph. I swear. I swear to God.'

'Good. But first things first: as soon as we're out of here, we're going to execute PST.' The childishly named 'Plan Stone Town' was the scheme they had concocted whilst lounging around in Zanzibar: they were going to get fake passports from a contact of Katie's in Mexico, and go back to HQ and resign. Assuming that they made it out of Caracas alive, they would buy a house somewhere in the north of Scotland – the perfect place, Edith claimed, to lie low – and live there under assumed identities for a couple of years until the heat was off. Then they would travel the world, frittering away their wealth. After that, who knew? Who cared?

Edith smiled. 'Yes,' she nodded.

Katie climbed off the bed.

'Where are you going?' cried Edith.

'I'm going nowhere.' She pulled the rubber band from her hair and started to undress.

11. Guilt

Christina Ortiz, head of OCC, took a last drag of her cigarette. It was down to the filter and burned her lips. She pinged it onto the grass, its embers hissing to death in the early morning dew. She immediately lit another and continued her pacing back and forth across the lawn. Light from the kitchen illuminated her as she walked, making her feel naked under the gaze of the silent, motionless Jorge, one of her two security men, who was observing her through the window. She realised that she was acting out of the ordinary – outside at five in the morning, smoking furiously, and appearing, she knew, decidedly edgy. Would Jorge report this to the Minister? She could easily explain her behaviour – she was simply worried, she would say, about her two girls, even though they were now, apparently, tucked up safe in their hotel. But, still, her behaviour would look highly incriminating if anyone thought that she could have been in any way involved in Anson's abduction.

For the hundredth time she ran down the list of the people who could, conceivably, jump to such a conclusion.

She dismissed Anson out of hand. Like the rest of her field agents, she had low cunning, to be sure; but she also had tunnel vision and an incurious, malleable mind, and would therefore believe that it had been Ray, and Ray alone.

Then there was Spendlove. Spendlove probably had the keenest mind in the service, which made her dangerous, and made Christina afraid of her – hence she had her running around chasing scraps, to get her as far away from her as possible. It was precisely because of this precaution that Spendlove could be discounted: she hadn't been in HQ for two years, and knew too little about the other operations to make it feasible that she could imagine that Christina had been behind it.

Then Raphael, her number two. But Raphael was as loyal and obedient as a puppy. It would never enter his wildest dreams that Christina might have been involved.

Lastly, she thought of the Minister himself. Now, *he* was distrusting and saw conspiracies and shadows everywhere; but, as there was simply no evidence of any wrongdoing or negligence on her part, and there was no one who would report any such suspicions to him and stoke his paranoia in the first place, he, too would surely believe that the blame lay solely with Ray.

She stopped her pacing and glanced up at the window. She couldn't see Jorge's face as the light was to the back of him, but his figure was just as it had been the last time she looked: dark, unmoving, obelisk-like. It was unnerving. She took a deep breath, plastered on a smile, and beckoned him to join her. The figure reacted slowly as if from slumber, and trudged its way out.

'Jorge,' she said as lightly as she could between pulls on her cigarette, 'why don't you go next door and have a rest. Help yourself to a drink if you like. You must be tired.'

'No thank you, ma'am,' he said in a monotone. 'Can I get you anything?'

'Could you put some coffee on, please? It doesn't look like I'll be getting any sleep tonight,' she added clumsily in explanation. She instantly realised that this, too, was out of character – she never explained herself to her subordinates; to do so now made it look like she had a big guilty sign around her neck.

But if Jorge suspected anything he gave no indication. 'Certainly, ma'am,' he said impassively. 'Will there be anything else?'

'No thank you.'

Jorge shuffled back in, and the light on the lawn flickered as he made his way around the kitchen. Christina threw down her cigarette and lit another. She was surely in the clear, she tried to convince herself: Spendlove had succeeded, after all, and so, by extension, had she. Thus, regardless of what happened to Anson and Spendlove now, she, Christina, would appear completely blameless.

She gazed up at the stars, the black eastern sky above the house beginning to melt into a navy blue as day dawned. If she could make it through the next twelve hours, she thought, she would survive. She just had to act normally – businesslike, unemotional – and calmly talk her way out of it if interrogated by the Minister. As for her covert activities? It was her instinct that they were done, at least for the time being – there was too much heat on her now, and one more misstep would mean her downfall. She was perhaps doomed already. Only time would tell.

She made a decision: if things got too hot – either today, or, in fact, ever – she would skip the country at once.

If, or when, it came to that, what, she wondered, would she tell Guillermo, her husband, who was upstairs sleeping? She loved him dearly and didn't want to leave him. But she loved herself more, and knew that, far from wanting to come with her, he would probably turn her in or kill her himself if she divulged her plans. She would tell him nothing, and would leave without a word, she resolved coldly.

She took a long pull on her cigarette and filled her lungs. 'Be calm,' she whispered as she exhaled. The Director would tell her what to do. She would be up soon, and would respond to the running commentary she had sent her during the night.

She would get out of this, she told herself resolutely. She threw down her cigarette and marched back in to check her messages.

12. Breakfast For Two

Katie woke to find herself just as she had fallen asleep – wrapped in Edith's strong arms and legs, breathing her air. The room was still dark, but Edith's eyes glinted back at her through the gloom.

'What time is it?' whispered Katie.

'Ten.'

'How are you feeling?'

'Sore.'

Her body jolted. 'Oh, no! I didn't hurt you?'

Edith chuckled. 'Of course you didn't. You were...' she paused. 'You were, and are, utterly spectacular.'

She hissed a sigh of relief through chattering teeth.

'No, *that* bit of me's fine. But it's about the only bit. My mouth, my head, my arms, my legs are killing me. I feel like I'm about to fall apart.'

Katie breathed deeply. The mere notion that she might have hurt Edith was terrifying. But as the fog lifted from her mind, she realised with certainty that she had been very, very gentle, just as Edith had been with her – far gentler than they had been with each other the previous year. She smiled, feeling slightly euphoric, and ran her fingers through her hair. 'Okay then, sweetie, let's get you fixed up.' She jumped out of bed, switched on the light, pulled on her jeans and jersey, and sat Edith up on the side of the bed. She fed her another two Advils, inspected her nose, then gently peeled off the bandages on her wrists and ankles. She sucked her teeth thoughtfully. 'No sign of infection,' she said brightly. 'I think you might just pull through.'

'Scarred for life though,' said Edith, reading her mind.

Katie swallowed and looked into her eyes. They were still circled with black, the edges of which were turning yellow. But the redness of the eyes themselves was dissipating somewhat, and the blue of the pupils was brighter. She engaged them, and said as clearly as she could, 'Yes. But you can get skin grafts.'

'Fuck that!' she smirked. 'I'm not getting a bit cut off my bum to cover my wrists!'

'Fair enough. But it won't be too bad anyway,' she said encouragingly. She took each hand and pointed to where the cuts were deepest, which were at the bone on the outer side of each wrist. 'You'll probably end up with white patches here, but they shouldn't be too noticeable.'

'I can live with that,' she said doughtily.

'I know you can, sweetheart. Now, run along and take a shower. I'll order up some breakfast. What do you want?'

'Your discretion,' she shrugged.

'Okay, leave it to me.'

Katie phoned down for some food then busied herself around the room, hanging their clothes and putting their underwear in the bedside cabinets, then called up room service to take their laundry. She took the gun and box of ammunition from Edith's holdall and put them in one of the carrier bags which had contained some of Edith's clothes. Also in the holdall was a thick roll of hundred dollar bills, which she left. She then opened the curtains and the balcony door to let in some air. It was bright and warm, the sky cloudless. They were in the heart of the city, the traffic busy on the road below. The buildings ahead were all four or five storeys and commanded views of their room, and each could, conceivably, be used by the Feds to observe them. But it was improbable that they would go to such lengths, she thought – if they knew where they were they would simply kick the door in and ship them off to Guantanamo Bay. She leaned over the side and stared down at the street below, and wondered why she was so unafraid at the prospect. Had her soaring confidence after rescuing Edith and burying the hatchet with her tipped her into arrogance, making her believe that she was now invincible and too good to get caught? No, she concluded. Her mind was lucid and she was seeing the situation as clear as the sky above. Getting apprehended had been, and remained, a very distinct possibility as long as she remained with her. Her complete lack of fear, she knew, came from the fact that she was resolved to share Edith's fate, whatever that might be. Besides – and she realised, with a grin, that this *was* arrogance – she was confident that she would be able to talk her way out of anything; not least because she was prepared to sell Cortez and OCC down the river. She would do so without any hesitation. In fact she knew, with something approaching glee, that what she had in her head might be enough to save both of them.

She went back in and strapped on her plastic blue Timex. It was 10.30. 30 minutes to go before their captives let themselves go – that is, if they were brainless enough to have believed Edith's story about leaving guards outside and had not released themselves long before now and raised the alarm. If they *had* let themselves go immediately, it had to be regarded as a plus, as heavy boots had not yet come storming down the corridor. On the other hand, if they *hadn't* released themselves, that meant that they had probably believed Edith, and, that being the case, the chances that they would come after them at the hotel were diminishing rapidly, as they would reckon that the two of them would be long gone, and San Antonio would be the last place they would start looking. Either way, Katie was confident about their chances of escape.

Edith re-appeared in black underwear, and sat obediently on the side of the bed as Katie re-dressed her wounds. Edith put on her blue Levi's and black V-neck top, and they sat in silence on the sofa, watching the local Fox News station. Breakfast arrived ten minutes later on a trolley pushed in by a young waiter, who was followed in by a man who took the bag of laundry. The boy, after a brief look of enquiry when he saw Edith's face, unloaded the food on the table on the balcony and Katie gave him a ten. Katie demolished hers, realising she had not eaten since before the card game – and only then it had been a rushed Wendy's from across the street from the casino. Once they were done – Edith having merely had half a bowl of cereal, a couple of bites of a bacon roll, and a cup of coffee – Edith lit a cigarette. 'You know, Anson,' said Katie, 'I'm feeling a bit out of shape. I really need to go for a run.'

'Doesn't look like I'm joining you,' Edith said glumly, nodding down at her bandaged wrists.

'What are you going to do if the police raid the room?'

She shrugged. 'There won't be much I *can* do. Trying to shoot my way out would be crazy. I'll take my chances with being arrested, and hopefully they won't torture me.'

'I'm glad you said that. I'm taking your gun, so they'll have no excuse to shoot you. Your credit card and phone's going as well – we'll use my laptop for comms, it's clean.'

'We might need the card, Spen – I've only got about ten K on me, and the room's going to cost at least two.'

'Don't worry – I've got about three and a half. Plus I've got a card, which is clean as well,' she said confidently. She knew it was: she had procured it herself, in the name of a friend back in Yeovil, as an insurance policy against the sort of situation in which they now found themselves. The chances of it having been red-flagged were zero. 'Now, I'm going to photograph every inch of your body.'

Edith thought for a moment, her brow taut as she tried to work out what Katie was driving at. She gave up with a shrug, to which Katie said, 'If you get taken in, you are going to tell them that your lawyer has photographs of your injuries, and that if you do not report to him every six hours he will release them to the press.'

'And just who am I supposed to be?'

'Whatever your real name is – assuming that it's not Anson!' she laughed. 'You're here on holiday. You got beaten up and tortured by the authorities, who accused you of being a spy for China. You managed to escape, so you barricaded yourself in your hotel room, afraid to go to the police or the British embassy in case they handed you back to your interrogators. Your intention was to wait until your face had cleared up, then make a run for it to Mexico, because they had stolen your passport. You can make up the rest.'

'And if I *do* get taken in? What will you do with the photos?'

'I'll tell HQ to do what you tell your abductors what your lawyer will do.'

'But no one's going to believe a word we say!'

'Of course they won't! But they certainly *will* believe that the Americans are capable of torturing a helpless young girl. And no one will believe *them* when they publicly accuse you of being a foreign agent. The revulsion at what they've done to you will override most people's logic. It will damage America very badly – perhaps even as much as Abu Ghraib. I mean, it's bad enough torturing a bunch of Arab blokes who look like they can handle themselves; it's quite another doing it to a white English rose who appears incapable of harming a fly. Whoever takes you will know the repercussions, and as soon as you hit them with the threat of releasing the pictures, they will panic and try to get a way out – probably by deporting you, or cobbling together a deal with the boss.'

Edith grinned. 'I've got to hand it to you, Spendlove: that's quite brilliant. But what happens if they take *you* as well?'

'We read from the same script,' said Katie. She was not ready, yet, to tell Edith of her intention to sing like a canary if necessary. She felt bad about hiding it from her, given what they had sworn to each other last night. But, despite the fact that Edith had agreed to leave with her, Katie was not 100% sure of her intentions, or if her loyalty was as flexible as hers: it was just possible, she thought, that Edith would denounce her to OCC if she thought she was about to turn traitor. For the time being, discretion was the better part of valour.

They went back inside. Katie closed the curtains, helped Edith undress, and stripped off the bandages and the plaster from her nose. Then, after removing the SIM card from Edith's phone, she turned it on and photographed every cut, every bruise in the minutest detail, and took full body shots, with Edith looking suitably miserable with her black eyes and cut nose. Katie redressed her wounds and helped her back into her clothes, and cuddled her and kissed her on the lips. Then she bluetoothed the photos to her notebook, hooked into the hotel's Wi-Fi, opened her VPN to put any snoopers off the scent, opened her Proton Mail account, and sent the following to the boss's email address:

> Hi mama!
>
> Thanks very much for the present. I'm afraid it arrived slightly damaged (see the attached photos). But with a bit of TLC I think it will be fine.
>
> We're intending to stick around for a few days to do a bit of sightseeing – will that be OK?
>
> In the event that we run into difficulties here, please pass the photos on to the appropriate news outlets and anyone else who you think might be interested in them.
>
> Best to get me by email. Will check every few hours.
>
> Love you,

Steph.

It seemed slightly ridiculous to couch the email in euphemistic espionage speak, especially given Proton's end-to-end encryption and her use of the VPN. But, still, in the event that the NSA had hacked either her or Artemis's account, it wouldn't do to overtly implicate herself with OCC (although the photos *did* thoroughly implicate Edith – a gamble she was prepared to take: she knew that Edith was finished as an agent, regardless of whether or not HQ had somehow managed to blitz her mugshots; and it would do them no harm if the Agency knew of the photos they had taken, and what they were prepared to do with them).

While waiting for the reply, she scanned news sites in San Antonio to see if there was any word of the action from last night. In the five websites she visited, there was, unsurprisingly, nothing. But one article grabbed her attention. It read:

SHOP GIRL SLAIN IN ARMED ROBBERY

Police are hunting the killers of a young store assistant from Comfort, Kerr County, who was gunned down in an armed robbery Tuesday.

Cheryl Denham, 17, who had been working in her father's store, the popular Bill's Mart off IS-10, was shot twice. She was declared dead at the scene.

Police have described the suspects as being two white males in their thirties. One is clean-shaven with thinning dark hair and is around 6'. His accomplice has short dark hair, is unshaven, and is of similar height. They were wearing dark suits and white shirts, and made their getaway in a 1970s black Ford

Mustang II, the plates of which had been removed. Police are urging anyone who may have seen them or has information as to their whereabouts to call 911 immediately. The suspects are armed and extremely dangerous and should not be approached.

Police are also anxious to trace an eyewitness, Julie McKay of Phoenix, AZ. Julie chased the suspects after Cheryl was shot. She is described as white, around 5'10", with shoulder-length blonde hair. She was wearing a grey t-shirt, blue jeans and tan boots. It is believed she was assaulted during the robbery and had sustained injuries to her face. Ms McKay was driving a red 2002 Dodge Intrepid, license 213 – MCR. Anyone who has seen or heard from Julie should contact law enforcement immediately.

Captain Loudon of Kerr County Sheriff's Office said at the scene, "The killing of Cheryl was completely senseless. She was working in her father's store to save money to go to college in Austin later this year. She had her whole life ahead of her, and that life has been tragically cut short. The perpetrators will be brought to justice."

Commenting on his concerns for Ms McKay, Captain Loudon said, "We are extremely worried about Julie. She very bravely set off after the suspects. However, it might have gotten her harmed. I would make this appeal to the suspects: if you are holding Julie please release her immediately. Holding or harming her will only make matters worse."

Cheryl's parents, Bill and Patricia Denham, said in a statement: "Cheryl was a wonderful daughter and the light of our lives. She was a talented artist and musician with limitless potential. We are utterly devastated that she is gone. Our family will never be whole again. We pray to God to care for her.

"We would plead with those responsible to give themselves up. We do not want any more blood to be spilled."

Accompanying the article was a photo of the Stetson-hatted, sunglasses-wearing sheriff, standing with his arms folded in front of 'Bill's Mart', which had yellow police tape around it, and one of its big front windows boarded up.

Katie took the laptop out to the balcony, where Edith was sitting staring into space, and set it down in front of her. 'I think you might want to look at this, Edith,' said Katie. 'I wonder if Julie has a fractured nose?'

As Edith read it, her face sagged. 'Cheryl,' she breathed. She sniffled and rubbed her eyes, then cleared her throat and said, 'Sounds like that Julie is really heroic – and I'd imagine quite pretty as well – apart from having black eyes and a busted nose,' she giggled. 'Although her taste must be poor, driving an old banger like that. Still, I hope she's okay.'

'And who, exactly, is Julie?'

'Haven't a clue,' she shrugged. 'Probably whoever they bought the car from, or had it registered to.' A thought hit her. 'If she exists,' she laughed, 'she's probably had the police round giving her a hard time.'

'Just when I thought there was nothing more you could do to surprise me, you go and do something like this. Yes, Julie is extremely heroic. My Julie.' She bent down and kissed her brow. 'I'm just glad you weren't killed. Did you catch up with them?'

'Yep.'

'And?'

'You know.'

'You killed them?'

'Well, one of them,' she said dispassionately. 'The other one's still alive. Or, at least, he was when I left him. With a bit of luck he'll have turned his gun on himself.' Katie said nothing, so Edith added defensively, 'The one I killed was the one who killed the girl in the shop. Cheryl.'

'And the other one?'

'He was the one who broke my nose. So I smashed his face in in return.'

Katie regarded her for a second. She didn't appear perturbed in the slightest, as if it was just another thing that had to be done, like brushing her teeth or going to the toilet. 'Violence doesn't really bother you, does it?'

'Nope. Not if they deserve it.' She said this with conviction. But then her eyes dropped to the floor and her face tensed with anxiety. She looked back up at Katie, biting her lip and shaking her head listlessly. 'I...' she began. But she seemed to think better of what she was about to say. She forced a smile. 'But what about you? You don't seem to be too concerned about it either.'

Katie inhaled sharply, as she realised that she had not given a second thought to the man she had executed only a few hours before. She felt a sudden rush of guilt; not so much for having killed him, but for the fact that her conscience had not been troubled by it for a single second since the rescue. She felt her face redden. 'I...good grief! I don't know what's got into me. I had forgotten about it. I...'

Edith stood up and hugged her. 'Shh.'

'I...I never thought I'd have to kill anyone. Ever. I'm a Christian! I never wanted to harm anyone!'

Edith pulled back and held her chin, forcing her to look her in the eyes. 'Listen, Spendlove,' she said sternly, 'you're neither a criminal nor a murderer. All you have done is carry out an execution – a quasi-judicial execution, but a legitimate one nonetheless – of a man who was guilty of treason.'

'But *I* didn't know that!'

She shook her head. 'Doesn't matter. The fact is that had you not pulled the trigger, someone else would have, sooner rather than later. You did what had to be done, what *would* have been done, that's all.'

'But…what about his friends? His family? I…I don't want to be responsible for that.'

'You're not. Ray knew exactly what he was getting himself into, and knew that to turn on us carried the death penalty. Frankly, if I had had any inclination of what he had in store for me, I would have killed him long before you had the opportunity. And if you had left him alive, the *very first thing* I would have done when I got to my feet was to carry out the execution, for which I had ample evidence and for which I would have been perfectly justified. So don't worry, please. It was our clear duty. You must consider yourself to have been the weapon, not the actual person pulling the trigger, which was the government of Venezuela.'

'You sound pretty convincing,' she said uncertainly.

'Good,' she beamed, and kissed her on the cheek. 'Just always remember: guilt in our game? It's for the birds.' But as soon as she said this her smiled evaporated and her eyes darted away. She pulled out of the clinch and sat down and lit a cigarette, and went back to staring out over the city.

Katie sat down on the other chair and touched her arm. 'What is it? You can tell me.'

She gave her a distant look, and shook her head. 'I…Steph, it's been a pretty traumatic 48 hours. I…I'm exhausted. I'm sorry. I'll be myself again soon, I promise,' she said with a bat of her eyelids and a flash of a smile.

Katie wondered if, despite the lesson about guilt, she was feeling guilty herself. Maybe about killing the bandit from the other night? After all, that seemed to have been merely a personal bit of revenge. Would such a distinction – the fact that she did not have official sanction for her actions – make any difference to her? She guessed not, especially given the two assassinations that had started her down this path. More likely – and with perfect justification – she was simply despondent after the events of last night.

Her computer chirped. The message appeared to be from the boss herself.

> Hi Steph,
>
> Thanks for the email.
>
> We are all extremely distressed about the photos. I heard you took care of one of the perpetrators. For that you have my eternal gratitude.
>
> Tell your sister I tracked down the photos of her from last night. They have been corrupted and will be of no use to anyone now.
>
> From what I can gather, I believe it is fine for you to stay in town for a few days, at least. I will let you know if the situation changes.
>
> Please be very careful – there are a lot of dangerous people out there, and I'm worried about you. At the first sign of trouble come back home immediately. I would suggest going north first.
>
> Stephanie, you have turned into a very fine young lady, and I am very proud of you. Take care of yourself and your sister. Tell her to stay positive.
>
> Mama.

Katie, thrilled at having apparently been formally exonerated for the killing last night and at Artemis's pep talk, passed the computer to Edith. She read it, but looked troubled. 'What's up?' asked Katie in bewilderment. 'I thought you would be delighted: she's managed to blitz your mugshots, and says the heat is off. So why the sour puss?'

Edith opened her mouth, but nothing came out. She shook her head slightly, stubbed out her cigarette, and lit another. Katie decided to leave it. She had given her a hard enough time already today. She would let it lie, for now. In the meantime, she would go for a run, clear her head and get rid of Edith's gear, then think properly about how and when they would make a break for it.

13. The Knot

Spendlove left five minutes later, taking the carrier bag with Tempany's gun, phone and credit card.

Tempany was ashamed to admit it, but she was glad she was gone. She needed time to think; to try to work out exactly what had happened. She was not sure her mind was up to it, which made her afraid. Yes, she had killed people. But planning to eliminate someone and then executing that plan was child's play: all it required was basic logic and a cool head. Trying to figure out the motives and strategies of the people who controlled her, and the people who controlled her enemies, was something else entirely.

She closed the balcony door, shut the curtains, turned off the television, and lay on the bed and stared up at the ceiling.

Her beliefs: were they all just fantasies, as the man had claimed? One thing was true at the very least: what he knew about where some of those beliefs had come from was on the money. When she joined up, she had been ordered by OCC to study Noam Chomsky and Gary Webb and William Blum; and their works had added an additional layer to her world view, which was this: the USA specifically – and not just capitalism, as she had originally believed – was, as a result of a fascistic foreign policy since the Second World War, responsible for most of the world's ills, up to and including Al Qaeda and ISIS. She had felt extremely smart when she had figured this out, thinking she had unlocked some great truth about how the world worked, a truth that most of the decadent, pampered fools in the West were blind to.

But she realised now that, by not questioning any of it, it had, in fact, been *her* who had been the schmuck. 'Brainwashed' the man had said. More like blind acceptance, she thought grimly.

She tried to put her finger on why she had allowed herself to have been so gullible. But then a terrifying thought hit her: maybe she had *always* been this gullible? She had liked to think she had a Socratic level of scepticism, not believing anything until she had verified it from multiple sources or seen it with her own eyes. But now she could see that this was a fiction she had concocted for herself, and that she had had a blind spot when it came to people she deemed to be right-wing. From a very early age she had immediately, foolishly, thought all such people to be evil. No ifs, no buts, no compromise. Evil. But now Rebecca's stinging words from that day in Hyde Park, when a jovial Scottish bloke was on the stage defending freedom of speech, were pounding her brain: 'Uh, Bells, are you *sure* these guys are Nazis?' In her childish hatred, she *had* been sure. But now? The man Collier, who murdered Rebecca? Definitely. John Barrett? Probably (or at least he was if Magellan's tale about him assaulting the Brazilian guy had been true, which she now seriously doubted). But the rest of 'fascist' crowd? The blacks and the Asians cheering the Scottish guy? The people cheering the theatrically homosexual man railing against radical Islam, which wanted people like him dead? She had screamed the most horrible things at them, just as she had screamed to other people at countless such protests before. But weren't they just a bunch of ordinary, working-class folk wanting to make their society better? Wanting to defend their basic, hard-won freedoms? The very sort of people she had been professing to be crusading for? And what the hell was wrong with most of the stuff that was said that day anyway?

John Barrett maybe crossed the line with his calls for mass deportations of illegal immigrants. But everyone else who spoke? No. In fact, nowhere near it. '*Jesus!*' she gasped as she recalled herself screaming obscenities as the 'fascists' sang God Save the Queen. She felt thoroughly ashamed of herself. 'How could I have been so stupid?' she whined. *Lack of a father figure*, she thought in reply, and laughed.

Yes, she had always been this gullible, at least when it came to 'the right'. And the cause of all this? There were two parts to it, she realised. The catalyst had been her parents, a couple of hotshot City bankers who, she thought, hated her; and she hated them in return, bringing with it a sizeable dollop of malice for *all* people of wealth (of which she was now one, she reflected with some amusement). But the thing that had given her ire form and focus was the neo-Marxist education system in Britain. It had fashioned her base instincts into a fanaticism which made her see anyone promoting even moderate ideas such as free enterprise, personal responsibility, freedom of speech, and small government, as well as anyone who so much as questioned multiculturalism and mass immigration and 'diversity', as Nazis who had to be destroyed. That is why she turned up at Hyde Park that day. That is why, against all sense and logic, she hated everyone there and wanted them dead.

Those were, indeed, the principal reasons for her gullibility. But when it came to OCC, she realised, there was one more important element to it, one more reason why she had swallowed hook, line and sinker every word, no matter how implausible, they had fed her all these years: she had simply not *wanted* to question. OCC had made her feel special. Made her feel like she was doing good. Made her feel like part of a family. OCC gave her life purpose. She did not want to question because she was scared of the answers – scared of the answers she was now getting. Scared that the world was not quite as black and white, good and evil as the Marxists and OCC had painted it for her, and as she had kidded herself into believing it was. She liked being Edith Anson; she liked being the Leninist Angel of Vengeance, as the man had quirkily put it. She did not want to go back to being the lost little girl she had been after Rebecca's murder, skulking around her flat, drinking herself to death.

She began to sob. She knew with certainty that the version of reality the man had shown her last night was true – or at least true enough to fatally undermine all her own, hitherto unchallenged, convictions. Could she carry on being Edith Anson knowing this? Knowing that the righteousness that had driven her thus far had been a load of infantile Marxist claptrap?

Her sobbing stopped and her body tensed as an even more alarming thought hit her. She had instinctively felt it last night when she looked down at the pool of her blood in the shed, but hadn't quite realised until now the full implication of it, which was this: Edith Anson was already dead, regardless of whether or not her world view was in tatters. For a start, there was the DNA she'd left. Secondly, her real name was blown. Thirdly, even if Artemis *had* managed to burn her mugshots, the two agents she had left alive would be able to provide detailed identikits of her, and, despite Zulu's trashing of their phones, it was more than likely their tech people would be able to salvage her photos from them. Nope. There was no escaping it. Anson was done. There was always plastic surgery, she thought. 'No way!' she said aloud, and laughed.

She wiped her eyes. Edith Anson already felt gone. Anson would never have broken down like she, Tempany, had in front of Spendlove last night. Anson would not be lying here now, crying like a baby. Still, at least she had Spendlove to look after her now. Yes. The prospect of being with Spendlove, if she could somehow extricate herself from this mess, was looking not only inevitable, but highly attractive.

But, then again, if she was no longer to be the person that Spendlove had first met – that is, a somewhat mysterious, stylish, danger woman – would Spendlove still like her?

She laughed long and hard at the bizarreness of her train of thought. Spendlove, she knew, did not like her because she was a swashbuckling adventurer. Or even a murderer. Spendlove liked her because she was smart, and pretty and…

She struggled to form the word in her head, because it made her feel weak, pathetic. But she knew what it was: vulnerable. Despite everything else that she was, despite the rock-hard exterior she had tried to construct for herself all her life, beneath the surface that's exactly what she was. Spendlove could see it, and that's why Spendlove loved her.

'*Stop it!*' she snapped, trying to wrench herself out of her self-pity. She got up, poured herself a vodka, took a seat on the balcony, and smoked a Marlboro while she drank. With an effort, she bent her mind to what else the man had said: the phoney operations. Was he telling the truth about those, too? She reckoned he was. Or, at least, he was telling the truth according to what he thought it to be (which was not to say that whoever had told *him,* were themselves telling the truth!). She trawled her memories of each of those missions. Her conscience was pricked at the thought of Mr Han, who had sued for mercy before she pulled the trigger. Her instinct now was that Mr Han was *not* one of their agents. The fear on his face was simply not the look of somebody in their line of work. People in their profession knew the score; knew that an assassin might one day track them down and liquidate them, so when that day came there should not be the look of pure terror as there had been on Mr Han's face. Her stomach clenched. She quickly stamped out the picture of him and turned to Raoul, the drug lord.

There seemed to be no question that he was, in fact, what she had been told – only what he was doing with some of the profits might have been different. If what the man had told her last night – that Raoul was funnelling some of the profits to the Venezuelan government – was a lie, it seemed clear that it had been concocted in order that her faith in her organisation would receive a mortal blow, given that the implication was that at least some of the proceeds were used to pay her salary, which was in US dollars. But she knew so little about Raoul and his dealings that it was impossible for her to speculate further as to whether or not the man's claims were true. As such, there seemed little point in worrying about it now. Besides, she thought, trying to alleviate her guilt, he was a drug dealer, and was probably responsible for turning hundreds of thousands of kids throughout the hemisphere into junkies, and therefore deserved it.

Then came Abdullah Jebreen. She had meant to kill him in Paris, but he had skipped the city three days before she got there. With her bloodhound, the awesome Stephanie Spendlove from SdI, she had trailed him, overland, to Dodoma. He had visited mosques in every town he stopped in. His route – avoiding airports – had raised no doubts in Tempany's mind that he was exactly what HQ had told her. As such, she had chosen to murder him in a gruesome manner in order to send a message to any other would-be terrorists.

But now she was not so sure, because she simply had no evidence that he *was* a terrorist, or was planning anything more threatening than a children's tea party. Indeed, it was possible, she reflected, that he was travelling overland because he was simply scared of flying, or for the even more mundane reason that he couldn't afford the fare. If the real reason for the hit was what the man had told her, she was guilty of a very heinous crime indeed. She could try to rationalise it, somewhat, by telling herself, as she had just told Spendlove, that she was merely the weapon, that the man pulling the trigger was the racist pig in the foreign ministry. But that didn't make her feel any better. She thought of how she had cruelly coshed him with a metal bar in order to stun him – she shivered as she recalled the horrible, hollow whacking noise as the bar hit his head. Then she was on top of him, her right knee rammed into his spine. Then she had the wire round his neck, his slight arms and hands trying desperately to pull it from his throat. She thought of his jaunty Hawaiian shirt. The musky aftershave. The mop of brown curly hair. The long, blank face. The face of a simpleton. The choking to death. The final gurgling as his life was snuffed out.

She ran to the bathroom and brought her breakfast and vodka up into the toilet.

After several minutes' retching, she washed her face and stared at herself in the mirror. The eyes that stared back looked thoroughly beaten. 'Get a grip of yourself, Bellman!' she growled. 'This could all be bullshit. Clear your head!' She filled the sink with cold water and ducked her head in, keeping it there until her breath ran out. Then she dried herself and went out to the balcony for another cigarette. After three drags, she stubbed it out, went back inside, and found hotel notepaper and a pen from one of the drawers beneath the television. Taking in a chair from the balcony, she sat at the sideboard and wrote in the middle of the top sheet: 'EDITH ANSON'. She drew a rectangle around it, then drew a line to the right, and wrote 'RAY WALKER'. From there she drew a line down and wrote 'CIA'. Then, under her own name, she wrote:

> Ray set me up.
> That is obvious.
> But…but he could
> <u>NOT HAVE KNOWN MY NAME.</u>
>
> And my activities?
> How could he possibly have known all the details?
> Could he???
> <u>NO</u>.
> It's impossible.

She sat back and stared at the page. Then she drew a line from 'CIA' and wrote: 'Magellan. Magellan's people.' She paused. Almost involuntarily her hand wrote:

ARTEMIS

She threw down the pen as if it were a hot coal, ripped the page into small pieces and threw it into the wastepaper bin. She jumped to her feet and banged her forehead with her fists. 'What the *fuck?!*' Why would Artemis set her up? And if it *had* been her, why would she have launched the rescue mission?

The rescue mission.

There was something off about it; she had sensed it the very moment she clapped eyes on Spendlove: why would they have sent *her*; and to lead it, no less? It should have been the last thing that one of the intelligence officers was sent on, it being assumed that they would make matters worse by getting either killed or captured. As far as Tempany knew, Spendlove had had no combat training whatsoever; it was entirely possible that she had never even held a gun before. It made no sense...

Unless...unless Spendlove was sent as a blind...in order that she would fail?

But if Artemis meant for Spendlove to fail, why would she have sent her – or anyone else, for that matter – in the first place?

The beacon in her watch. She wasn't supposed to be able to activate it, hence the reason Ray had grabbed her wrists when she was abducted, then took it to prevent her hitting the buttons later on.

But, that being the case, why would he have kept it with him? He should have thrown it in a dumpster or something just to be on the safe side. The fact that it was still there only made sense if Ray did not know about the beacon, and was simply stealing it, as she had initially thought. Or maybe he had thought she hadn't activated it?

It was a mystery, to be sure, the answer to which had probably gone to the grave with Ray. But, whatever his game was, she *had* managed to press both buttons, and the beacon *had* worked, of that there was no doubt.

She tried to piece together a possible scenario. For whatever reason, Artemis had offered Tempany up to the CIA. In exchange for what – the men stewing in Gitmo, perhaps? – did not matter. The main point was that Tempany was never to be heard from again. Ray was in on it, obviously, and had been instructed, either by Artemis directly or by the CIA, to stop Tempany from activating the beacon. But by getting out of Ray's clutches just long enough, she had managed to hit the buttons and her predicament had flashed up on one of the tech guy's computers. Who in turn told his supervisor. Who in turn told Raphael. Who in turn told Artemis. Artemis had to do something – there were too many people who knew that Tempany was in trouble. As luck would have it, an operative who could not possibly be expected to succeed in extracting her was in the vicinity. So Spendlove was sent, and Artemis could be seen to be doing something, without *actually* doing something. But Artemis had underestimated her.

She got up and went into the bathroom, turned on the light, and looked at herself again. Her face was pale, and her eyes squinted back at her. 'But this...it doesn't make any sense. If it was a trade – me for someone, or something else – why were they trying to turn me? If I was placed back into HQ working for the Agency, and Artemis had already been doubled, what the hell would be the point of putting me in there as well? Unless...unless it's to muddy the waters? To provide cover. For her.'

She gasped as the realisation hit her.

'It was her who blew the operations.'

She shook her head, her jaw dangling. The whole thing was just too fantastic. 'Good grief, Bells. That knock on the head last night has made you as paranoid as anything. Ray's behind it all. He'd already been doubled, and was offering you up for cash, probably, and stealing the Omega into the bargain.'

But she wasn't buying her own argument. Her name. Her name gave it away. Additionally, if Artemis had, indeed, lied to her about the latter assassination missions, and if the real reasons for them were as reprehensible as the man had claimed, she was certainly capable of ratting Tempany out to the CIA. Moreover, given that Tempany's fingerprints were on those crimes, and that she was a direct link back to HQ and Artemis herself, it would make sense to get her out of the picture sooner or later.

And then there was Artemis's note of a few minutes ago. Tempany knew with certainty that the CIA were on their way. Which meant that, unless Artemis's intelligence was wonky, Artemis, too, knew that they were coming for her, and she therefore wanted Tempany to stay there; wanted the Agency to continue to try to turn her.

Why hadn't they come? She had been expecting them at dawn. Even though her head had been spinning when she was rescued, she had known instinctively that the Agency was the only place she was likely to get answers; and, perhaps, were the only people who could keep her alive if someone in OCC was, indeed, out to get her. That was why she had insisted on coming back to the hotel. That was why she was still there. That was why she had whispered the hotel's name into the man's ear. That's why she slipped her penknife into his trouser pocket when she was pretending to frisk him for a phone. That's why she left the door to the shed unlocked.

'Shit! Spendlove!' They had been waiting until they were split up before coming for another try at her. 'You idiot!' she groaned. She had thought she was being smart with her little spot of subterfuge. But because she had gone so long without having any external pressure points, she had completely forgotten about her. They would surely abduct her, and then they would have all the leverage they needed...

Then again, that was assuming that they had known Spendlove was with her. They would have had no way of knowing, she thought – unless, of course, Artemis, or someone else on the inside, was priming them.

It felt like her head was going to explode. She poured the last of the vodka and slung it down her throat. Then, right on cue, there came three sharp raps on the door.

14. Playing The Field

'Miss Worthington?' came the man's voice friendlily. 'Are you decent.'

'Yeah, I'm decent,' she answered morosely, and shuffled up to the door. Without bothering to look through the spy hole or put the chain on, she opened it to find the man and the woman from last night. They were both in a fresh change of clothes – he in a navy suit, white shirt and pink tie; she in a black pin-stripe trouser suit and white cotton blouse. Marring their smart appearance was the absence of their eyebrows, presumably having been ripped off with the gaffer tape that had been covering their eyes. The woman had tried to compensate by pencilling hers in. The only other sign of the excitement of earlier were light scratches on the side of the man's face, which would probably heal up in a couple of days. They were smiling at her. She couldn't help but smile in return: there was a bond of shared experience between them.

'It's good to see you in one piece,' grinned the man. 'I must say, you're looking rather better than you were last night. I thought...well, you had us worried for a moment. Here.' He handed her back her penknife.

'Thank you,' she said. 'And sorry about the eyebrows. Please understand, it wasn't my choice to tape you up like that. I would have just shot you both.'

They laughed. 'Thank you for your concern, I think,' said the man. 'But we're fine – the eyebrows will grow back. And, other than that, I've only this small memento,' he pointed to his cheek.

The woman, speaking for the first time, said, 'And my ears are ringing,' and jerked her head a few times as if to expel water from them.

Tempany, not smiling, said, 'And you gave me this.' She held up her bandaged wrists.

'Shit,' hissed the man. 'I suppose it's too late for "sorry"?'

Tempany shrugged. 'You suppose right. But I appreciate the sentiment. Come in.' She opened the door wide. 'Sit by the balcony,' she said, guiding them to the sofa. Tempany pulled over the chair from the sideboard. Addressing the man, she asked, 'How did you know I had someone with me?' taking care not to mention Spendlove's name or gender, lest she be barking up the wrong tree.

They glanced at each other, and the man said, 'I don't know what you're talking about.'

Tempany shook her head. 'Don't play games. I am certainly not in the mood. You knew I had company, and waited until they were gone. How?'

'The hotel's security cameras,' he said automatically. 'Do you think we would come in here, unarmed, without knowing that you were here alone? For all we knew, you could have been luring us into a trap. We might be stupid,' he chuckled, 'but we're not suicidal.'

This sounded plausible. She figured that the scenario could have been that they had freed themselves within 15 minutes of her escaping, and had immediately sent people round to the hotel to check the CCTV. From the recording, they had noted the two women with baseball caps, their heads hung low, walking in a short time earlier. Then it was just a matter of monitoring the images from the camera in the corridor until someone emerged from the room. By the time Spendlove came out, they would have had lookouts stationed at each of the hotel's exits, and the person watching the CCTV would have radioed down a description: Caucasian female, 25-30, 5'8, tied back brown hair, blue Nike baseball cap, red Adidas t-shirt, black leggings, orange Asics running shoes, blue plastic watch, carrying a plain blue carrier bag. Outside, Spendlove would have been apprehended. As soon as they realised it was not Tempany, they would have informed the man and woman, and here they were. That seemed to be the most logical explanation. But she did not trust it, and she did not trust him. They might have gone through these motions as cover. But Tempany was certain that HQ was guiding them. What had more likely happened was that Zulu and Alfonso had reported what had happened back to their handlers, and they, in turn, had relayed that to HQ, and someone there had then told the Agency, meaning that the Agency knew Spendlove was with her without even looking at the CCTV. 'What have you done with my associate?'

The man shook his head and held his hands up in innocence. 'Nothing. Absolutely nothing, I swear. She's away for a run. I'll tell you, she's in mighty fine shape. Although you probably knew that already,' he said with a suggestive wiggle of his eyebrows.

Suppressing a sigh of relief, Tempany shot back, 'Ha! I'm disappointed in you. I had thought you were a gentleman. But you're nothing but a dirty old pervert.' She said to the woman, 'You enjoy working with a deviant like this?'

She shook her head. 'Em…he's not usually like this,' she said with forced levity.

'Whoa! Hang on, ladies!' he said, slightly panicked. 'I was only yanking your chain, Miss Anson. Suffice it to say, Miss Kirkwood is safe. And will remain so.'

Kirkwood! Was that Spendlove's name? If it was, the final sliver of possibility that Ray could have been behind it all was blown to bits: there didn't seem to be a cat in hell's chance that he would have known *both* their names – if he had even known of Spendlove's existence in the first place, which seemed unlikely. It was Artemis. The bitch.

She managed to keep her face set hard. 'She'd better. You owe me big time. I saved your lives last night. My men' – she said 'men' deliberately, remembering that her two guests were blindfolded and therefore could not be sure that it was Spendlove who had murdered Ray – 'were going to kill you.'

The man meekly nodded his agreement. 'Yes. And it's much appreciated, I can assure you. I rather enjoy being alive. But why let us go? And more curiously,' he said, sitting back and looking up at the ceiling, 'why tell me where you were?'

'Isn't it obvious? I want answers. Or, more precisely, I want *an* answer: how did you know my name?'

He swallowed. 'I don't know what you mean. Your name is Miss Anson – or Alison Worthington – as far as I know.'

'You said my real name. My name is Tempany Bellman. And you knew it. Who told you?'

'I don't see the significance of this,' he floundered.

'Well, that's good. I don't *want* you to know the significance of it. I just want to know how *you* know.'

He scratched his neck, glanced at his colleague, and said, 'Look, Edith, you're a smart girl. You know how this game works. I – we – are given intelligence and are supposed to act on it. *Where* that intelligence comes from is irrelevant. In fact, as you well know, the less we know about our sources the better, because if we are ever caught by the opposition, the less we will be able to tell them. So, yes, I know your name. I know where you live. I know where your money is, and I know how much you've got. But where that information came from? I honestly don't know.'

Tempany doubted very much that they knew about her money. They probably knew about the account in the Virgin Islands where her pay was sent. But the others, where the bulk of her fortune was stashed? Jersey, Zurich, and Grand Cayman? She seriously doubted it – she had been extremely careful in how she shifted her money around, and had created an intricate web of aliases and front companies to handle it. No one else in the world besides her knew exactly where everything was. Still, she made a mental note to change all of her accounts at the earliest opportunity. 'Funnily enough,' she said, 'I believe you. But someone in your organisation *does* know. So here's the deal: provide me with a name and I'll work for you as requested, and will do so for half price.'

His eyes widened. 'I…I can only agree to see what I can do. Like I say, *I* don't know the information you want. And I don't know…' He paused and shook his head. 'Frankly, I don't know if you working for us will be worth giving that information to you. That's the call my superiors will have to make.' His eyes narrowed. 'Would you mind if I just rowed back here a second, Miss Anson? You've obviously got it into your head that somebody other than the recently deceased Mr Walker has burned you. But, if it wasn't Ray, it is possible that some of our own people have been able to piece together who you are just by good old-fashioned detective work. You might not have been betrayed at all. And by that I mean that the person you're looking for might be one of the computer geeks in our basement.'

That's exactly what they would say had happened, thought Tempany. He would come back tomorrow with a dossier on her, showing how the tech guys had uncovered her identity. But it would be a lie. She was nowhere on the Internet. No photos, no name, no stupid social media accounts, nothing. True, she had a National Insurance number and a driving licence, but neither had ever been used. There had also been a passport in her real name, but that had expired two years ago. Her flat in London, meanwhile, was rented in the name of Abigail Norman – a name she had appropriated from the local registrars; the name of a girl who would have been Tempany's age, had she not died when she was five. It was the name that was on all her bills and her London-based Santander current account. To all intents and purposes, 'Tempany Bellman' did not exist.

Still, she nodded and said, 'Fair enough. If you provide me with a satisfactory answer, I'm in. Six months only, and then I'm out, for good, with five million and your protection, for life, from my employers.'

He nodded.

'Also, I want a written contract.'

He gave a dismissive snort. 'No chance.'

'Then no deal.'

'It simply can't be done. The United States Government cannot put its name to something like this.'

'Look, I want a contract. And I couldn't give a toss if it's in the name of the US Government or one of your fronts. Just as long as I can take it before a grand jury if you do not hold up your end of the bargain. And I want written on it the specific tasks that I am to carry out for you.'

He sighed, shaking his head. 'My people are going to say no, I can assure you. But I'll ask them.'

'Well, that's a start. And don't you dare,' she warned, jabbing a finger at him, 'try to pull the wool over my eyes.'

'What do you mean?' he asked innocently.

'I mean putting it in the name of someone who is not authorised. Or someone who doesn't exist. Or otherwise invalidating it. Believe me, I know contract law like the back of my hand, and if you try to dupe me, I will know, and I will be most unhappy.'

'Miss Anson, please, trust me. Regardless of whether or not we can commit anything to writing, we will not deceive you. You will be one of our employees. And we look after our employees. To the end.' The woman nodded vigorously.

'We'll see,' said Tempany. 'There is one more condition: my friend Miss Kirkwood is to be part of the deal. She gets protection as well.'

'I...I don't quite understand,' he said, his brow knotting in confusion. 'Are you going to bring her in on it? I would, frankly, advise against it. The fewer people who know about our arrangement the better, and safer, it will be for all concerned.'

She shook her head firmly. 'No. Miss Kirkwood is going to be no part of it. However, she and I are partners, and I intend to tell her, when my contract with you is about to expire, that I am leaving OCC, and give her the opportunity to come with me. That will be up to her. But whatever she decides, she must be part of the deal now, and her name must be on the contract. Might I suggest a clause along the lines of: "Miss Kirkwood will be pardoned for any suspected and actual crimes hitherto committed in the United States, and she will be provided with the same protection accorded to Miss Bellman-slash-Miss Anson until the end of her life".'

He barked a laugh. 'Jeez! This is growing arms and legs! You want a *pardon* for her as well?!' He shook his head. 'You're one hell of a negotiator, Edith. Remind me to never buy a car from you.'

Tempany grinned. 'I take it that's a "yes"?'

'That's a "yes", we'll look at it.'

'Good. Might I have your number?'

He handed her a plain white card with the name 'Irvin McDowell', a telephone number and a Gmail address on it. 'Any time,' he said. A vibration came from inside his jacket. He pulled out his phone and read the message. 'It appears your friend is on her way back. We'd best make ourselves scarce. We'll contact you tomorrow.'

Tempany thought. 'What day is it?' she asked.

'Thursday,' he said.

'Could you leave it until…I don't know, could you give me until, say, Tuesday? I want to recuperate properly before I commit myself to anything – you know, my head needs to be crystal clear for this, and I'm feeling a bit dopey due to someone having tranked me last night.'

The man gave her a wry smile, and said, 'Won't you be missed? And Miss Kirkwood?'

Tempany shook her head. 'We've already got approval to hang around here until I'm well enough to travel. There will be no questions asked.'

'Fine,' he said. 'That will give me time to straighten all this out with my people.'

'Don't put a tail on me. I need time to relax and think, and I don't want to be followed when I'm doing it. Don't worry, I'll be here on Tuesday.'

He nodded. 'I'll see what I can do.'

'That applies to Miss Kirkwood as well.

He nodded again. 'Tuesday, then, Edith.' They both shook her hand and he gave her a small bow, and they left.

Half an hour later Spendlove returned, sweat dripping off her. She kissed Tempany, turned on the television and put up the volume, then went into the bathroom. She reappeared dabbing her face with a towel, and said softly. 'They're onto us.' Tempany looked blankly at her in return. 'You don't seem altogether shocked?'

'How many?'

'Three cars, two in each. At least.'

'Do they know you spotted them?'

'Ha! *Please.*'

'And the gear?'

'I gave them the slip. Went into the basement of an apartment block, put three bullets into the phone, and dumped it, the credit card and gun down different drains. It's all good.'

'Well done. You'd better sit down.'

'Sounds ominous.' She sat on the sofa, and Tempany sat on the chair in front of her.

'Apropos...'

'*Apropos!*' laughed Spendlove. 'Did you just use the word "apropos"?'

'Em...yeah. What of it?'

'Who on earth in the 21st century uses the word "apropos" in conversation?'

'I do,' she shrugged with a grin. 'Now, *apropos* our conversation last night about being honest with each other…well, the first test of this is here. But you should understand, Spendlove, that what I'm about to tell you might be difficult.'

'It's okay, Anson,' she said with an encouraging smile. 'You can tell me.'

'I was wondering if I could take a guess at your name?'

Her eyes scrunched; then opened wide as the meaning of the question hit her. 'Oh, no,' she groaned.

'I'm sorry, Spendlove: is it Kirkwood?'

Spendlove put her head into her hands and rubbed her eyes. She looked back up, her face sagging, and whispered, 'How?'

She told her everything: that their identities had been blown; of the conversation she had just had; that she suspected that Artemis was the mole. By the time she finished, Spendlove's face seemed to have turned a shade paler and her head was shaking. 'I…I can't believe it. There are too many holes, Anson,' she protested weakly. 'It could be anyone. Raphael?'

'I've thought of that. It is true that I provided detailed verbal reports of my jobs to both him and the boss. But would he know our identities? More to the point, *why* would he know? I'm not aware of my real name being anywhere, either on paper or on the server in HQ. My pay gets wired to my business account in the Virgin Islands, which doesn't have my real name attached to it. Can you think of your name being anywhere in writing?'

She thought, and shook her head.

'And given that it was not my man Magellan who recruited you, it seems highly unlikely that our names could have come from him. Which leaves only Artemis. Granted, it might be possible that there are personnel files somewhere which contain all our details, and it is possible, just, that Raphael or Artemis could have written up my reports and put them on the server, and that these could have been hacked by the Agency, or, indeed, by suspect number one, our friend Ray.' She paused and shook her head. 'But I don't buy any of that. Our identities should not have been divulged to anyone in HQ who didn't need them, or kept on file, for the simple reason of protecting us in the event that anyone *is* turned or our systems *are* hacked. It would simply be insane to keep them *anywhere* if not necessary. And our names, our true identities, are not: they are meaningless to anyone other than our ourselves and our enemies. Likewise, why on earth would they have written up my reports? It doesn't make any sense, because it would leave information on the Venezuelan Government's systems implicating them in a whole slew of illegal activities. No, that would be idiotic. And neither Artemis nor Raphael are idiots.' She shook her head. 'But we can forget about Raphael, Spendlove. It's Artemis. Or, at least, I'm 90% convinced it's her, simply because I know with certainty that she knows my name, and I do not know if Raphael does. Also, it must have been Artemis who sent you on the raid last night – Raphael would not have had the authority for something that serious. Of course,' she reflected, 'Artemis could be on the end of a setup herself with someone trying to make us think it was her. But the trail that has led us to her just seems too imprecise to have been laid by someone else. I mean, even the fact that they know our names was not guaranteed to make us think it was her. We might not even have noticed it, and might have carried on believing it was Ray. No. This is Artemis's game, and Ray was her patsy. Artemis is not somebody else's.'

'It's still a bit of a stretch,' said Spendlove. 'I mean, what can she hope to gain by this?'

'Who knows?' she shrugged. 'Money? Maybe she's being blackmailed? But I intend to find out.' She quickly ran over the bones of the plan she had been forming in her head. 'Are you in?'

Spendlove stared at the carpet and said nothing.

'Look,' said Tempany, 'if you don't want to help me, just say so. I don't want to put you in any more danger if you're not up for it. And I won't hold it against you, I promise.'

'It…it's not that. Seriously, I couldn't give a damn about the danger. If I did I wouldn't be here with you now. It's just…I don't know.' Katie wanted to tell her about her plan to talk in the event that they were captured; and that that plan now seemed to be in ruins, given that they were blown and that it had to be assumed that the CIA already knew all that she could tell them. But she couldn't spit it out – it made her feel like a snake and a coward, and she didn't want Edith to think that of her. She just looked up and shook her head. 'Being compromised like this. It feels as if I'm naked in the middle of the street. And…well, this is going to sound a bit soppy, Anson, but I have something approaching a life outside of this madness. I've been able to live under my own name and stay in my home town. But now? If my identity's blown, that's done.'

Tempany moved next to her and put her arm around her. 'Darling, that's not soppy in the slightest. Indeed, I wish *I* had somewhere to call home. I wish I could be myself for a while…if I even knew who the hell I was in the first place!' Spendlove giggled at that. 'Just out of curiosity, where is home?'

Spendlove gave a doleful chuckle. 'If we're going to be BFFs, I don't suppose there's any harm in telling you. It's Yeovil. Ever been?' Tempany shook her head. 'It's…well, it's nice. It's quiet. It's home. My family and friends are there. Not to mention all my stuff. But I guess I'll not be able to go back any time soon.'

'I'm not going to lie to you, Spendlove: our predicament is precarious, to say the least. But you must know that there is no reason for you to be involved. You don't appear to be the target here. I could give you the slip, and you could report that back to HQ, and carry on as if this conversation never took place.'

'But that won't help. If the Agency knows who I am, that means the NSA does, which means the British do, which means *anyone* could. I might not have killed anyone – until last night, that is,' she said grimly, 'and I might not have as many people after me as you, but I've been involved in operations where people have died, and a lot more unsavoury things besides. My knowledge of all of that, and just by being an operative of OCC, is enough for any number of people to want to hurt my family or me. And remember, if what you're saying is true, the boss, or someone, essentially tried to have me killed last night. I'm in this up to my neck, Edith. We both are. The only way I'll be able to go back home safely is if your plan comes off. So I'm in. I'm in till the end.'

'Good,' beamed Tempany. 'It's a two-woman job. By the way, you never did tell me your first name?'

'It's Katherine...um, Katie...with a "K".'

'Your middle name had better not start with a "K" as well, or else I'm going to have to have a chat with your parents.'

She shook her head, smiling. 'It's Madison.'

'*Katherine Madison Kirkwood.* How delightful!' She thrust out her hand. 'Katie, my name is Tempany Bellman. No middle names. Delighted to make your acquaintance, at long last.'

Her brow creased. '*Timpani?*' she asked in faux bafflement.

'Very funny. *Temp*-any.'

Spendlove burst out laughing, to which Tempany said, crossly, 'It's not that funny, is it?'

She took a second to control herself, then said, 'No, no of course not. It's just that I had got it into my head that your real name was Diana, given that you would never shut up about Diana Rigg.'

Tempany giggled. 'I didn't go on about her *that* much, did I?'

'You did, a bit. But never mind: "Tempany" suits you better. And it's a hell of a lot better than "Edith", that's for sure,' she laughed.

15. Spinning The Web

'So, where do we start?' asked Katie.

'Getting to Caracas shouldn't be a problem once we get over the border. It's getting out of the hotel: we have to assume that the CCTV is being monitored; and obviously the entrances and exits are being watched.'

'Not that I want to leave you or anything, but I think it would be best if we split up, on the basis that it will be harder for them to track us separately. Also, although it's less likely that they will pay me much attention, I might just be able to peel one or two off of you.'

Tempany thought, and nodded. 'Agreed.'

'We can meet outside the safe house in Piedras Negras tomorrow.'

'I'm not sure the safe house is a good idea – if anyone's in it and looking out at that moment, we'll be screwed. There's a Holiday Inn Express a couple of miles from the bridges. Know it?'

'Yes.'

'If you go first, book in there. I'll be there within 12 hours.'

'Fall-back?'

'On the path between the road bridges at eleven tomorrow night. Okay?'

'Check. I'll book into the hotel under Rachel Johansson.'

'Check. If I happen to get there first, it's Abigail Norman.'

'Check. There's a flight every morning to Mexico City at 11.45.'

Tempany nodded. 'Got any photo ID?'

'I doubt we'll need it. But if we do, I'll offer them a hundred bucks. Which they'll take,' she added confidently.

'Check. But if they don't go for it, we'll just have to get a cab and tell them to put the foot down.'

'Check.'

'Your passport guy: does he know you're OCC?'

'No. He thinks I'm with the cartel out of Guadalajara. Well, that's what I told him, at least, and he should have no reason to think otherwise.'

'Can you contact him before we get there? It would be handy if we could shave some time off.'

'Yes. We can take mugshots on the laptop, and ask him to deliver them to the airport.'

'How much?'

'Probably a thousand bucks each. I'll offer to throw in an extra grand to get them done quickly and get them delivered.'

'Brilliant...but, um, what are we going to do about my face?'

'Not a problem. Take the plaster off, we'll take a picture, and I'll 'Shop it.'

'Okay.' She went into the bathroom, gently pulled off the plaster, and held the laptop up to her face to photograph herself with the webcam. She took three, and handed the computer to Katie, who set to work on the best one. After ten minutes she said, 'There...' sounding pleased with herself, and handed the laptop to Tempany. She found herself looking at her completely unblemished face. The photo wasn't perfect, looking blurred and smudged, but it would do.

Katie took her own picture then typed an email to her passport dealer in Mexico City, Lucero Martinez. It read:

Hey, Luca! Been a while.

165

I'm needing two done – British or Irish, please. Failing that, Australia, Canada, New Zealand, or USA, in that order. It's rather urgent, I'm afraid – need it done by this time tomorrow. Also, we would like them delivered to the airport.

Can this be done?

If you can do it, I have attached the photos we need them in. Can you please put them in the names of:

Rachel Johansson (my one), DOB 30 August 1992;

Abigail Norman (the other girl), DOB 28 December 1989.

Obviously real addresses. Doesn't matter where.

I'm prepared to offer $1,500 each, cash, given the rushed nature of the job and the requirement to deliver.

Please let me know by return if you can do this. If you can't fit me in, can you suggest anyone else who might be able to help?

Many thanks. Hopefully see you tomorrow.

Clara Von Blomberg

'Here goes nothing,' she said as she hit the send button. 'Any ideas about how we get out of here unmarked?'

'I'm working on it.'

'I think the first thing to do is sew confusion.'

'Any suggestions?'

'Yes. Firstly, I contact the boss again, right now, and tell her that you've asked me to leave. I'll protest that I shouldn't, and ask her to decide. If she tells me to go, that will provide more ammunition to your theory, because it would suggest that she knows that you've agreed to cooperate with the Feds, and she's therefore wanting me out of the way; just as she'll assume *you* are in asking me to go. Alternatively, if she tells me to stay, it would suggest you might be barking up the wrong tree, as, if she was wanting to protect you, she would want at least one babysitter around until you're well enough to make a run for it.'

'Makes sense.'

'Secondly, we try to get the tails off us. If the boss agrees to letting me go, you email your man telling him I spotted them this morning, but you managed to talk me out of reporting it. Then you request that they lift the surveillance so that I won't immediately blow the whistle if I spot them again.'

'Good thinking,' Tempany smiled. 'But what happens if the boss comes back telling you to stay put? Does that not pretty much kill everything?'

'To a certain extent. What I would propose is that we just hang around here until Tuesday, meet with your man as arranged, agree to anything he asks, and then make a run for it once we hit Mexico.'

'You mean do the dirty on the CIA, *and* have OCC come after us at the same time?'

'I would suggest that that would be safer than going deep cover in OCC. You'll almost certainly be detected, and when you are they will take you down to the basement and murder you. I think I'd rather take my chances on some Pacific island on a false passport.'

'Or we can just do PST and go back to Caracas and resign, working to the assumption that the boss has had nothing to do with all this? At least then we'll only have one group of homicidal maniacs after us, and, you never know, OCC might offer us some modicum of protection, especially if we tell them that we were trying to reel the CIA in in order to uncover a mole in OCC. Besides, don't I now have the perfect excuse for packing all this in, you know, having been blown and all?'

Katie nodded. 'Okay. But we can deal with that if it comes to it. First things first.' She grabbed the laptop and typed the following to Artemis:

Mama!

Sorry to bother you, but sister's acting up. She's telling me to leave her in case I catch her infection. I'm adamant that I'm not going, but she's being rather insistent about it.

I think she's crazy, but I said I would ask you to decide. If you wish me to leave her in order not to catch what she's got, could you please let me know by return.

Sorry to have to burden you with this, mama, but she seems to be pulling rank on me – her own sister!

If you don't want me to leave her, could you please talk some sense into her? I think it's a terrible idea!

Love you! Steph

She showed the email to Tempany, who nodded her approval. She hit send, then drafted the following, with 'URGENT' as the subject matter:

Dear Irvin –

Miss Kirkwood knows that she was followed this morning, and came to the conclusion that it was your firm. She was going to contact OCC to alert them, but I managed to convince her that she was imagining things and talk her out of it.

During this conversation I tested the waters with regard to our proposed deal. Suffice it to say, the waters were decidedly frigid! She is utterly loyal to OCC and, I fear, would betray me in a heartbeat if she had the slightest inclination of what I was planning.

At any rate, I used the situation to tell her to go, claiming that, even though she probably wasn't being followed, it was too dangerous for her to remain, with a good chance that she would be shipped off to Gitmo if she was caught with me. She was foursquare against the idea, and went over my head to Artemis herself. Artemis, though, agreed for her to go.

As I type this she's in the shower getting ready, and will head off imminently. What her destination is I've no idea – I would guess she'll be going north and into Canada. But I'm not going to ask her.

I'm not going to blame you for this near miss. After all, this all happened before I asked you not to put us under surveillance. That said, if you do feel the need, for whatever reason, to follow her now, I would suggest keeping yourselves thoroughly incognito – although she's somewhat pliable, she's also smart, and if she spots a tail again she will immediately raise the alarm with OCC, which will alert them to the fact that you know I'm here, and will ruin everything.

I expect she'll leave within the next hour.

As for me, I'm going to spend the next few days sightseeing and kicking back, so please don't bother me unless it's something really urgent – like you finding out that Miss Kirkwood guesses what I'm up to and rats me out to OCC, and that there's a hit squad coming to get me!

Incidentally, when I'm out and about, I will, as a matter of routine, change clothes regularly. This is not to give you the slip, you understand. Rather, it is my standard tradecraft when in this part of the world: for some bizarre reason, a large number of people want me dead, and a big proportion of those – ie, the Cuban exiles and the Central American fascists – are located here.

If I don't hear from you, I'll see you on Tuesday. Can we say midday, please?

Many thanks,

Edith

'Why tell them about changing clothes?' asked Tempany as she read it.

'Well, for a start this sort of thing is standard tradecraft, so it's not as if we're giving the game away. But the reason is is that, if they're alerted to the fact you've changed, they won't automatically assume you've done so in order to try to escape *them* – otherwise they would either run you in, or ramp up the surveillance so tight you wouldn't be able to pick your nose without them knowing about it. Also, it's a display of good faith, which will hopefully convince them you're committed to them, and to go easy on the surveillance...although,' she shrugged, 'that's perhaps wishful thinking. But it's worth a shot, at least.'

Tempany grinned. 'I like it, Steph. I'll send it once we hear back from the boss.' She sat next to Katie on the couch and put her arm around her. 'I really don't want you to go. It doesn't feel…oh, Christ, look at the state of me!' she sniffled.

'We'll be okay, darling,' she said soothingly. 'Just stay focussed.'

Presently Katie's inbox rang with a message from Artemis.

Hi Steph,

Your sister's condition must be very bad if she wants you to leave. Tell her I'm not comfortable about this, but, as she is the one affected, I'll leave the decision to her. Ask her if she wants anyone else to come look after her.

As for you, Steph, I would suggest you come back to see your brother. I will tell him that I think you are due another holiday.

Again, thank you so much for looking after Edith.

Take care,

Mama.

'Oh, boy,' giggled Katie nervously. 'It's not looking good for her.'

16. The Ringer

30 minutes after Katie left, Tempany was still crying. She had rarely felt an emptiness and loneliness like this. She felt utterly bereft. And terrified. Her first instinct was to get some more booze up and sit and get drunk. She had to bend all her willpower to resist the temptation, knowing that if she was going to make it through the next few days she would have to keep her head as clear as possible. Instead, she picked up the phone and ordered a chicken salad and a fruit bowl. It was as this arrived that the laptop chimed.

Hey, Edith,

Nice meeting you this morning. (And last night!)

Apologies for the near miss. It won't happen again.

(On a personal note, I'm glad that Miss Kirkwood is out of this. It was an unnecessary complication and would almost certainly have opened the two of you up to greater peril.)

I have raised some of your points with my people. Initial feedback is VERY positive – it turns out I might have been a bit too negative in my assessment of what might and might not be possible. But I'll come back with a full response on Tuesday. If my people have any questions in the meantime, I'll email you at this address. Likewise, if you have any further questions please don't hesitate.

We also hear your concerns about bumping into unfriendly characters during your stay here. If you do, phone me immediately: I will fix it.

If you need anything – ANYTHING – cash, clothes, or even just some company, let me know. We want to help.

Yours with the greatest of respect,

Irvin

PS This goes without saying, but please delete this immediately!

Tempany stroked her chin. *It won't happen again?* Did that mean that the surveillance had been pulled? She had to assume that it didn't, and that they had put a tail on Katie, just as they would put one on her when she left the hotel.

Regardless, she had to forget about Spendlove, she told herself harshly.

Christ! I could use a drink!

'*No!*' she barked, and punched herself on the leg. She went out to the balcony and munched into her salad and fruit, then smoked a Marlboro. When she was done, she went for a shower and dressed again in the blue 715s and black top.

She had a vague idea of what she was going to do: hire a changeling to sit in the hotel room, then get several taxis to Eagle Pass and swim over when it was dark. But where to begin? She rang room service and asked for someone to come back up to take the plates away. Five minutes later, 'Andy', the young Latino waiter, turned up pushing a trolley. Tempany ushered him in and he went out to the balcony to clear up.

Tempany asked him awkwardly in Spanish, 'Andy, this is going to sound a bit odd, but I wonder if you or any of your friends in the kitchen would know where I could...um, find myself a *good time?*'

Andy turned to look at her. He was slack-jawed. 'Um...what? Ma'am,' he added nervously.

'Andy, I'm, um, gay, and I'm looking to...look, I'm looking to hire a prostitute, okay?' she said, getting red in the face.

'I...oh, ma'am. I don't want to get into trouble,' he said, and put his head down and quickly had the table cleared.

As he pushed the trolley back into the room Tempany pulled a hundred from her pocket and held it in the air. 'You're not going to get in trouble. I swear. If you can just tell me where I can possibly find a woman for some company, I shall keep my mouth firmly shut. And this is yours.'

He shuffled in and stopped in front of her. 'I...I can get you some numbers?'

'No thanks, Andy. I'd rather go and see the goods before I buy, if you catch my meaning. Can you tell me where I should go?'

'Um...you could try the junction between Guadalupe and Zarzamora. Although there's probably not much choice at the moment. Better waiting until it gets dark.'

'Thank you,' she grinned, and gave him the 100. As he left, she called after him, 'Andy! If this turns out to be a crock of shit, I'll be down to the kitchen for my hundred.'

Andy sniggered. 'It's good – unless the cops have cleared it out since last week!'

'We'll see,' said Tempany. She closed the door and turned her attention to her last lines of defence. She logged back into her Proton account, and typed a reply to McDowell which read:

> Many thanks, Irvin. This is a real comfort. Miss Kirkwood left earlier this afternoon. I'm still slightly worried about what she suspects. So, again, if you would be so kind as to let me know if you hear anything it would be appreciated.
>
> If I need anything else I'll let you know. And if anything else comes up in the meantime, email me or phone the room.
>
> Yours, Edith

She left the message open and unsent, then in another typed the following to Artemis:

> Mama –
>
> Thank you for giving sister the all-clear to go earlier. You might have suspected my motivation: two bodies are easier to spot than one, and I feared that with both of us here there would be a greater danger of our acquaintances latching onto us. I think sister was a bit hurt, especially in light of her bravery last night, so it would be appreciated if you could do whatever you feel is right to make amends with her. (Far be it for me to tell you what this might be, but perhaps an early birthday present could be in the offing!)
>
> At any rate, I'm feeling a lot better, and am hopeful of being able to come home early next week – say Monday or Tuesday – Wednesday by the latest. I'll come straight to you.

If you hear anything, email me.

Thank you, mama. Love you.

Edie

Again, she left the message open and unsent, and put the laptop to sleep.

Ten minutes later, with Spendlove's black jacket and red baseball cap on, she went down to reception and told the girl at the desk that if anyone called to tell them that she was away out sightseeing and would be back in the evening. She then walked out of the Riverside Walk side of the hotel, went across the zebra crossing on Commerce Street, and into the shopping centre on the other side. She went into Macy's, bought a blond, shoulder-length wig, green and blue pullovers, a pair of stonewashed jeans, dark blue and black baseball caps, and big D&G sunglasses, the thick bridge of which covered most of the plaster on her nose. She went back out and hailed a yellow cab to take her to the bus station. In the back, she put on the wig, the black cap, new jeans, green pullover and sunglasses, and turned the Macy's carrier bag inside out. From the bus station she wandered around a bit, went up a side street, took off the wig and changed caps and pullovers, then hailed another taxi to take her to the place Andy had mentioned. It took 15 minutes to navigate out of the city centre and onto Guadalupe Street, which was straight as an arrow and stretched off into the distance. Unlike the impressive and immaculate central area, Guadalupe Street was rundown, with abandoned, graffiti-daubed buildings everywhere, and chain link fences and electricity poles lining the sides. Adding to the depressed feel, hunched Hispanics trudged around looking thoroughly miserable. She thought again of Britain. Of the miles-long stretch of sandy beach near her parents' home in Sandwich where she used to play. Of Perth and Dunkeld. Of walking in the Highlands; of conquering the Three Sisters and a bunch of other Scottish mountains with Rebecca. Those were the best days of her life. She felt again the sting of homesickness; but it quickly gave way to a burst of pride as she recalled how, under pretty extreme duress, she had stood up to the man when he had insulted her country.

Holy shit! she thought. *Am I turning into a nationalist?*

Up until 24 hours ago the mere notion would have sickened her; after all, and just as the man had guessed, a key component of her belief system was the age-old Marxist trope that Britain and her Empire, the most successful incarnations of capitalism in history, had been cancers on the world. She looked at herself dolefully in the window as clarity continued to drill through her brain. Hating Britain and its past had always troubled her, because, deep inside, there was the unanswered question: how on earth could a country that is so welcoming, free, at the forefront of culture and science, the country that had crusaded heroically and selflessly against slavery, be as evil as academia – and a big chunk of the media – would have her believe?

It wasn't, of course. Britain was, in fact, a beacon of justice and freedom and civilisation itself. She now realised that, just as the 'progressives' and feminists who controlled education in Britain had duped her into hating everyone to the right of Fidel Castro, they had duped her into hating her own country – a country that she actually loved! She had been guilty of *1984*-style doublethink...which made her wonder if the people who had twisted her mind thus were equally as guilty of it? Or did they really believe what they were saying when they were trashing Britain and her history; when they were depicting the Empire as a white-supremacist racket which had enslaved and plundered much of the world; when they were smearing Winston Churchill, one of Britain's (and Tempany's!) greatest ever heroes, as a genocidal, racist drunk? More broadly, did they really believe it when they were pushing their man-hating radical feminism and their identity politics; when they were suppressing free speech, guilt-tripping white people, promoting the cruelty of 'body positivity', championing open borders and illegal immigration; when they were sexualising young children, and making them believe that they could change sex at will, sterilising themselves in the process? Most, she concluded, had probably been conned, just like she had, and were simply parroting neo-Marxist quackery that they neither understood nor believed.

But whether they had been hoodwinked or not, she knew, didn't really matter. What *did* matter was that each and every one of them was – just as she had been up until this very moment – actively complicit in the insidious Marxist campaign to kick down the pillars of Western civilisation – Christianity, freedom, family, morality, decency, the rule of law – and replace them with degeneracy and immorality and nihilism and moral relativism, the end point being to create such cruel and grotesque societies that the working classes would finally get it into their thick skulls that communism was their only salvation. This decades-long crusade, which had been initiated in the 1920s by Italian Marxist Antonio Gramsci, was, she now grasped, quite insane. Destroying a perfectly good and decent country in order that it might, in the Marxists' demented fantasies, be replaced by a communist utopia in which all private property is stolen, the middle and upper classes – including her! – murdered, and anyone left enslaved? It was the purest form of evil she could imagine. And capitalism, the thing she thought she had been fighting all her adult life? She realised now that, despite its inevitable iniquities, capitalism was positively benevolent compared to this wickedness; a wickedness which was, together with its witting and unwitting boosters, the real enemy of civilisation.

She grimaced at her idiocy for never having questioned this madness; for having blithely gone along with it in the silly assumption that it was all for the ultimate greater good – despite knowing instinctively, and ever since she had first read Marx and Gramsci and learned about their acolytes in the so-called Frankfurt School – the vehicle chiefly responsible for the poisoning of academia – some ten years ago, that everything about it was utterly warped.

She felt lost. Her entire life had been a waste of time. Worse, she had been a willing tool in the hands of evil men peddling an evil doctrine. She reflected with heartbreaking regret how she had thrown the Christian values her parents had tried to impart to her back in their faces; and how she had been too feeble and too ignorant to resist the cynicism and hatred of the corrupted education system which had indoctrinated her. And she now knew beyond all doubt that had the scales fallen from her eyes five years previously – or had she been just a little bit smarter; smart enough to have seen through all the 'white privilege' and 'social justice' and 'intersectionality' bullshit she had had rammed into her – she wouldn't have been within a million miles of Hyde Park that February morning. And she wouldn't have dragged Rebecca along. And Rebecca wouldn't have been murdered.

Which brought her to Spendlove.

Was it possible that her attraction to her was down to the Marxists' undermining of the West all these years? Had same-sex relationships not been normalised, while at the same time Christianity and family values were being traduced, would she and Spendlove have ever even thought about each other that way? Was their attraction entirely synthetic, the product of skilful propaganda designed to make it feel real, normal, natural? As Tempany well knew, propaganda can make anyone but the most strong-willed believe in and do almost anything, and it was entirely possible that the basis for her feelings were communist lies designed to bring down the West.

But did it matter? It did to the extent that, if their feelings for each other were a result of those lies, they would find themselves incompatible and their relationship wouldn't last. That was the worst-case scenario. And the best? She smiled. The best would be that she would spend years with this amazing woman who was her soul mate, her best friend, her equal...nay, her better! And if that happened? Well, she would maybe have Marx and Gramsci and all their Frankfurt School dipshits to thank. *Perhaps Marxism ain't so bad after all!* she thought, and barked a manic laugh.

'You okay, miss?' asked the driver, glancing at her in his mirror.

Chuckling, Tempany sat forward, and said, 'Mr Rashid,' reading the driver's name from the permit on the dashboard, 'have you ever felt like you're Jeff Goldblum in David Cronenberg's version of *The Fly?*'

'Uh...miss...is that a movie?' he said in a thick Indian accent.

'Sure is.'

'Don't think so.'

'You'd remember if you had. Let me put it another way: have you ever lived through a day, and while you're going through it, you just *know* that your life is changing.'

He thought for a moment, then nodded, 'Yes. When I was coming to America.'

'How did that work out for you?'

'Fine, miss, thank you for asking.' The perfunctory nature of his reply made it sound as if things were far from fine. 'Um...is that what is happening to you, miss? Today?'

Tempany nodded. 'I believe so.'

'And how is that working out?'

Tempany smiled. 'Put is this way: it's all rather confusing. But I'm optimistic.'

'Well, good luck,' he said cheerily.

A couple of minutes later they came up to the junction with Zarzamora. It had somewhat more life to it than the road leading there, with a McDonalds, a pizzeria, a supermarket and a Chinese at each corner of the crossroads. As they slowed, Tempany glanced around. 'Look, Mr Rashid, I'm not going to beat around the bush: I'm looking to hire a hooker, and was told that this was the place to come. Any ideas where?'

He shifted in his seat, grinned nervously, and took a left at the junction. After about 400 metres, he started to slow, and just ahead of them to the left was a handful of women spread out at random intervals, mostly looking at their phones or smoking, or both.

'Drive past,' said Tempany, 'and take the next left.' He drove up the next side street, and Tempany told him to take the next left, telling him to stop about 50 metres further on. She checked around for following vehicles, but nothing appeared. 'Just stay here for a few more minutes, please. I'm going to get changed. Keep an eye out for any other cars. If you spot anything suspicious let me know.'

'Yes, miss.'

She changed caps and tops again, and said, 'Mr Rashid, if anyone asks about me, you've never seen me in your life. Okay?'

'Okay, miss,' Rashid nodded.

'Thank you.' She paid and gave him a $100 tip, which he accepted gleefully. She got out and walked back the way they had just come. When she turned back onto Zarzamora she walked up to the row of hookers. First she came up to a fat black woman in a short leather skirt and plunging black top. 'Good time, ma'am?' she said speculatively to Tempany. 'No thanks,' she smiled, and carried on. Next was a short Latina, who was sitting on a low wall, and paid her no heed. Then came the one that Tempany had marked when they drove by: a white, thin girl, also propped up on the wall, smoking a cigarette. She was wearing a black bustier, black miniskirt, black fishnet stockings and black high heals. She had long, straggly blonde hair, which would have to go, as would her bright red lipstick and blusher. But, other than that, she would do. As Tempany approached she pretended to look over to the buildings opposite…and walked straight into a telephone pole on the side of the pavement. She fell onto the sidewalk with a yelp, the sunglasses flying, and cupped her face with her hands. After a moment she pushed herself onto all fours, groaning, and the girl was next to her and had her hand on her shoulder. 'You okay, sweetie?'

'Uhhh,' groaned Tempany. 'Could you help me up, please?'

'Um…sure, sweetie. Sure.' The girl hooked her hand under Tempany's armpit and pulled her to her feet. Tempany doubled up and wheezed, then straightened up and rubbed her face where she had apparently been hit, then walked over to the pole and booted it with the sole of her trainer. 'Bitch!' she snarled. When she turned back, the girl, who had picked up the sunglasses, was regarding her through gimlet eyes. 'Are you okay, ma'am?' she asked suspiciously as she handed them back.

'I think so – my pride's just a little bruised, is all. Miss, I can't thank you enough. Can I take you for something to drink, or eat? Don't worry, I'll pay for your time.'

The girl glanced around, then stammered, 'Uh…it…it's a hundred an hour, ma'am.'

'No problem. Anywhere you would like to go?'

She nodded up the street. 'Wanna go to McDonald's? Or there's a pizza joint across the road?'

'McDonald's?' she shrugged. 'I'm Tempany, by the way.' She offered her hand.

The girl shook it cautiously. 'I'm Chloe, ma'am.'

'You trying to make me feel like your granny? It's Tempany.'

'Uh. Okay.'

'Would you like to lead the way?'

'Um, sure.' Chloe grabbed a bag and a black leather jacket from behind the wall, and led Tempany back up towards the junction.

'So, tell me about yourself, Chloe.'

'Ain't much to tell, Miss Tempany.'

'You're not from around here, are you?'

'Not to begin with.'

'Kentucky?'

The girl laughed. 'Not bad, Miss Tempany. Tennessee. My dad came here for the oil. But…he got killed a few years ago. My mom…' Her voice trailed off.

Tempany could guess from her countenance what had happened: dad died, mom went off the rails, couldn't cope. Chloe ended up neglected and failing at school, and now had nothing but her body to make ends meet. 'Aren't you a bit young for this sort of thing?' she asked.

Chloe sighed. 'Look, I hope you ain't some Good Samaritan tryin' to make me see the error of my ways. I know you mean well, but could you people just leave me alone?'

'No, Chloe. I'm not one of those people. In fact,' she smirked, 'I'm probably the opposite of a Good Samaritan. What you do with your body is entirely up to you. Indeed, under different circumstances I might well have resorted to that myself.' Chloe glanced at her and smiled. 'It just wouldn't be on the top of my list of things to do.'

'It's not on mine either,' she moped.

'Did you not go to college?'

'Ain't smart enough. Dropped out of high school,' she said, her voice catching and her stride faltering.

'Well, you seem smart to me,' said Tempany brightly.

'That's very kind of you, Miss Tempany. I…I hope you don't mind me asking, but what's an English woman doin' here, in this part of town, talkin' to me?'

'Just doing a bit of sightseeing.'

'It's a mighty queer place to be doing sightseeing, if you don't mind my saying. Have you seen anything you like so far?' she added suggestively.

'I'm not sure yet.'

Chloe laughed.

'How old are you?'

'Old enough.'

'20?'

'Ha! I'm flattered. 23.'

'Want to guess mine? Be honest, now.'

'I'd say you were about 30,' she mused. 'Though it's kinda hard, what with your eyes and that Band-Aid and all. But you seem to be in pretty good shape. So 30.'

'I should be offended!' she laughed. 'But I'll let you off. Especially with the bit about my body. I'm 28. 29 in a few months.'

'What do you do?'

'I'm in the oil industry, like your dad.'

'It's mighty dangerous, Miss Tempany,' she said in awe.

'Not for me,' she shook her head. 'I'm in sales. For the government of Colombia.'

'Really? Wow. Do you like it?'

'It has its moments. I'll tell you more when we get there.'

They crossed the road and went into McDonald's, Tempany buying them chicken burgers and Diet Cokes. They sat opposite each other at a centre table away from the windows, Tempany facing the door.

'Thank you,' said Chloe, as she bit into hers.

'You're very welcome.' Tempany leaned across and, dropping her voice, said, 'Chloe, would you be interested in making a lot of money? An *awful* lot of money.'

Chloe smirked. 'If you tell me what you mean by an *awful lot* of money, I'll tell you if I'm interested.'

'$5,000 tonight, cash in hand. And *300,000* next week if things work out for me.'

Her mouth popped open. She blinked several times and shook her head. 'What?'

'305 grand all in.'

'*Jesus!*' she whispered. 'Is this a sting?'

'Do I look like I'm a cop?' said Tempany with a laugh.

She shook her head slowly. 'It's just...that amount of money. You're yanking my chain.'

'Believe me Chloe, I'm not. I...well, suffice it to say, I'm a woman of means.'

She looked down, then up, and said, 'What, exactly, am I to do for this money?'

'It's the easiest cash you'll ever make. All I need you to do is to put on my clothes, go to my hotel in them tonight, and stay in my room until 5.00am on Tuesday, or until such time as I phone giving you the all-clear.'

She shook her head again. 'What...what's this all about? I don't want to get in trouble.'

'You won't,' she said assuredly. 'It's all rather simple. I have a meeting with an asset management company at the hotel on Tuesday, during which they are going to try to make me rat on my employers. This is something I want to avoid, so I'm planning to make a run for it this evening. The problem is, they have the hotel under surveillance, and if I don't return tonight they will send out a search party and try to stop me leaving the country; and, if they catch me, they will make me talk. This is where you come in. If you agree to go back dressed as me, I'm banking on them not noticing the switch, and just sitting on their asses and not alerting anyone.'

'These people...' Chloe nodded at her. 'Did they hurt you?'

She shook her head. 'No, Chloe. This was something else. As you saw earlier, I'm rather clumsy. This is nothing to worry about.'

'But...why do they want you to rat on your employers?'

'It's basically industrial espionage,' she said airily. 'I know all Colombia's pricing and production strategies for the coming year, and this is something these people are desperate to get their hands on so that they don't lose money in the futures markets – which they will if Colombia ramps up production. They've been harassing me for this information all the while I've been here these last few weeks, offering all sorts of bribes and getting more threatening each time I refuse to play ball. I managed to put them off until Tuesday by telling them I don't have all the information they need at the moment, but that I'll have it on Tuesday morning. By the time they turn up, you'll be long gone, and I'll hopefully be safely back in my HQ in Bogota.'

'But…why are they picking on *you?*'

She shrugged. 'Probably because I'm here. They see me as an opportunity to satiate their greed. Also, I…' she paused and said sheepishly, 'I met their top guy at a party two weeks ago…and, um, I might have been rather indiscrete and offered information I shouldn't have. They…they're a bit upset about it.'

'Can't you go to the police?'

'And say what, exactly?'

'I…okay,' she nodded. 'But…why not just tell them what you know, if they're offering you money?'

'That would be insider trading,' she said with a straight face. 'Besides, I'm loyal to my employer. And my employer pays very, very handsomely. That's how I can afford to give you 300 grand.'

'But what's to stop them from just kicking the door down and trying to make you – or me – talk before the meeting?'

'Because it would be impossible for them to do so without drawing attention to themselves. That's why I'm sure you'll be safe. They know that if they were to try to use force in the hotel I would scream my head off. No, they won't try anything.'

Chloe frowned doubtfully.

'Tell you what: if you're worried, get one of your friends to come with you – but I'm not paying for them,' she said adamantly. 'Also, if you bring someone else in, they are not to leave, under any circumstances, until you go on Tuesday morning. Deal?'

She smiled weakly. '305's a lot of money, Miss Tempany.'

'Certainly is.'

She took another bite of her burger, chewed thoughtfully, had a drink, then looked Tempany in the eye and asked, 'When do you want me there?'

'First things first: tell me where you live and I'll meet you there,' she glanced at her watch; it was half past three, 'at seven. But go back to work for a couple of hours first as if nothing's happening – it's quite possible we're being observed even now. If anyone comes and asks you what we've been talking about, just say we were chatting about where we're both from and stuff, and that I asked you how much it would be for a night. Tell them you said you don't take female clients, and I just left it at that. Okay?'

Chloe nodded.

'When you're going home tonight, take three cabs in different directions, and walk a couple of blocks before jumping in each. When you get dropped off in the last one, make sure it's a couple of blocks from your house, and use side streets to get there. I'll give you money to pay for them. In the event that you're convinced you're being followed, either by car or people on foot, don't go home. Go sit in a diner or something. If you don't turn up by eight, I'll know you've been followed and our deal will be off.'

'Okay,' she nodded.

'What's your address?'

She gave her an address on Ware Boulevard.

Tempany repeated it. 'What is it? An apartment or house?'

'Apartment.'

'Which floor?'

'First.'

'Of how many floors?'

'Just the two.'

'Is it north or south of the city?'

'South.'

'Good,' said Tempany. 'I'll be there at seven. When we get there, I'm afraid you're going to have to cut off your hair and dye it black.' She took off her hat and pointed. 'Just like this. I'll get the dye. You're also going to have to put a plaster on your nose and blacken up your eyes. Then you will put on the clothes I've got here in my bag, and I will wear some of yours, and you will go to my hotel and wait there until Tuesday. Don't worry about food and drink – I've paid 500 bucks into room service, and they'll give you anything until it's spent.'

'Wow. Thanks. What's the hotel?'

'Marriot River Walk. The room's been paid up till the end of next week...but I would suggest not using it beyond Tuesday morning. Just leave when I tell you, and leave in your own clothes. Again, when going home, don't go directly. Take a few cabs and go for breakfast somewhere. If all goes to plan from my side – that is, if I make it safely to Colombia and there's no mishap – I'll phone you to arrange the transfer of the 300.'

She took a sip of her Coke. 'Miss Tempany. This all sounds a bit...well, a bit fucking crazy.'

'You're right to be sceptical, Chloe. You wouldn't be human if you weren't. But all you've really got to know is this: you will be paid well, starting with the five grand tonight.'

'I know I'm going to regret this,' she sighed, 'but, what the hell: I'm in.'

They grinned at each other. 'Thank you. Now, there is one other thing, which is most important: once you get to the hotel, don't answer the door to anybody except room service or housekeeping, and when they turn up try not to let them see your face. And if anything happens out of the ordinary – if, for example, anyone comes to the door who is unexpected, you are to call me immediately – I'll give you the number tonight. Clear?'

'Yes,' she nodded, her blue eyes focussed.

When they finished eating Tempany gave Chloe a hug and 200 dollars. 'Later.'

'Later,' Chloe smiled, and skipped across the road and back down towards her spot.

Tempany sat for ten minutes with a coffee, then hailed a cab to South Park Mall, which was about three miles due south on Zarzamora Street. There, she bought a black backpack, black trousers, a black pullover and black underlayer, black beanie hat, a pair of black boots, a torch, a roll of gaffer tape, black hair dye, and a burner phone. She managed to cram everything into the backpack, then jumped into a cab and gave the driver the address of Chloe's apartment. When they got there, she asked her to drive on and drop her a half mile further along the road. Before getting out, she changed clothes again. She then walked in a series of turns through the various blocks of houses on the way back, ending up across from Chloe's apartment complex at 6.30. It consisted of two blocks of two-storey flats facing each other across an access road at right angles to the main road. She had half expected it to be a dump, but it, and the surrounding area, was all neat and tidy, which gladdened her, for Chloe's sake. The problem was that there wasn't any place for her to hide and observe Chloe when (or if) she appeared. This was rather critical, because while she was sure that she was not being followed, she had no idea if they had latched onto Chloe. She looked around, then sauntered across the road, and walked up the access road between the blocks, marking Chloe's flat on the upper floor of the one on the right. There was no one else about, though lights were on in most of the flats. She walked to the end of the road, which led to a big turning circle surrounded by parking spaces. Beyond that was an area of waste ground, which she walked on to, and carried on walking until she reached a clump of trees at the end. She couldn't be seen here, so she lit a cigarette and stood and smoked. Then she walked slowly back. About halfway to the turning circle, she saw Chloe walk up the stairs to her apartment. She unlocked her door, but before entering kneeled down to tie her laces, and glanced surreptitiously back down the street. *Good girl!* thought Tempany. When Chloe went in and the door closed behind her, Tempany waited ten minutes. Two cars entered the cul-de-sac, both of which parked at the side of the turning circle, and their drivers got out and went into different apartments. There was nothing and no one else. Tempany walked back onto the circle, back down the street, and, as sure as she could be that Chloe hadn't been tailed, went up to her flat and rapped on the door. It opened instantly, and Chloe chirped, 'You made it, Miss Tempany! And, um, you've changed.'

'Yep,' she grinned.

'Come in, come in!' Tempany found herself in a living room with a computer desk with a laptop on it on the right, a sofa facing a TV in the corner, and a kitchenette to the left. There were two open doors on the left leading to a bedroom and a bathroom. The walls were painted cream, with a few posters of bands she didn't know, and above the TV a poster of the film *Titanic*, with Leonardo DiCaprio and Kate Winslet embracing each other above the imposing prow of the ship. The main thing that struck her was that the flat was spotless and smelled of air freshener.

'Make yourself at home. Want anything to eat?'

'No thank you, Chloe. Any problems?'

'I don't think so.'

'Anyone speak to you?'

'No one out of the ordinary. There was one usual client, but that was all.'

'Good.' She produced the box of hair dye, handed it to Chloe, then took off her hat to remind her of the job. 'Okay?'

Chloe squinted, and nodded slowly. 'Yes, ma'am.'

'Do you want a hand?'

She shook her head. 'I should be fine.'

'What size of shoes do you take?'

'8 ½.'

'Perfect. Could you wear these as well, if I can get a pair of yours, please?' she said as she kicked off her trainers. 'Hopefully they don't smell too bad.'

'I'm sure they'll be fine,' she smiled. She went into the bathroom, leaving the door slightly ajar, and turned the shower on. Tempany fished from the Macy's carrier bag her 715s, black pullover, and Spendlove's jacket and baseball cap, and laid them out on the back of the sofa. She then sat down and switched on the TV, finding a rerun of *Star Trek*. She heard the shower turn off, and the faint sound of scissors chopping hair.

'These accountant guys,' Chloe said from the bathroom. 'They sound a bit heavy duty.'

'You'd be amazed,' replied Tempany.

A moment later, Chloe said from right behind her, 'I *am* amazed.'

Tempany turned with a start to find Chloe standing behind the sofa with a towel wrapped round her, her greasy, frizzy hair chopped off, and her red and blue makeup washed away. Tempany could only stare. Her pale skin was clear and there was a youthful, innocent beauty to her. 'You...you're beautiful,' she mouthed.

'Thank you, Miss Tempany,' she smiled bashfully. Then she frowned and said, 'Yeah, I'm amazed at these friends of yours. That they would be such a bunch of psychos. That it would be worth 305,000 for you to get away from them. In fact, Miss Tempany, I'm so amazed that I know you're lying to me.'

Tempany got to her feet. Before today she would have automatically tried to lie her way out of it. But now? Faced with this beautiful, broken young creature she was putting in harm's way? She couldn't do it. She took a deep breath and said, 'You're right, Chloe. The story I told you was a lie. I know you're brave and that knowing the truth wouldn't stop you, but the thing is, if you know the truth, and things don't work out, you could be an accessory to what I'm...well, my situation, and you could therefore be sent to prison for a very long time. As it is, if you know nothing, or only know the story I've told you, they can do nothing, I mean *nothing* to you.'

'And who are *they*, Miss Tempany?'

'Just saying who they are would make you an accessory. So I'm not going to tell you.'

She thought. 'Well, it's obviously the law. And obviously not local. So I'd say it's the Feds or the CIA.'

Tempany just shook her head. 'Look, if I get out of this, I promise I will tell you, at some point.'

Chloe nodded slowly. 'Okay, Miss Tempany. I won't trouble you no more about it,' she said, and went back into the bathroom.

Tempany sat down again, trying hard not to cry, but failing to stop a solitary tear running down her cheek. She cleared her throat. 'So, Chloe,' she said over her shoulder. Chloe was standing at the sink staring at the instructions for the hair dye. 'How much are you for a place like this?'

'500 a month, all in.'

'That's not bad.'

'Yep. Not bad at all. I can make that in good a day,' she said proudly.

'Wow. What do you do with the rest of it?'

'Save.'

'What for?'

'Dunno.'

'You don't know what you're saving for?'

'Not really. I would maybe like to go back home sometime. My grandparents and a few aunts are still around. I think.'

'You never think about going back to school? It's never too late these days.'

'I...I ain't very good at reading.'

'Do you need glasses?' offered Tempany.

'I don't thing so.'

'Have you ever been tested?'

'Not recently.'

'It's maybe worth a try.'

'Maybe,' she said morosely.

On an impulse, Tempany got up and went into the bathroom and sat on the edge of the bath. Chloe was filling the sink and had the various bottles of the kit laid out in front of her, and was putting on the throwaway plastic gloves.

'Chloe, what happens when you try to read?'

'I…um,' she sniffled.

Again, Tempany had to struggle not to cry. 'It's okay, Chloe,' she said haltingly. 'You can tell me.'

'The…the letters are all jumbled and stuff. I can make them out for a bit, just about, but I can't read a newspaper or a book or anything.'

'Have you been tested for dyslexia?'

'I was supposed to. A few years ago.'

'And?'

'And…well, I never got an appointment. Then my dad died and things just went bad. Besides, I just thought I was dumb. That's what everyone told me.'

'Oh, God, Chloe. You're *definitely* not dumb. You've probably just got dyslexia, and it's treatable. You should have been seen years ago. You've been failed. By everyone. *Jesus Christ!*' she spat. She wanted to hunt down Chloe's mum – if she even still existed – and rip her fucking head off. As it was, she started to sob. She quickly grabbed some toilet paper and dried her eyes and blew her nose.

'I think I've always known it, Miss Tempany,' said Chloe. 'I'll be fine. Especially if this job comes off.' She smiled at Tempany in the mirror, then went to work on her hair. 'Don't waste any tears on my account.'

'I'm so sorry, sweetheart,' she said, and trudged back out, feeling wretched about everything.

In between application of the hair dye, Chloe rumbled around her bedroom then made some toast and a cup of coffee, and sat next to Tempany. She asked where Tempany came from and about her family, and Tempany answered fairly truthfully, though leaving out the bit about her parents hating her. Then Chloe went back into the bathroom to finish the job. Ten minutes later she reappeared with short jet-black hair. 'How do I look?'

'Bingo!' she cried. 'Need a hand with the face?'

She shook her head, 'Nope,' and went back into the bathroom. When she reappeared she had simulated black eyes, a plaster over her nose, and was wearing Tempany's clothes and Spendlove's red baseball cap. Tempany sprang to her feet, delighted with her choice of ringer: Chloe would easily pass for her from more than a few metres away, and might even pass for her up close in a pinch.

'Perfect! Perfect, Chloe. You're a star!'

'Thanks, Miss Tempany.'

'Could I get some of your clothes, please?'

She nodded, went into her bedroom, and came out with a pair of faded jeans and a grey sweatshirt and gave her a pair of white Converse trainers. 'These do you?'

'Great.' Tempany pulled off her top and jeans and put on Chloe's. They were ever so slightly tight, but would do until she changed into the cat burglar gear. 'Don't suppose I could trouble you for a bin liner and a towel, Chloe?'

'Sure,' she said, and produced a towel from the bathroom and a bin liner from the kitchen, both of which Tempany stuffed into the backpack.

Tempany gave her the number of the burner phone, and Chloe gave Tempany hers. 'Chloe, please don't be offended by this, but are you able to text?'

'Sure. If it's short.'

'This is short. I want you to send me a text message every morning at seven and every evening at seven saying only "okay" in the event that nothing untoward happens. If I don't hear from you I'll know something's happened, and I'll attempt to contact you. If anything untoward does happen –

that is, knocks on the door or calls to the room you're not expecting, or anything else worries you – call me immediately. If my phone's not on, send me a text saying only "no". And delete each message as soon as it's sent. Okay?'

Chloe nodded, 'Yes, Miss Tempany.'

'Good. Another very important thing: whenever you're in the public areas of the hotel – the lobby, the corridors – basically anywhere that's not my room, have this cap on, have your face done up, and never, ever look up to the ceiling.'

She nodded.

'Have you any belongings you need to take?'

'You did say I should take a change of clothes? And I guess my toothbrush.'

'Yes. Put them in this,' she said, handing her the Macy's bag.

'What about your clothes?'

'They're yours if you want them.'

'If you're sure?'

'I'm sure.'

Chloe dumped Tempany's clothes on the bed, then quickly filled the bag with a pair of trousers, a couple of t-shirts, and some underwear and toiletries.

Tempany handed her her keycard. 'Room 1036. Repeat it.'

'1036.'

'Again.'

'1036.'

'Good. The room is booked in the name of Alison Worthington. That will be your name while you are in the hotel. You will answer to it, and give it as your name if anyone asks. Alison Worthington. Repeat it.

'Alison Worthington.'

'There is one further task I need you to perform when you get there. I have left a laptop in the room. There are two email messages open on it. I want you to hit the send button on both of them. Send the first about half an hour after you get in, and the other about 15 minutes later – it doesn't matter the order. If the computer's offline, use the hotel's Wi-Fi to log back on. Also, make sure that the laptop's VPN is not on. If it is, turn it off before you send them – I want the recipients to think I sent them from the hotel. Okay?'

'Yes, ma'am.'

Tempany handed her a scrap of paper with the passwords for the laptop and her email account written on it. 'Can you make these out?'

Chloe squinted and said slowly: 'Laptop: tor…torpedo,' pronouncing the 'e' 'eh'. 'Proton Mail: Di…ana…Diana1938.'

'Good girl,' grinned Tempany. 'If any responses come back, take a photo of them on your phone and send them to mine. Don't do anything else unless I tell you.'

Chloe nodded solemnly, then said, 'Say, Miss Tempany, you ain't some sort of secret agent?'

Tempany chuckled. 'What do you think?'

'Um…about as much as you're a cop,' she laughed.

'Are you taking anyone with you?'

'Haven't decided yet. I, um…well, there's not really anyone else, except my co-workers.'

Goddammit. She hated Chloe's life. 'Ask round whoever you want,' she sighed. 'But remember: they are not to leave before you do on Tuesday.'

'Understood.'

'Good. By the way, the laptop's yours if you want it.'

'Gee, thanks!'

'And you can take the clothes I left there as well. Plus, and keep your eyes open for this, I've some clothes in the laundry. With a bit of luck they'll be back already, but if not, someone should be up with them tomorrow. Just let them in and run into the bathroom or something.'

'Will do.'

Tempany unzipped the backpack and gave Chloe a roll of $100 bills. 'Here's the first instalment. You'd best count it.'

She pulled the rubber band off it and expertly riffled through the bills. 'Perfect. Thank you, Miss Tempany,' she said, and went into the bedroom to stash it. When she came back out she was beaming. 'Is it time?'

Tempany nodded. She engaged her clear blue eyes and put her hand on her shoulder. 'You said you didn't want a Good Samaritan. Not that I could ever be that person, but if you do decide you want help, with anything, I would be honoured if you would allow me to try. And if you don't, just let me be your friend.'

Chloe bit her lip. 'I...I guess I would like that, Miss Tempany.'

'Problem is, I can probably never come back here. Would you like to come and visit me? My...' Her voice caught in her throat. She swallowed and said with an effort, 'My girlfriend and I are planning on heading to Scotland.' Why it was an effort wasn't shame, she knew. It was just that it was no one's business other than her and Spendlove's.

'I...wow...your *girlfriend?* I was sure you were straight!' she laughed.

'I...well, I am...kinda,' she blustered.

Chloe chuckled, 'I believe you,' and winked.

'Well, would you like to come and see me or not?' she said testily.

She nodded slowly. 'Yes. Yes, Miss Tempany. I would like that very much.' She took off her hat and threw her arms around her, childlike, and nuzzled her head into her chest. Tempany thought fleetingly, ludicrously, of adopting her. 'I hope she likes me,' said Chloe.

'Oh, she'll like you, sweetheart. She's even nicer than I am. And prettier, too, if that's even possible.'

Chloe pulled out of the clinch, laughing. 'I can't wait to meet her. But I don't have a passport.'

'Better apply for one then.'

She nodded. 'Will do.'

'That's a date.' Tempany kissed her forehead. 'Ready?'

She pressed her lips and narrowed her eyes. 'Ready.'

PART III

17. Rio Grande / Rio Bravo

Tempany was scared. She had crossed the river once before, and had sworn that she would never try it again: being a lousy swimmer, she had been sucked under, and was only saved when she hit one of the concrete legs supporting the southern road bridge. Yet, here she was, slipping down the bank at the edge of the golf course between the two bridges in Eagle Pass in the early morning darkness, flipping the torch on and off intermittently, and about to plunge into the water. She had changed into her all-black gear in the back of the first taxi, before switching cabs in the town of Devine. Chloe's clothes were sealed in the bin liner and zipped up in her backpack.

She hit the water – which was cold but, mercifully, not cripplingly so – and was up to her waist in two steps. She turned off the torch, clamped it between her teeth, and started to wade across. After about five metres the water was up to her chest and starting to drag her downstream. She turned into the current and began to breaststroke into it to stop herself being pulled off course. Three more steps and the water was up to her neck. *This is it, Bells! Focus. Focus.* She tentatively took her feet off the bottom and began to kick. The current became more powerful with each stroke, and she was soon struggling to keep her head above water. She swallowed a mouthful of it, causing her to splutter and spit the torch into river. She looked up at the streetlights flanking the bank ahead, but they appeared to be no nearer than when she had plunged in. She had a clear vision of being swept under again, but this time drowning. Panic gripped her, and she thought of turning back and running away. *Come on, Bells! Come on!* She gritted her teeth and splashed on. But soon she was gasping for air and her legs and arms began to tighten. She focussed on the streetlights and counted ten more strokes…but then an excruciating stab of cramp hit her right thigh. She put her feet down, but they found nothing but water, and she had no choice but to let the current take her for a few seconds while her breathing steadied and limbs cooled. Then, with a grunt of pain, she started pulling and kicking again. *Ten strokes! Ten strokes!* She got to six, and her foot hit a rock. Immediately she stood up, to find the water only up to her chest and the stream less turbulent. '*Thank God,*' she puffed. With leaden legs she waded towards a clump of trees silhouetted in the streetlights about 15 metres ahead. She pulled herself up the grassy bank with trembling arms, staggered towards the thicket, and collapsed. She lay there for two or three minutes, wheezing and shaking, then got to her feet, stripped down, ripped open the bin liner, and dried herself with Chloe's towel. She put a fresh plaster on her nose, got into Chloe's clothes, then checked the pockets for her remaining cash and cigarettes. She was about to light up, when she told herself what a stupid idea it would be, given how much her lungs were still hurting, and impulsively threw the packet towards the river, hearing a small splash as it hit the water. She left the backpack and wet clothes under the trees, and walked stiffly onto the riverside path, which was deserted. She hobbled towards the north bridge, then walked up onto the plaza backing passport control. She spotted a cab parked near the bridge's exit and asked the driver if he would take dollars. He nodded enthusiastically, and ten minutes later she was at the Holiday Inn, feeling sickly from a mixture of relief, exhaustion, and fear that Katie hadn't made it. If she hadn't, she would just have to get a room and hunker down and wait. And if she didn't come at all? She was in no state to even consider this eventuality.

On reception was a black-haired, dark-skinned man staring into a monitor. When she presented herself with a cough, he jumped to his feet, and grinned, 'Si, Señora?'

'I'm meeting my friend here, Rachel Johansson. Can you tell me her room number, please?'

'One moment,' he said, and started typing. He apparently got a hit, and asked, 'Name please?'

'Abigail Norman,' she said as calmly as she could.

He picked up his phone, spoke briefly, then smiled as he put down the receiver, 'Room 125,' and pointed to the lift.

When she got to the room, she gave three knocks, paused, then another two. A moment later the door opened, and Katie, bare-footed with a pair of blue tracksuit bottoms, a white t-shirt with a large teddy bear on the chest, and wet hair straggling to her shoulders, stood smirking. Tempany jumped in and threw her arms around her. 'You made it!'

'Good to see you, too, Abbey,' giggled Katie as she kicked the door shut.

'When did you get here?'

'About two hours ago.'

'Any problems?'

'Not that I know of. If I was being tailed they must have the Invisible Man working for them,' she laughed, and ushered her into the room. A Mexican football match was playing on the TV, and there was an open laptop on the bed. Katie sat cross-legged in front of it, and Tempany sat on the chair under the cabinet with the TV. She nodded at the laptop. 'The insurance policy?'

'The insurance policy.'

'How's it coming along?'

'Not too bad, I think. I sent the emails an hour ago. I doubt we'll get any acknowledgements until about ten or eleven CET. If we're busted in the meantime, we'll still hopefully be able to talk our way out of it – the lawyers have got the dirt now, and as long as they think they can get money from us, they'll use it as per my instructions…that's the theory, at least,' she shrugged. 'Everything okay with you?'

'Not bad…apart from that bloody river!' she laughed, then told her about Chloe.

'What happens if she gets run in?' asked Katie.

'God knows. We might not have enough blackmail chips to spring her. But, even if we don't, as she knows nothing of our business they won't be able to pin anything on her. Legitimately, at least. She'll be fine.'

'You *hope* she'll be fine,' she said sceptically. 'And I'm not sure about you getting her to text you. If they take her in, they'll pull her phone records, and they'll be able to locate us, more or less.'

'I have thought of that, and it's a risk worth taking to know we're not busted.'

'But there is a possibility that, if she is pulled in, she'll tell them of her alerts to you, and it could be the Agency sending them, not her.'

'Good point. Just after she texts me this evening, I'll phone her to make sure she's okay. Also, I don't plan to have the phone on all the time. I'll just switch it on at seven, and off as soon as I've heard from her, and I'll get rid of it before we hit Caracas.'

'And if they do bust her, or otherwise know you've left, and there's a reception committee waiting for us when we get there?'

'We tell the truth, up to a point: that the Agency were onto us and we decided to make a run for it, and were on our way back to HQ for debrief. And if that doesn't work we've got the insurance policy to fall back on. We'll be fine,' she said breezily.

'And the 300 grand? Where's that coming from?'

'Me.'

'Don't you think it's a bit steep?'

Tempany shook her head. 'Not really. Suffice it to say, it's pretty much loose change, and it'll be worth it if all this comes off. Besides, I...' Her voice trailed off and she gave Katie a squint smile.

'I don't need to be jealous, do I?'

'Don't be silly. I just feel...well, kind of protective of her. She's a lovely kid who's had a rotten time of it, and I, well, I want to look after her. Must be my maternal instinct kicking in.'

They looked into each other's eyes for a few beats. They both smiled, as if coming to the understanding that this would be a conversation for another time. Katie got up and kissed her on the cheek. 'You know, apart from the odd lapse of judgement, you're not half as bad a person as you think you are.'

'I'm trying.'

Katie sat back down and said, 'Sorry for nitpicking. It's just the details I'm trying to get straight. Other than that, I think it's rather brilliant.'

'Thanks,' she said softly. 'That means a lot.'

'I'm glad. Now, I've emailed Cortez and told him I'm going north to Canada as per the boss's instructions. I've told him I'll contact him again once I get there. That should give me a few days before he starts getting twitchy.'

'Where were you going to meet him?'

'Acapulco.'

'Nice work if you can get it. Any joy with the passports?'

'He can deliver them tomorrow...well, today, but you know what I mean. Providing we can get on it, and it's on schedule, the plane should land in Mexico City at 1425, then there's a plane to Caracas at 1630, which changes in Panama, and gets in at half one in the morning. I'll ask our man to show up at about half two, which should give us plenty of time to sort ourselves out.'

'The time's not very good for getting into Caracas. It means we'll probably have to hang around all day, because we simply won't have time to do everything before it gets light.'

'Should we go to your flat?'

She thought, and shook her head. 'No. I'm not staying there a second longer than I have to. I only want to be in – grab the gear and my bits and pieces – and out. I vote we get a hotel, I'll go for the stuff during the day, then we do the jobs later on. How does that sound?'

'Good,' she nodded. 'I'll confirm with Luca and get our tickets and a hotel booked. Get some sleep.'

Tempany kicked off Chloe's trainers and jeans and threw herself on the bed. She was fast asleep even before Katie had turned the lights off.

18. Raphael

Katie woke her at nine. She immediately switched on her phone, to be greeted by three text messages from Chloe, the first sent at 2225, the second at 2305, and the third, which read 'OK', just after seven. The first contained a photo of a reply from Irvin McDowell, which read simply, 'Will do, Edith. Keep in touch.' The second was from Artemis, which read, 'I hear you, Edie! I'm relieved you're getting better. We'll pull through, I know it. If you need anything get back to me immediately.' She showed all three to Katie, who seemed pleased. They went down for breakfast, then Tempany went out to buy more clothes. The hotel's shuttle bus took them out to the airport at 1030. Just as Katie predicted, the woman on the desk merely took their order number and didn't ask for ID. The plane – a small Aeromar turboprop with about 50 seats – was only half full, and Tempany and Katie sat at the back, several seats away from anybody else. Tempany was feeling hot and claustrophobic. She desperately wanted a drink. As they were climbing into the air, she was on the verge of asking the stewardess in the jump seat behind them for a beer and a wine to straighten herself out, but Katie held her hand and whispered in her ear, 'What's up?'

'I...I'm drying out, Kat. I need a drink.'

Katie snapped round to her. 'When was the last time you had one?'

'Um…I don't know…yesterday, when you were out for the run. I think?'

'How much do you drink a day? Honestly, now.'

'Um…I don't know…a half bottle, maybe?'

Katie, with her lips pressed tight and brow crinkled, put her hand on Tempany's forehead. She looked uncertain for a few moments, then smiled faintly and said, 'You'll be fine. Stick your head between your knees and take some deep breaths until we're level. If you need anything later we'll sort it.'

Tempany took 'anything' to mean either alcohol or diazepam, or whatever else they could lay their hands on. She put her head down and breathed deeply, and Katie gently massaged her neck and shoulders until the seatbelt alert pinged. As soon as it did, Katie turned to the stewardess and asked for some water, which Tempany glugged down gratefully. When she sat back, she was over the worst. Still, to take her mind off the rest of the flight, she put her seat back and her head against the window and tried to sleep, which she managed fitfully. When Katie shook her awake as they descended she felt ultra-groggy, almost delirious, and drank another bottle of water. It straightened her out again, slightly, but she was worried: she might have to drink just to get through the next couple of days; it might be the only way she could function, and would probably be a better fix than diazepam, which would knock her out. She wrenched her mind from the problem, and started chatting to Katie about Yeovil: how was it? Where did she hang out? Who were her friends? She didn't process any of the answers, but it was distracting enough, and by the time they walked off and got their bags she was reasonably stable again. Coffee, she told herself. Lots of coffee. And some cigarettes.

When they walked through arrivals, a black-suited chauffeur was standing holding a sheet of A4 with

'BLOMBERG' written on it in red marker. Katie bounded over, spoke to him briefly, and he led them through the thronging concourse and to the taxi rank outside. His was a big black sedan parked near the back. He got into the driver's seat and Katie hopped in the passenger side, leaving the door ajar and Tempany standing on the pavement with their bags. The man reached into the glovebox and gave Katie a brown envelope. She said, 'Do you mind?' and before he could answer ripped it open and took out two blue Australian passports. Katie methodically examined the covers then each page, paying particular attention to the ID pages at the rear. 'Good,' she said at last, and gave the driver a roll of dollar bills, which he quickly counted. 'Thank you,' he said.

'No, thank *you*,' smiled Katie, and kissed him on the cheek. 'Tell Luca I said "hi".'

'Yes, ma'am,' he said, blushing.

As they made their way back into the terminal, Tempany asked, 'How do you know so much about passports?'

'I don't,' she smirked. 'Well, not really. But you just have to make out you know what you're doing when dealing with these people, otherwise they'll skin you alive.'

'Good point,' she laughed.

'As it is, the stuff I get from Luca hasn't failed me yet, and these look like they'll do the trick…fingers crossed.'

'They'll do,' she said confidently.

The next flight was a Copa Air Boeing 737, which, although almost full, was far more comfortable than the lumbering turboprop, and Tempany's DTs from earlier were, aided by a substantial dose of nicotine and a handful of stress relief tablets from the airport, wafting away by the hour.

She had bought the issue of *Cosmopolitan* she had been thumbing through the other night in Bill's Mart, and found herself staring at it with the ghoulish fascination of a witness to a car crash. On the cover was a scantily-clad Emma Roberts, followed by an infantile cavalcade of titillation, make-up and hairdos. She eventually nudged Katie – who was reading *Heart of Darkness*, and looking baffled – and said, 'Have you read this recently?' Katie shook her head. 'I…I used to like it. But…it's just *awful*.'

'What's changed? It or you?'

'It…and me. *God!*' she moaned. 'Is this what it's like being red-pilled? Hating everything?'

'Don't ask me,' she laughed. 'I took the blue one.'

When they were changing in Panama, Tempany switched on her phone again, to be met with another *OK*. She phoned Chloe, and was answered after three rings.

'Hi!' she chirped.

'Hey, honey. Just thought I'd check in. Everything all right?'

'Yes, Miss Tempany. I love the room!'

'It's not bad, is it. Have you ordered room service yet?'

'Um…I've had a few things,' she said sheepishly.

'Did the waiters say anything to you?'

'No. I made sure I was in the shower each time and just shouted at them to come in and leave the food in the room.'

'Good thinking. Has anyone phoned the room?'

'No.'

'Has anyone phoned your cell?'

'No.'

'Anyone email you or anything?'

'No.'

'Any more emails to my account?'

'No.'

'Anyone else come to the door?'

'Your laundry turned up about eleven. But there's been nothing else. I've got the do not disturb sign outside.'

'Well done.'

'How…how are things yourself, Miss Tempany?'

'Not bad so far. I don't want to tempt fate, but I'm reasonably confident things will work out. And if they do, I might be able to phone you early Sunday morning that you can go.'

'Really?'

'Really. But that's a best-case scenario. Hang tight in the meantime, and I'll phone you tomorrow morning at ten. It will be from a different phone, so don't ignore it when it rings. Okay?'

'Yes, Miss Tempany.'

'Thank you, Chloe. I…well, thanks.'

'No, thank you, Miss Tempany.'

She was smiling when she turned the phone off, and Katie said, 'You really do have a soft spot for her.'

'What can I say,' she shrugged. 'I'm *going* soft.'

The connecting flight took off on time at 2200; but landed at Simón Bolívar half-an-hour late after being held up by air traffic control. This flight had only about ten people on it, so they were out with their bags and through immigration – the man at which simply waving them through disinterestedly without even checking their passports – within 20 minutes, then were in their room in the plush, multi-story Marriott on the Avenida Venezuela 40 minutes later.

They got breakfast delivered at nine, after which Tempany got a taxi to her flat on Calle Sucre. As she stared sullenly out at the city going by, it seemed, at first glance, to be much as it had been when she first arrived five years ago: bustling, alive, pulsing with traffic and people. But even though central Caracas wasn't, yet, the Dante's Inferno of the Venezuela portrayed by the Western media, it wasn't nearly as bustling as it had been, and the other scabs that had since formed over it were too ugly to ignore: litter everywhere, refuse sacks piled high on street corners; at least half the shops shuttered; the people, where once there had been joy and verve, now looking as miserable and downtrodden as their peers in San Antonio. The sky, laden with thick, cobalt rainclouds, only added to the feeling of oppression. Again, Tempany thought of the pointlessness of her life and of her misguided crusade on behalf of these people, and how much she had failed them.

No! she chastised herself. It wasn't her who had failed. The thing that had failed, and always had, always would, was the ideology of Karl Marx. The ideology of envy. Of brigandry. Of greed. Of slavery. The ideology of Genghis Khan given a faux-intellectual bent.

And as for his disciples who had tried to force this evil onto the world? Trotsky and Lenin and Mao and their myriad groupies like Gramsci and the Frankfurt School? They were, Tempany concluded, one and all, workshy, indolent frauds. Indeed, for all their professed love of the working classes, Tempany suspected that they secretly despised them, as the proletariat knew the dignity and honour of a hard day's work and the simple pleasure of competence – feelings utterly alien to all those covetous quacks, who wouldn't have known the inside of a factory if it caved in on their heads.

Granted, I've never done a hard day's work, or, indeed, seen the inside of a factory, thought Tempany with a smirk. *But at least I'm competent at something: I'm competent at killing people. And if I had had half the chance, I would have killed every last one of those scoundrels. For what they've done to humanity. For what they've done to me.*

She told the driver to wait, and punched her codes into the keypads on both the main door and the door to her flat on the second floor. She went straight to her bedroom, where she opened the combination safe in her wardrobe and stuffed all the gear she needed into one of her two black holdalls. Into the second she put two changes of clothes and her combat gear and her personal effects – her bank and credit cards and passport in the name of Abigail Norman, and the keys to her flat in Soho. She took one last look around the Spartan flat which had been her sometime bolthole for five years, shrugged emotionlessly, and left. She bought another burner phone from the electronics shop across the street, and phoned

Chloe. The 'Hello?' in reply was tremulous, but she gave a squeal of delight when she heard Tempany's voice. She reported, again, that all was quiet. There was nothing in her tone to suggest otherwise.

Tempany threw the bags into the boot of the taxi, told the driver to wait, and loitered on the pavement, watching the traffic. She hung around for ten minutes, when at last she could spot a black and yellow delivery van coming towards her. As it neared, Tempany kicked out her cigarette and jumped onto the road and waved it down. The driver, a big man in a black baseball cap and corporate black and yellow t-shirt, stopped, jumped out, and checked his tyres. When he could see there was nothing wrong, he confronted Tempany and said brusquely, 'What is it?'

Tempany smiled. 'How would you like to make 300 US for five minutes' work?'

The man's face lit up. 'What's the job?'

Back in the their room, she dumped the contents of the bags on the floor, and Katie burst out laughing. 'Good grief! Are we going to war?'

'Let's hope it doesn't come to that.'

They lay on the bed watching television for most of the day, Katie intermittently firing off instructions and agreeing fees with her various lawyers, while waiting for the call that might or might not come. If it didn't, they agreed to gamble and do the raid anyway. But a little after four Tempany's new phone rang, and her taxi driver from earlier, whom she had paid to sit across the street from Raphael's flat, complete with a headshot from his Facebook page under his real name, said excitedly, 'He's here!'

'Is he alone?'

'Yes!'

'We'll be there in 20 minutes. As soon as we appear drive away for half an hour and come back and wait for us. If he leaves, phone me again, and try to follow him. Okay?'

They got up and left, each carrying one of the black holdalls and Katie a black backpack. As they got into a taxi outside, Tempany called the delivery driver and said, 'Be there in 20.'

As soon as they arrived at Raphael's apartment block in Altamira, Tempany's other taxi on the opposite side of the street pulled out into the traffic and drove off. Katie paid their driver and, laden with their bags, they stepped into the side of the bottom floor of the white, six-storey building and waited for a few minutes until the delivery van pulled up. Ignoring the traffic behind him, the driver parked on the road, jumped out, took a parcel from the back, and went up to the main entrance. He hit one of the buttons, and after a moment there was a buzz as the door was unlocked. He went in, and stood behind the door and held it open for them. They rushed in, their heads bowed, and they all went into the lift. The driver hit the button for the fourth floor. Nothing was said between them, but Tempany gave him $300, which he took with a grin of acknowledgement. When the doors pinged open, they followed the man out and along to apartment 415. The women took up position at either side of the door, the driver knocked, and a few seconds later it opened. 'Hello,' said Raphael cheerfully. 'What have you got for me today?' Before he could answer, Tempany slipped in in front of him, hooked her right foot behind Raphael's ankle, and gave him a palm strike to his sternum. He yelped and fell flat on his back. 'Clear,' she said, and Katie jumped in and past the prostrate Raphael, dumping the holdalls at the end of the hall. Tempany gave the driver a nod and a thumbs up; the driver nodded and smiled in return, and left. Tempany kicked the door shut, jumped past Raphael, and whipped out her gun and aimed at him. He was wheezing, his face crumpled in pain. He rolled onto his side, clutching the back of his head.

'You alone?' asked Tempany.

'What…what the fuck?' he moaned.

Katie took her gun out of the backpack, pushed open the five doors around the hallway, did a sweep of each room, and declared, 'Clear,' after the last one.

Raphael continued to writhe. Tempany asked concernedly, 'Are you okay?'

He looked up. '*Anson?*'

'Yes, Raphael. Are you okay?'

He rubbed the back of his head some more and checked his hand for blood. Then he pushed himself onto his knees. '*Fuck*,' he groaned. 'What the hell are you doing here?'

'I'm sorry, Raph, I didn't mean to hurt you.'

'Then why the fuck did you rush me? And why are you pointing *that* at me?' he bristled.

'Security,' she said shortly.

His eyes moved to Katie. '*Steph?*'

'Hey, Raph,' she grinned with a wave. 'Been a while.'

'Uh, hey, Steph.'

'I'm sorry, Raph. But we need to ask you some questions,' said Tempany. 'Let's go for a seat.' She motioned with her gun for him to get up, and he obeyed shakily. He was dressed in a pair of striped blue and red pyjama bottoms and a white t-shirt. He passed his hand through his damp black hair, and wiped it on the bottoms.

'Slowly now,' Tempany warned. He put his hands behind his head, and shuffled towards them. The door on the right led into the living room and kitchen. Katie went in first, and took up position in front of the television on the far side of the room and covered the door. Tempany edged back into the room, and as soon as Raphael was in her sights, Katie said, 'Got him.' Tempany backed off into the kitchen area, and told him to sit on the brown leather settee facing a matching chair to its right, a wooden mantelpiece, and Katie and the TV to its left. Raphael walked slowly round the back of the sofa, and flopped down on the middle cushion. 'Okay, ladies,' he said gruffly, trying to assert some authority. 'What's going on?'

Tempany sat down on the chair next to the settee, resting her gun on her thigh. She looked Raphael in the eye and said slowly, 'Colonel, it's my unpleasant duty to inform you that we're on a mole hunt.'

'*Oh, shit!*' he hissed. He looked from one to the other, panic-stricken, and pleaded, 'It's not me! I swear to God!'

'Easy, Raph. You're not under suspicion.'

'I…I'm not?' he said in astonishment.

She shook her head.

'But…why the Gestapo tactics?'

'We can give *no one* forewarning of what we are investigating, or even that we are here, lest our targets discover we're onto them. Because if they do, they will cover their tracks or try to eliminate us before we can unmask them. Therefore, we have to arrange our meetings in this rather unconventional manner. I'm so sorry Raph,' she said, her voice catching. 'You're the last person I wanted to scare like this. Can you forgive me?'

Raphael nodded slowly. 'Of…of course I can forgive you, Edith. It's just…well, your turning up like this is a bit crazy.' He thought for a second, then his jaw slackened and eyes widened. '*Fucking, hell!* Were you even *in* the US? Was all that shit from this week even real?'

'I'm afraid we can't tell you much about our investigation, including our movements, Raph. It's mostly classified for, the time being.'

'And you, Spendlove? Were you there?'

'Sorry, Raph. Classified.'

'By whom?'

Tempany shook her head firmly.

He rubbed his face. 'But…why come to me? I don't know anything.'

'You might think that you can't be helpful,' she smiled, 'but the people we are investigating might have said or done something in their dealings with you or the boss that could help.'

He took a deep breath and relaxed slightly. 'It might help if I knew who your target was?'

'We can't say, yet. Suffice it to say, our client believes that this person's activities have been causing the whole organisation, up to and including the boss, to make catastrophic blunders – the sort of blunders which have resulted in the blown operations in Sacramento and Bogota, and God knows where else. In other words, none of our failures have been accidental, as we've been made to think they've been.'

'I...I don't believe it.'

'I think the fact that we've got a bunch of guys stewing in Gitmo can attest to it. There's a cuckoo in our nest, Raph.'

He hung his head and stared down at the rug. 'I don't believe it,' he repeated.

'Raph, I want to ask you about Magellan's activities.'

His head snapped back up. '*Magellan?!* Are you kidding me?'

'We never said it was him. All I want to know is where he is now.'

'Um...England.'

'Doing what?'

'Recruiting.'

'Who?'

'A group of students in Cambridge. Or so he says.'

'Has he been in contact with you or the boss over the past week?'

'Not me. I...I can't say for sure about the boss, but certainly nothing has come through me or the office.'

'And all emails and calls go through you first?'

'Yes,' he nodded. Then said, 'Well, mostly.'

'What does that mean?' asked Katie.

'Obviously there are some things that are classified which the boss handles herself.'

'Such as?'

'Dealings with the Minister; things above my pay grade.'

'Spendlove's emails to Artemis on Thursday,' said Tempany. 'Did they go to you first?'

'Yes.'

'Then what?'

'I sent them straight through to her and went into her office to draw them to her attention.'

'The responses: did you see them?'

'Yes.'

'Did she write them?

'Yes.'

'Anyone else see them?'

'Not that I know of.'

'Artemis said she blitzed my mugshots from the Agency database. How did she do it?'

'There is a…contact who we can call on for favours now and again.'

'The boss also alluded to the fact that it was safe for me to stay put. Was it from the same source?'

Before he could answer, Katie broke in, 'Raph, how senior is this contact?'

He looked at her, thought for a second, and said slowly, 'I…I believe it's analyst level.'

'You "believe"? Don't you know?'

'Um…this is one of those things that is beyond my pay grade. I know there's a source, an analyst, but that's about it.'

Katie looked up at the ceiling, then looked back down at Raphael. 'Is it the boss who controls this analyst, Raph?'

He nodded.

'What's her tradecraft? Phone? Email? Carrier pigeon?'

Raphael laughed. 'Email, I assume,' he shrugged. 'But I don't know. I never see the product. And, frankly, I don't want to.'

'Did you see or hear what was said between them on Thursday?'

'No. She had been in contact with him before she got into the office at seven.'

'Doesn't seem very likely, does it, Raph?' said Katie, her eyebrow cocked sceptically. 'The head of OCC being the controller of some low-level analyst, and their communications with each other being classified above you?'

'Uh…it never seemed peculiar to me. But,' he shrugged, 'that's the boss's call.'

'Of course it is,' said Katie, grinning. 'Thanks, Raph.'

Tempany couldn't quite grasp what Katie had stumbled upon, so she disregarded it for the time being and continued, 'Now, I want you to think about Wednesday night. My beacon went off. Who was first alerted to it?'

'Juan Jimenez on the duty desk.'

'What did he do?'

'He called me.'

'Where were you?'

'In bed.'

'What did you do?'

'I phoned Artemis.'

'What did she say?'

His eyes narrowed. 'She said there must be some mistake, and to double check with Juan. I had him holding on the other line, and he confirmed it. She then asked me if we had any assets in the area. I told her that there was obviously Walker and our other local bagman, Zulu. Other than that, the only person anywhere near was the lieutenant,' he nodded at Katie. 'She then asked me to try to get hold of Zulu and set him off in pursuit, and to phone Steph to do the same. If her phone was off – which it was – I was to try her runner, Alfonso, and get him to deliver a message, which she dictated, and get him to go with her. If Alfonso couldn't be reached, we were to try getting him through his boss at the embassy. I asked her if we should try contacting you and Walker on the off chance your phones were on. She told me that, if you had been abducted – as seemed likely – it was probably Walker who was behind it. She told me to try your phones anyway.'

'She suspected Walker, even at that point?' asked Katie.

'Uh…it seems so.'

'I take it,' said Tempany, 'there was no answer when you tried our phones?'

'None. We tried eight times each until Steph got there. They were both off.'

'Then what did the boss say?

'She told me to go to the office and coordinate things from there. Before I left I passed all the instructions to Juan to deal with while I got there.'

'Did she come down to the office?'

'No. But I was in contact with her all night telling her what was happening.'

'Where was she?'

'At her house.'

'How was her tone?' asked Katie.

'It was, um…' he thought for a few beats. 'She was shouting to begin with. But by the time she was giving us our orders she was back to herself.'

Katie gave Tempany the briefest of winks.

'Spendlove's man, Cortez.' said Tempany. 'When was the last you heard from him?'

'He's had some email correspondence with the boss in the last couple of days, about Steph and the job she was on. Well done, by the way,' he said with a smile to Katie.

'Don't mention it,' giggled Katie. 'I'm just happy I didn't blow it all, or I would have been for the high jump!'

'Apart from the phone call, how has the boss been over the last few days?' continued Tempany.

He opened his mouth to say something, then closed it and shook his head.

'Look, Raph, I think I'm at liberty to say one thing: it's not the boss who is the subject of our investigation. We are trying to discover who is putting the screws on her. So you can speak freely. None of this will get back to her, and none of it will get back to anyone else, I promise.'

He inhaled deeply through his nose. 'It's, just, well, an observation. She...she's not been herself, exactly.'

'What do you mean?'

'She...look, it's probably nothing, but she's shut herself up in her office and hardly spoken to anyone.'

'How was she looking?'

He shrugged. '*Old*. Older than usual. She's had rings under her eyes as if she's not slept. On Thursday she turned up with the same clothes she'd had on the day before. It's just...you know how she is, Anson? She's usually so immaculate it was just a bit of a jolt to see her, well, not. But I didn't really pay it much attention, on account that I thought she was just worried about the two of you, and perhaps guilty about what had happened to you, Anson. I mean, she wouldn't be human if she wasn't. Your injuries looked horrific.'

'Did you discuss who had abducted me?'

'Yes. When she came in on Thursday morning she took me into her office and confirmed what I'd already pieced together from the reports from Alfonso and Zulu: that it had been the Agency, and they had flipped Ray and had been trying to flip you. Her source obviously hadn't known anything about it beforehand, and therefore couldn't warn us.'

'This source of yours, Raph,' said Katie, 'who is being handled by the boss, and who can tamper with the database at will, and who knew all about Anson's abduction so soon after the fact. This doesn't sound like a low-level analyst, does it?'

'Why not? Edward Snowden was just a contractor, and he had the keys to the entire castle.'

'Yeah, right,' chortled Katie.

'Other than Spendlove and Cortez,' said Tempany, 'who has she been in contact with this last week?'

'It was all routine meetings and calls until Thursday, when, after she spoke to me, she dictated a memo to Julia to the Defence Minister outlining what had happened during the night.'

'What did it say?'

'Basically that you had been abducted, that a rescue had been effected, that our man in Texas had been suspected of defecting, and that he had been executed.'

'Did it mention Spendlove?'

'Not by name, no.'

'Did they talk?'

'Not as far as I know.'

'What has she been doing today?'

'I don't know. She was locked in her office most of the day.'

'Any calls or emails for her?'

'None.'

'Is that unusual?'

'Not for a Saturday.'

'Do you normally work on Saturday?'

'Now and again. She asked me to come in today given the danger you two were still in. It…it didn't seem particularly necessary, but I didn't question her, again assuming she was just feeling guilty, and wanted us in the office on the off-chance something went wrong again.'

'Anyone else in today?'

'Jennifer Santos on the duty desk; Sanchez and Dominique on the door; and the cleaners, who were in until twelve.'

Tempany stared him in the eye. He stared back for several seconds, then wilted and cast his eyes to the floor. 'Raphael, I need you to think very carefully about the following questions before answering. If you are in any way liberal with the truth, I must warn you that the consequences shall be severe.' He nodded weakly. 'Have you ever given anyone, either inside or outside the firm, details of Spendlove's or my assignments?'

He shook his head vigorously. 'No. Absolutely not.'

'Did you ever write up details of our assignments after the event?'

'*What?!*' he cried. 'Are you crazy?! Of course not!'

'Are you aware of any such details existing anywhere on the server, or on hard copy anywhere in HQ?'

'No. We don't keep *anything* like that. That would be insane.'

'It sure would be,' said Tempany stonily. 'Have you ever given anyone outside the firm our work names?'

'No.'

'Have you ever given anyone, either inside or outside the firm, our real names?'

'*What?!*' He turned his palms upwards, shrugged his ignorance, and said exasperatedly, 'I don't even know what your real names *are!*'

'You're joking, right?'

'No! No one ever told me, and, frankly, I don't want to know.'

'So, Magellan never told you?'

'No. He…he deals mostly with the boss about recruitment. As it should be,' he added defensively.

'So you never thought to Google me when I came on board?'

'And Googled what, exactly? I didn't know the first thing about you. And still don't.'

Tempany smiled and said, 'Thanks, Raph. That's been most helpful.' She sat forward, and said softly. 'Is her security detail with her tonight?'

He nodded.

'Still two?'

'Yes.'

'Do they still stay in the house when she's there?'

He nodded.

'Are they both up all night or do they take shifts?'

'Shifts.'

'When do they change?'

'I'm not sure.'

'What do they do when they're off shift?'

'I don't know. They've got the use of the spare room.'

'Which is where?'

'Uh…off the hall, under the stairs.'

'And the General? Is he home?'

'I don't know.'

'What's she doing tonight?'

'She said she's staying in, and if anything urgent comes up to phone her there. Edith, if she's in danger I need to warn her.'

Tempany shook her head. 'Absolutely not. We believe that the people who are controlling Artemis are going to meet her tonight. What their intentions are, we don't know, but we are going to be there to stop them and capture them. But we cannot, under any circumstances, let the boss know, in case she might do anything that tips these people off. Everything must appear normal. Don't worry about her, Raph, we know what we're doing. Plus, she's got her gorillas with her. She'll be as safe as houses.'

'I don't want anything to happen to her. I've got to tell her!' He began to get up.

Tempany raised her gun, and he shrank back down. 'I'm sorry, Raph. I know how much affection you have for her. But you're going to have to stay out of this. And I'm afraid we're going to have to immobilise you for the evening to ensure that you do so. Lieutenant, watch him, please.'

'Check,' said Katie. Tempany got up and scanned the room, then the kitchen, then went out to the hall and checked the two bedrooms and the bathroom, drawing a blank in each. She looked at the living room door. It was of panelled wood. 'Raph, have you got a drill?'

He jumped to his feet, shrieking, '*Are you fucking kidding me!*'

Katie raised her gun. 'Careful, now, Raph. I like you, but…' She gave him an apologetic smile and shrugged.

He put his hands up and flopped down again.

'Don't be an idiot,' said Tempany. 'I'm not going to take a drill to you. Have you got one?'

'What the hell for?'

'I'm about to make a small adjustment to your door. Don't worry, I'll pay for the damage.'

Raphael shook his head in bemusement. 'In the cupboard. In the hall,' he said.

'You got drill bits?'

'Um…in the case…beside it.'

She went to the cupboard and, on the floor under the bottom shelf, was a lime green Ryobi cordless drill and a black drill bit case. She tried the drill for power, attached a 16mm spade bit, opened the living room door as far as it would go, then drilled a hole through the right-hand stile, about a foot from the bottom and three inches from the side. She stood back to inspect her handiwork.

'Good thinking,' said Katie, twigging on to what she was up to.

'Thanks. Okay, Raph,' she said, pointing her gun at him again. 'Up, please and hands behind your head.' He looked mystified, but did as he was told. Katie laid her gun on the floor and frisked him. 'Clean,' she said, and stepped away. Tempany pointed at the wall next to the door. 'Here, please, and sit on the floor.'

He stumbled over and sat down with his back against the wall.

'Right hand next to the hole, Raph,' said Tempany. He obeyed meekly, and Katie took a set of handcuffs from her backpack, snapped one side shut through the hole, and locked his hand in the other. Raphael's confusion cleared and he gave a sigh of relief.

'I know you could easily break out of this if you wanted,' flattered Tempany. 'But please don't even try. I beg you. The stakes this evening are extremely high, and believe me when I say that, if we succeed, we might have found the key to saving the revolution.'

Raphael brightened up. '*Really?*'

Tempany nodded. 'Don't get your hopes up. But, possibly.'

'*Fucking hell,*' he breathed.

'That's the carrot, Raph. Here's the stick: if you try to interfere tonight, you will be fired and court-martialled. I don't need to spell out to you what that will mean.'

He shook his head slowly.

'Good man,' she smiled. 'All being well, we'll be back later to let you go, after which we should be free to speak. I would hope to be back by four at the latest. Do you want any food left out?'

'Um…I don't know…some bread…and some butter and cheese and stuff from the fridge. And some water, please?'

Katie went into the kitchen and returned with a tray with a loaf of bread, a pack of ham, slices of cheese and butter, a plate and a bottle of Perrier.

Tempany tossed over the remote for the TV. 'Want anything to read?'

'There's a book by my bed.'

Katie went through to his room and handed him Hemingway's *For Whom The Bell Tolls*. 'Enjoying it?' she asked. He nodded. 'Bit boring though, isn't it?'

'If you've got no patience it would be,' he said sourly.

'*Touché!*' laughed Katie. 'Just sit tight, and we'll be back in a jiffy.' She bent down and gave him a lingering kiss on the cheek.

Raphael looked up, smiling, his eyes glinting. There was hope in them. Not hope of getting released; not hope of Artemis being saved from whatever phantoms he thought Edith and Stephanie were about to battle. It was the hope that he might, someday soon, screw Spendlove. Tempany felt a stab of jealousy. But it was gone in an instant. She realised that Katie had just rendered them an almost invaluable service: his hope of bedding her would ensure that, even in the unlikely event that he could break free, Raphael wasn't going anywhere. He would sit there as obedient as a puppy, dreaming of Katie's naked body next to his as his reward. She almost burst out laughing, but managed to check herself, and gave Raphael as tender a smile as she could muster. 'We'll be back soon, Raph. I swear.'

When they got to the lift, Tempany asked, 'What was all that about? The stuff about Artemis being the mole's controller?'

'Ah, Artemis, you have been clever,' said Katie to herself. She looked at Tempany, grinning as if she was Archimedes in his bath. 'Have you ever read *Tinker Tailor Soldier Spy*?'

'Uh, no.'

'Anson, I'm shocked! But Artemis evidently has. Not that it particularly matters – it really just boils down to her tradecraft, after all – but I would speculate that what she's done, both to increase her kudos with the regime, and to allow her to communicate with her controller at will without raising suspicion, is to claim she's running a mole in the CIA – when, in reality, it's the other way around. I would imagine she'll get some chicken feed from him in order to give the setup credibility – probably a low-level runner here or there, such as the clowns setting fire to the factories in Maturin; while, in return, she delivers the big stuff, like the blown operations in Bogota and Sacramento, and you the other night. It's rather fiendish,' she said admiringly, 'all the more so because she's pitched her source as being merely some computer nerd who couldn't possibly know about the moves against us beforehand, and therefore couldn't forewarn us. Also, as a side benefit, the apparent low-level nature of the source reduces, dramatically, the possibility that either the Minister or Raphael – or anyone else for that matter – would guess that the source is controlling Artemis, and not the other way around.'

'I…I don't understand,' said Tempany dumbly.

'The supposed mole, Anson, isn't some spotty intern with a Che Guevara poster on his bedroom wall, as Artemis would have us believe. No. I'd guess it is someone very senior indeed. Perhaps even the Director himself – or herself...I think it's a woman now. Anyhow,' she shrugged modestly, 'that's my theory, at least.'

'Holy smoke,' murmured Tempany. 'This is nuts.'

19. The Raid II

It was exactly one hour since the lights at the front of the house had gone out, and ten minutes since they had scaled the wall to the rear. They were crouched in the bushes bordering the back of the swimming pool and tennis court-sized lawn. There were no lights on save the one in the kitchen straight ahead. The blinds on the windows were half closed, through which they could see one of the bodyguards moving around. The other one had yet to make an appearance. Tempany looked again at her watch, the luminous hands reporting half past midnight. 'What do you think?' she whispered.

'I think we should go now. The longer we leave it, the more chance there is of his sidekick turning up.'

'Check,' said Tempany. 'Two stones only, about a minute apart if he doesn't respond to the first. If he doesn't come to the second, I'll try the door. If it's locked, you go round the front with the kit and I'll keep an eye on him.'

'Check.'

'Okay, sweetie. Good luck. And remember: don't do anything silly. If things get too hot, leave them to me.'

Katie pulled up her balaclava, pulled up Tempany's, and kissed her gently. 'Good luck, darling,' she whispered, her voice a frisson of excitement. 'Let's do this.'

'Go.'

Katie scrabbled around in the dirt beneath her, picked out two small stones, and pushed her way through the bushes. In her black combat gear she was, apart from the eyes glinting through the holes in the balaclava, a mere shadow as she scampered down the edge of the pool and lawn until she was within range of the windows. Tempany skipped down the darkest section of the opposite side – noting with disgust the dozen or so cigarette butts that were tarnishing the otherwise pristine lawn – and soon found herself on the concrete path beside the kitchen door, which jutted out at right angles from the rest of the house. She took the dart gun from its holster under her right arm and a pencil torch from one of the pockets on her vest. She flashed it once, and five seconds later there was a crack as a stone hit one of the windows. Tempany kneeled, the pistol steady in her outstretched hands. The silhouette of the man projected onto the lawn, disappeared, then a floodlight above the door came on. It was stronger than she had anticipated and showered her with light, forcing her to jump back to the border wall. The doorknob turned, the door opened, and the man appeared, holding his gun in both hands at the side of his head. Tempany pulled the trigger. The pistol responded with a low metallic thud, and the dart hit him in the stomach. She whipped out her Beretta from the opposite holster, and aimed at his head. At first he didn't notice her; he was staring down, quizzically, at the large tranquiliser dart with blue hairs sprouting from it that was sticking out of him. Just as Katie appeared with her pistol drawn, he batted it off. Then he looked at the black-clad, balaclavaed figures pointing guns at him. 'Shh!' warned Tempany. His mouth fell open and he let his gun fall to the ground, the clang of which as it hit the doorstep muffled by music coming from inside. Tempany motioned for him to come out. He dopily obliged, stepping down onto the path with jelly legs. Then he crumpled to his knees with a groan, and fell flat on his face. Katie took off her backpack and quickly wrapped gaffer tape over his mouth and eyes, then trussed him up with plastic cable ties, using three each on his wrists and ankles. She then frisked him, pulled a phone from his pocket, and threw it and his gun into the bushes. Tempany holstered the Beretta, fished another tranquiliser dart from the pocket on her vest, pulled off the plastic cap on the needle with her teeth, snapped open the dart gun and reloaded it, then jumped into the kitchen to check for the other guard. It was clear. She stepped back out and made to shoot the man in the back. Katie touched her arm. 'No,' she whispered. 'There was enough in there to put down an elephant. He should be out like a light in a couple of minutes.'

Tempany nodded, handed her the pistol, and armed herself again with her silenced Beretta. 'You do the next ones.'

'Check.'

They left the man, who was moaning softly, lying on his front and went into the kitchen. It was spacious and modern, with shiny black and white units on all the walls, a red Aga against the far wall, and an island unit with a worktop and sink in the centre. Just beside them at the door was a large yellow SMEG fridge, on the top of which sat the radio from which the music was coming. The kitchen gave way to a large dining area, which had a big rectangular wooden table in the middle and a dozen chairs around it. There was a white door on the far wall at the point where the kitchen met the dining room. Tempany rushed over and gently pushed it open. She flipped on the light to find a big utility room. She glanced around, and found what she was looking for high on the far wall. She nodded to Katie, who retreated behind the fridge and turned off the radio. Tempany was in and out of the room in a minute. She turned off the light, closed the door, and motioned to Katie. Katie went outside to check the bodyguard. He was breathing noisily, but out for the count. She gave Tempany an 'OK' sign, and gently closed the door behind her. They crept through the dining area and pushed open the glass door at the far end. There were two doors on either side of the carpeted corridor ahead. A stab of light came from beneath the second one on the left. They went up to it, and Tempany stood aside, letting Katie take the lead. She pushed the door open and walked in. The second bodyguard was lying on a bed against the wall, his clothes in a pile on the floor and a white sheet drawn up to his chest. He was reading a paperback from the light of a lamp on the cabinet next to him. He looked up slowly, obviously expecting to see his partner. Katie put her index finger to her lips and shushed him menacingly. His head jolted back. He let the book drop onto his chest and held his hands up in surrender. Katie marched over and shot him in the neck at point blank range. He groaned like his partner, but application nearer the brain worked far quicker than the stomach, and almost immediately his breathing became laboured and his head flopped to the side. Katie passed the gun to Tempany, who reloaded, and went to work with the tape and cable ties. When she was done she removed the dart from his neck and they rolled him onto his side lest he vomit and choke. Tempany handed the dart gun back to her, took out her torch again, and went back out into the corridor. They followed it to the end, where it opened up into a large vestibule and the front door, moonlight streaming in from the semi-circular glass panel above it. Doubling back upon the way they had just come was a broad staircase with balustrade on the left. Tempany turned on the torch and led the way up. At the top there were doors all around a cavernous landing. Tempany went straight for the one on the left. With the torch's beam on the handle, she turned it slowly, gently pushed it open, and flashed the light onto the double bed ahead of them. There was a bulge on it. She flipped the light switch, and a huge chandelier burst into life. The bulge was two bodies, both of which began to stir. Katie skipped round to the far side, and promptly shot the stirring bald man in the back of the neck. At the near side, Tempany whipped the sheet off of Artemis, roughly cuffed her right hand to the wrought iron headboard, then pulled the pillow from under her to check for a gun. There was none. There was a phone by the bed, which Tempany ripped out of its socket and threw on the floor. Artemis, gaining her senses, screamed. Her left arm shot up to the wall behind the bed, and her fingers found and pressed a small silver button. She shouted in Spanish, 'You're dead. My men will be here in seconds.'

Tempany threw the fuse she had just taken from the utility room over to her. It landed by her head. Her eyes smarting, she picked it up with her free hand and examined it, bemused. 'Next time,' said Tempany, 'you install a panic button, tell your idiot electrician not to mark the fuse box, "panic button".'

As Tempany spoke, the fear and confusion drained from Artemis's face. Before she could say her name, Tempany and Katie removed their balaclavas. '*You!*'

'Who were you expecting? The Easter Bunny?'

Tempany and Katie glanced at each other and creased up laughing.

Artemis glared open-mouthed. 'How the *fuck* did you get here?!' she blurted.

'Public transport, ma'am,' giggled Katie.

Artemis took a deep breath, and a long, ragged sigh rushed from her mouth. Looking from one to the other, she shook her head and groaned, 'I should have known.' She pulled herself up with her cuffed hand and sat facing them. Sweat had beaded on her face and was showing through her gold negligee. She turned to her husband and gasped. But then, setting her face hard, she coolly put her hand back, pulled the dart from his neck and tossed it on the floor, and felt for a pulse. After five seconds her body relaxed, and she turned back to them. She shook her head, gritting her teeth. 'You can tell your boss to go fuck himself,' she spat.

'Our boss?' laughed Katie. 'What the hell are you talking about? We're working freelance tonight, ma'am.'

'Watch her,' said Tempany. Katie gave the dart gun back to her, and pointed her Beretta at Artemis's chest. Tempany made her way across the bedroom to two red doors adorned with gold sun motifs. She took the one on the right, which led into a large dressing room; the General's clothes and shoes on the left, Artemis's on the right. At the far end were two full-height mirrors and a dressing table, on which were the usual cosmetics and dozens of bottles of perfume and aftershave. She took the chair from underneath, returned to the bedside, and laid it down facing Artemis.

'Where's mine?' asked Katie.

'There's only one.'

'Well, what are you going to sit on?'

'Uh…I was intending to sit on this.'

'Only kidding,' she said. She took off the backpack, dropped it on the floor, and rested her back against the wall while holstering her pistol. As Tempany sat down she was about to draw hers to threaten Artemis, but decided against it: shorn of her make-up and expensive clothes, and with her normally beautifully coiffed hair straggling sloppily down the sides of her head and into her face, Artemis looked old and frail, her usually sharp eyes sullen, her pale lips drooping. She already looked beaten. Tempany looked up at Katie. 'I think the boss knows exactly what the situation is. So let's play nice. Would you mind releasing her?'

Katie arced an eyebrow at her, but quickly had the key out and undid the cuffs. Artemis rubbed her wrist with a grimace.

'Should have known what, ma'am?' asked Tempany.

'Excuse me?'

'You said, *I should have known.*'

'I…' she hesitated. She gave her hair a regal flick with her left hand, then smiled broadly as if it was just another day at the office. 'I should have known that you would be paying me this delightful visit. My female intuition seems to have deserted me.'

'I must say, ma'am, you're taking this far better than I thought you would.'

'And exactly how *did* you think I would take it?'

'I...well, I'm not entirely sure, but I had come here prepared for the worst – which would have meant torturing you. I trust that won't be necessary?'

She raised her eyebrows. 'That would be a little extreme, don't you think? I mean, harming me because you cannot live with the shame of having blown your assignment. There's nothing wrong with failing now and again, Edith. You're only human. Let me phone Raphael. We can help you. Both of you,' she smiled, looking up at Katie.

Tempany rocked back in her chair. 'Brilliant, ma'am,' she laughed. 'Brilliant.' She sat forward and glared at her. 'Ma'am, I don't think you quite appreciate how unbelievably pissed I am.' She took off her right glove and pulled up the sleeve of her black cotton underlayer to display her bandaged wrist. 'I'm going to be scarred for life, you piece of shit.' She pointed at her nose. 'And you're getting the blame for this as well, because if I hadn't been on your wild goose chase, this would never have happened.' She felt her temper about to explode, and had to take a deep breath to check it. 'I'm not messing around here,' she snarled as she put her glove back on.

Artemis gave a snort of indignation. 'And you think *I* am? If you think I'm going to tell you anything you can forget it. You've come here to kill me,' she said, nodding at their all-black garb, replete with tactical vests and body armour.

Katie put a hand on Tempany's shoulder and gave it a comforting squeeze. 'No, ma'am, I swear,' she said. 'This is us,' she grinned, 'trying to be stealthy. Plus, we thought we might have to fight it out with your gorillas.'

'What have you done with them?' she snapped.

'Don't worry, ma'am,' said Tempany, 'they're just enjoying a well-earned nap, like the good General here. Believe me when I say that they would not still be breathing, nor would your husband, had we been intent on killing you. In fact, we would have been in and out already, you would all be dead, and the fire brigade would be trying unsuccessfully to put out the blaze we had started before we left.' Katie smirked.

Artemis's brow creased. 'Let's suppose for a second,' she began slowly, her eyes fixed on the wall behind them, 'that I believe you; that you've not been sent by the Minister, that you're not here to assassinate me. Why, then, *are* you here?'

'Two reasons. Firstly, we know you sold me out to the CIA, and we – I – need answers.' She paused for the denial they expected would come; if it did, they had agreed that Tempany would slap her a couple of times and Katie, the good cop, would pull her off. As it was, Artemis blinked several times, bit her lip, and said nothing. Whether this was an admission of guilt was impossible to know for certain – it was possible, just, that Artemis realised the danger she was in, and was keeping quiet in order not to trigger Tempany to put a bullet in her head. Tempany continued, 'Secondly, we realise that if we *do* let you live, you might feel a bit sore about us coming into your home and putting you on the spot like this. As such, I'll need certain assurances from you as to our future safety. That's all,' she added lightly.

Pursing her lips, she looked first Katie then Tempany in the eye. 'And what do I get in return for this generosity? Apart from my life, of course.'

Katie answered, 'I would say that your life is probably enough, wouldn't you, ma'am? But in case it's not, Miss Anson and I are agreed that if we are satisfied with your answers, not only will you get to retain all your body parts, neither the Minister nor anybody else will hear the rather fascinating tale we've got to tell about our adventures over the past few days. Which means, just in case I need to spell it out, you get to keep your job.'

Artemis's eyes widened. She looked at them both, then looked down at her right wrist, which she rubbed some more. At last she said, 'Are either of you wired?'

They shook their heads. 'The fact that we might be wired is the least of your problems, ma'am,' said Tempany. 'But I can assure you we are not.'

She breathed deeply. 'How did you get here?' she asked again.

'Don't try dragging this out, ma'am,' warned Tempany. 'My patience is already very close to breaking.'

'I'm interested. Genuinely,' she smiled. 'I should have been told as soon as you entered the country.'

'Think about it, ma'am,' said Katie. She slid down the wall and sat on the floor, casually crossing her arms and legs.

'The fence,' she said. 'New passports in Mexico, then here.'

'Close,' said Katie. 'Swam over at Eagle Pass.'

'Did you?' said Artemis, raising an eyebrow at Tempany. 'I thought you said you were never going to swim over again?'

'I say a lot of things,' she said flatly.

'Well, "swim" is a bit of an overstatement,' said Katie. '"Waded", more like: the river's bone dry at the moment. And, yes, we got new passports, but didn't need them – we got waved straight through. Didn't even have to offer a bribe.'

'You ought to do something about the security here, ma'am,' said Tempany. 'It really is shocking. I mean, any old psychopath can get in.'

'It would seem so,' said Artemis mirthlessly. 'And my house? Let me guess – you slept with Raphael for my address?' She tried to make light of this, but her smile was strained and there was an edge to her voice: the thought of Tempany and Raphael evidently riled her.

Tempany and Katie tittered and glanced at each other, Tempany's cheeks turning scarlet. 'Um...not quite, ma'am – Raphael's not really my type. I simply followed you from time to time. You see, I realised some time ago – call it *female intuition*,' she mocked, 'that someday I might need an insurance policy, just in case a situation ever arose that meant I'd have to pay you or any of your associates a house visit. It was the logical thing to do. And here's a tip: if you want to remain inconspicuous around here, don't drive around in a chauffeur-driven Merc with two gorillas always in tow.'

'I must say, that's not very trusting of you, Anson,' she scolded. 'And your equipment? You can't have got it from the quartermaster,' she said haughtily.

'It did come from him, as it happens. Only, I have a nasty habit of not returning all of my stuff after jobs. This was another part of my insurance policy – if anyone was to come round to the flat, whether sent by you or the opposition, I would have gone down fighting. You really should run a tighter ship. The fact is, no one, once, asked me where the missing equipment was. You're not a very good custodian of taxpayers' money, are you?' she sneered.

'Apparently not.'

'Anything else you would like to know, ma'am, or would you like to string this out a bit longer?'

She shook her head slowly.

'Good. Ma'am, why have you committed treason?'

20. Treason / Patriotism

She stared Tempany in the eye, unblinking, her face expressionless. She then took a deep breath through her nose, and released it in a long hiss through her teeth. 'Ladies,' she said, 'I don't think you quite understand what's going on here.'

'Then please enlighten us,' said Tempany, crossing her arms.

'Treason,' she said mildly, 'depends upon one's point of view. *You* might think I've committed treason. *I* think I'm a patriot who has been fighting for her people.'

'A *patriot?* Artemis, ma'am, are *you kidding me?!* You've burned your operatives. You betrayed me to the CIA. You sent Spendlove to what you thought would be her death. How can that be defined as anything other than treason?'

Again, Tempany prepared to leap forward and hit her. But, instead of denying the charges, Artemis sat up straight, tilted her head back to look down her nose at her, and said with an air of righteous indignation, 'You're a fool, Anson. Treason is propping up an incompetent and corrupt regime which can't provide the basics for its people.' Her face twisted into a snarl, and she spat, 'Treason is not even being able to provide fucking toilet paper! Treason is keeping your people in a perpetual state of poverty. Treason is being responsible for economic chaos. For bread lines. For riots. Treason is living

238

in opulence…' she looked round her luxurious bedroom: the dazzling chandelier, the heavy red velvet curtains over the two large balcony windows, the intricate cornicing and ceiling rose, all painstakingly painted in golds, reds and blues, the deep pile blue carpet with white fleur de lis motifs, the expensive burgundy and blue wallpaper; Tempany imagined that the taps in her en suite were gold-plated, '…while those at the bottom starve.'

Tempany should have expected this answer – it was, after all, the version of reality that she had crashed into over the past few days. Still, she could hardly believe that Artemis, a rabid socialist and the woman responsible for indoctrinating her with all the anti-American propaganda, could have reached the same conclusion. Out of a lingering sense of loyalty, her immediate instinct was to defend OCC, as well as herself. But she found she couldn't, and said weakly, 'You…you sound like we're no better than the fascists were.'

'*Fascists?* Ha! The people we booted out weren't fascists. They were just people with whom we disagreed.'

'But…but you and Magellan, you *told me* they were fascists!' she bleated.

'I've told my people many things which I thought were true at the time, but I've since come to realise are not. But what those people might or might not have thought is rather beside the point. The real point – the point that matters – is that we *are* no better than them. Because things are worse. The poor are poorer, our public services, infrastructure, the government machine, are falling apart. All we've achieved is replacing one elite with another – us – and our elite is worse, because at least they had some business acumen about them and had pretty much made their own money before they got into power. How did we get ours? How did we manage to pay the two of you millions of dollars? By leaching it off the state. By sucking it from the people, many of whom can hardly afford to eat – the very people we are supposed to be helping!' She threw her hands up in exasperation. 'Can't you

239

see it, girls? We have *failed*. We have been criminally incompetent. It's an obscenity, and we have committed treason against the people of Venezuela.'

'When did you arrive at this conclusion, ma'am?' asked Katie.

She gave a condescending smirk. 'It wasn't some Damascene conversion or anything like that. I could just see that things were getting worse: the queues, the shortages, the inflation. And it gradually dawned on me that *we* were the problem, not the solution.'

'But...why turn?' came in Tempany again. 'Why not just...I don't know, resign?'

'Because I could see a way of actually helping my people. Of making things right. If I could destabilise OCC it would follow that the anti-communists would grow more powerful, which would undermine the whole regime. Also, the stronger and better organised the anti-communists became, the more credible, effective and stable a government Venezuela will have when the Marxists finally lose control. And it's working. The country is coming to a standstill. It's only a matter of time before the regime falls and sanity reigns once more.'

'*Jesus,*' breathed Tempany. 'I thought you had been bribed or something. But *this?*' She shook her head. 'You're insane! Don't you see that your little scheme isn't making the slightest bit of difference? In fact, if you and your friends in the CIA are behind the unrest, it's having the opposite effect. It's making the regime stronger. It's tightening their grip, and you're going to end up with a full-blown communist dictatorship. Is that what you want?'

'Of course not. The regime's grip is not nearly as tight as you think it is. Time, Anson. Time. And then the whole rotten structure will come crashing down.'

'If resignation wasn't an option, ma'am,' chimed in Katie, seemingly unsurprised by any of this, 'why did you risk bringing the Agency in? You could have trashed the operation yourself just by, well, just by doing as little as possible, or doing it badly.'

'If I'd done that I wouldn't have lasted. No. I had to be seen to be doing my job, because, although there is plenty of incompetence above me, there are people in my organisation who are not,' she flashed Katie a smile, 'and they would have known I was deliberately sabotaging it. Hence I sought out the Agency. Not only could they help undermine OCC without my fingerprints being all over it, they could fund and strengthen the anti-communists. Also, the Agency are past masters at this type of thing. I needed their expertise. So, when I met my...um, contact in Manila two years ago, I offered my services. And the rest is history.' She tilted her head to the side and narrowed her eyes. 'Not that it really matters, but I wonder if you could reciprocate by telling me how you knew.'

'Haven't you guessed?' said Katie. The cool way she was interacting with Artemis made Tempany realise that Katie was far better equipped for this sort of thing than she was. Tempany was smart enough, she knew, but in this particular game she was little more than a blunt instrument – a hotheaded one at that, she thought despondently. But then, looking down at Katie's keen blue eyes and the dimpled smile, her spirits soared.

Then something odd happened. Her breath caught in her throat, and she was aware that her whole body was tingling. She had never felt this sensation in her life. And then it hit her, like a hot streak of lightning through her brain: she was in love. Deeply, madly, in love with her. Katie glanced up and gave her a flutter of her eyelashes. Tempany felt as if she had turned to a pile of mush. With her jaw trembling, she could only smile weakly in return. *Get a grip!* With an effort, she bent her gaze back onto Artemis, who, if she had noticed anything, wasn't letting on. She was regarding Katie while tapping her lips with her index finger.

'It must be...' she looked at Tempany. 'It must have been your operations. I gave them too many details.'

Tempany took a deep breath. 'Yes, you did, ma'am. But it wasn't that that gave the game away. They knew my name.'

Artemis groaned and sunk her head into her hands.

'Only you and Magellan and a handful of his runners knew it, and I knew it is not on the system. Then it turned out that they knew Spendlove's as well. I knew it was unlikely that Magellan or any of his team would have known it. And then, thinking back to my operations, given that only you and Raphael are supposed to have known the details, it was too much of a stretch to believe that Ray – or the Agency, for that matter – had independently managed to discover those *and* discover my name. You were the only one all this could have come from.'

She shook her head. 'These people are supposed to be the best in the world. Why the *fuck* would they let you know they knew your names?' she asked rhetorically.

'I think,' mused Katie, 'they used Anson's in order to try to chip away at the last of her defences. The *coup de grâce*, if you will, to let her know she was completely at their mercy. But why would they use my name, ma'am? That doesn't make any sense?'

'Agreed,' said Artemis. 'Although it is possible they wanted to let you know, via Anson, that you were blown too. Maybe they were using their initiative and thought it a good idea to try to turn you as well since you were on the scene. I simply don't know. Whatever the case, they have been completely brainless.'

'Perhaps not,' said Katie. 'According to the agent the other day, he did not know where Miss Anson's name had come from. Now, if no one had told him our names had come from you – in order, you know, to protect your identity from the rank and file – they would not feel any particular need not to use our names as leverage, probably thinking that they came from somebody lower-level, whose intelligence did not need to be treated as delicately as that which had come from someone higher up.'

Artemis thought for a moment, then said, frowning, 'I suspect you might be right.'

'But why tell them our names at all?' asked Tempany. 'It just seems so unnecessary – or, at least, unnecessary if you wanted to protect yourself as the source.'

She shook her head and gave a deep, frustrated sigh. 'Like you, Anson, I take out insurance. This was against me being uncovered, or getting hit by a bus, or otherwise being unable to finish the job. Amongst other things, I gave them a list of all our intelligence officers and field agents, including work names, aliases, real names, addresses and ages. The idea was that, if my employment was to be terminated, for whatever reason, the Agency would have more than enough to continue to hurt us. My agreement with my controller...'

'Who doubles as your supposed mole,' broke in Katie matter-of-factly.

Artemis stared at her, then cracked a smile and said, somewhat venomously, 'Clever girl.'

'Not that clever, ma'am. I just happen to have read *Tinker Tailor.*'

'Of course you have,' she sighed.

'Your agreement?' prodded Tempany.

'My agreement with my controller and her predecessor was that the list would remain in their safe until such time as I was no longer able to operate – then they could do whatever they wanted with it.'

'And you trusted them?' Katie asked, askance.

'Yes. Which turns out to have been rather unwise, wouldn't you say? It now seems possible they distributed it around Langley as soon as they got it. Which,' she looked up at the ceiling, 'implies that my caution the other night in not wanting to reveal myself might have been unnecessary, because if the people in Langley knew about the list, some of them might also have guessed it came from me – assuming my controller hadn't explicitly told them already. What a mess,' she groaned, shaking her head. She gave Tempany a grim smile. 'It turns out we've both been played.'

'It would seem so,' said Tempany. 'I want to know, ma'am, if the reasons for half the kill jobs were lies.'

'I'm sorry, Anson. The operations were exactly as you were first told. All of them. The stories you heard the other night were all concocted. By me, my little Leninist angel of vengeance,' she laughed.

Trying to resist the urge to slap her, Tempany massaged her temples. 'But…why me?' she said softly. 'And why now?'

'In answer to the second question, the Minister wanted to get Army Intel down to HQ to try to find out how our operations were being blown. I managed to convince him to call off the dogs by claiming it was all down to our agents bungling things on the ground. But the net was closing in on me. So my controller and I came up with a plan to give me cover and allow me to operate freely again: we would turn one of my field agents, who would then be my sacrificial lamb if and when Army Intel came in, taking the fall for the blown operations, as well as anything else that went down in the meantime. I selected you for this high honour, believing you to be the most rational of the five, and therefore the most likely to see through all the propaganda we filled your head with. Also, not only do you not have any personal skin in the game, because of your background it was going to be easy to paint you as a capitalist, thus giving you motive. And, as a bonus, you are quite an effective weapon, and getting rid of you would have hurt the organisation badly – probably more so than had it been any of the other four.'

'Flattered, I'm sure. But why not just use Ray? He had been turned already. If you needed a patsy, he would have been ideal.'

She shook her head. 'He could not possibly have known about the blown operations, and Army Intel would have known it. You, on the other hand, have an office in HQ. Even though you don't know everything, it was going to be easy to make it look like you did.'

'But if she was to be turned,' said Katie, 'why send someone to rescue her?'

'Because I had no choice.'

'Because of the beacon,' said Tempany.

Artemis nodded. 'Because of the beacon. No one here was supposed to know you had been taken. When your watch was in for servicing two months ago, I sabotaged it by cutting the beacon's power supply to the battery. It was quite a delicate operation, I should add,' she said proudly. 'Simply put, it wasn't supposed to work. So you can imagine my shock when I was told it had gone off. I thought I was going mad, so I looked up the service manifests, and it turned out the idiots had given you back the wrong watch. The one you've got is Theresa's.'

'Holy shit!' gasped Tempany. She looked down at Katie, who was giggling. She'd had no idea that the watch she had on wasn't hers. She took it off and examined it closely, then looked at the engravings on the back. She couldn't spot any difference at all...save the serial number on the lug: it was one out. She thought of Theresa. Little, beautiful, Theresa, who had come up from the favelas. Theresa, the maniac who had killed at least ten civilians. Tempany decided right then that if she ever saw her again she would kill her; and she would take her time about it. 'Let's just hope poor Theresa doesn't need the beacon any time soon, or she'll be screwed,' she laughed. Artemis shrugged. 'And I guess,' said Tempany as she strapped it back on, 'that the moral of the story is that, in future, you give different watches to your agents.'

'The tech guys told me they needed to be the same model to save them having to redesign the system over and over again. And, um, we had found a consignment of those

Omegas in customs, so I thought, two birds, one stone. That'll teach me for trying to do the right thing.'

'When I came to in the shed, the watch was gone, and I found it in Ray's pocket. Why did he take it? Assuming Ray knew it wouldn't work, what was the point?'

'So that your suspicions would not be aroused when no rescuers came. Ray's instructions were to take it as soon as you were abducted, and return it to you on your release – basically so that you wouldn't have to explain what had happened to it when you got back. Ideally he would have got to it before you had a chance to hit the buttons; but, even if you had, by giving it back to you, you would have just assumed Ray had switched it off, or you hadn't pressed them hard enough, or hadn't pressed them simultaneously, or that it was faulty. It would never have entered your mind that someone had tampered with it.'

Tempany's eyes narrowed. 'But if Ray knew about it, why sabotage it in the first place? Why not just get him to switch it off?'

'Because I would have had to send out a search party, even if it had been activated only momentarily. That would have killed the operation stone dead, because there would have been too many questions as to your movements, and as to why and how the beacon had gone off, as they are almost impossible to trigger accidentally. The only guaranteed solution was for it not to work at all. But the beacon was merely a safety net in the event of Ray not being able to stop you from hitting the buttons in the first place. How did he fuck it up?'

'Well, he'd drunk a fair bit, which probably didn't help him. And he obviously wasn't expecting the old one-two combination: a knee in the balls and a hard rap in the face.'

They all laughed.

'So once you knew the beacon had gone off you made the decision to send Spendlove,' Tempany continued, 'because you thought she would fail.'

'There was really no decision to be made. The lieutenant was the only officer in the vicinity. I *had* to send her. If I had left Zulu to do it himself, and made no effort to send Spendlove, I would probably have been arrested the next day for negligence, at the very least. Of course, it was lucky it was Spendlove who was there and not anyone else – I mean, if it had been one of your team, it would have ended in a bloodbath, and my controller would have been very cross indeed. As it was, Spendlove was perfect, because I knew, or at least I thought, she would fail.'

'By "fail", you mean, "killed",' said Katie stolidly.

'I hoped it wouldn't come to that, which was why I gave you as much of an out as I could in the message.'

'But you underestimated me, because you did not know that I was – I am – in love with Anson,' she declared proudly. 'So you did not know that I was prepared to kill for her, and, if necessary, be killed. So there was no question of me not going. And my motivation to save her made up for my lack of experience at the sharp end. So, far from being the ideal candidate for your little charade, I was actually the worst you could possibly have selected.'

As Katie spoke a grin spread over Artemis's face. Tempany, fearing that she was going to mock them, readied to jump out of the chair and give her a spear strike to the windpipe. As it was, Artemis beamed, 'Ah! It all makes sense now. When you came back last year,' she said to Tempany, 'you seemed to be…well, more withdrawn than usual. I was going to get Raphael to speak to you, but you appeared to snap out of it when we sent you on the next job. So I left it. But at the same time Cortez reported that you,' she said to Katie, 'were depressed when you eventually reported back in. I suspected you'd fallen out or something. But here it is! Well, girls, I wish you well, and I mean it with all my heart.'

Tempany laughed. 'We're talking about you sending Spendlove to her death, and you're making a pitch for a wedding invite?!'

'Hang on,' giggled Katie. 'Who said anything about a wedding?'

Artemis didn't join in the revelry. 'You must understand,' she said earnestly to Tempany, 'that this is not personal. None of it is. I meant what I said. I like both of you very much, and it made me sick – really, it did, physically sick – knowing that I was sacrificing you. But I'm engaged in a cause that is far bigger than any of us: the destruction of Marxism in this country. I want to see it, and the people behind it, ground to powder. We're all expendable in that.'

'Fair enough,' said Katie equably. 'But if *I* was supposed to be expended, why on earth were your people not ready for me when I arrived?'

Artemis smirked. 'It's not as if I have a hotline to my controller or anything. And even if I did, she is someone who only the...' She paused, seemed to think better of what she was about to say, and said, 'She is someone who can be woken by only a very small number of people. It did occur to me to contact Langley directly. But that would have meant everyone in Langley knowing I was working for them, and then I would have been blown to bits – which it turns out I probably was already.' She gave a mordant chuckle. 'All I could do was send her an email and hope that she was up so she could direct her men accordingly. Besides,' she shrugged, 'I didn't feel there was any need to panic.'

'Didn't you try to contact Ray?'

'Not personally – and his phone was off, so it was academic. And what, exactly, could I have said to him anyway? That a rescue attempt was about to be made and that he and the Agency boys had better get ready to stop it? Of course I knew Ray had been doubled. Indeed, it was me who was still controlling him – although he did not know it. But I wasn't about to reveal it to him for exactly the same reason I couldn't call Langley. Also, I made the mistake of assuming that he and the Agency boys would be smart enough to leave lookouts. But they weren't – probably lulled into a false sense of security by the knowledge that the beacon wasn't supposed to work. If you want something done properly…' She rolled her eyes and shook her head.

'I don't understand,' said Tempany, 'what was going to happen if Spendlove *had* failed? HQ would presumably have concluded that I had been abducted by the Agency, and there is not a cat in hell's chance that anyone would have believed I had escaped under my own devices and made it back here without the collusion of my captors. It would have been obvious I had been doubled.'

'Assuming that Spendlove and her men were killed, it had been my intention to tell you, via the Agency, to tell us that you had managed to escape in the shootout and had killed your captors, who were not Agency, but Cuban exiles looking for revenge for you killing their men in Miami. Then you were to go ahead and deal with Señor Carranza as originally planned, which would have made it appear doubly certain you were still loyal to us. That was how the plan was supposed to have played out in the first place: you were to have been turned, then taken out Carranza, but with the help of the Agency as an indication of their good faith. Then you would have been back here as if nothing had happened. If we had to add in an escape story, we would have made it plausible.'

'So the Carranza job was real? I had assumed it was a ruse to get me into the clutches of your new friends.'

'The job was real. I couldn't have sent you north on something I had invented. And this was the first opportunity since you were selected.'

'But I actually *was* rescued. So the plan, I take it, was to continue to try to turn me?'

'Yes. I had thought the whole operation had failed. Then, when I knew you had decided not make a run for it, you provided us with another chance to have a crack at you. This was the reason I told you the heat was off and to stay where you were. When I got word that it looked like you would agree to work for us, it seemed like it would all come off after all. But I guess you had us all fooled.'

'And my mugshots? Have they been destroyed?'

'What do you think?' she scoffed.

'There's something I still don't get,' continued Tempany, ignoring the jibe. 'Even with the mugshots supposedly destroyed, I would have been fatally compromised, as it would have been assumed by everyone here that their agents knew my face. Plus, they had my DNA. Also, our people couldn't be sure of what I had told them prior to being rescued. I could have sold everyone and everything down the river. I would have been damaged goods. I couldn't have been sent out in the field ever again.'

'That occurred to me the moment I knew the lieutenant had succeeded. But then an even better plan came to mind: in recognition of your bravery, I was going to get Raphael out of the way and promote you to be my number two – a promotion you were to accept at the Agency's behest. If and when I unmasked you, I would declare that I had suspected it was you who had been blowing the operations, and I had therefore appointed you deputy in order to feed you false information, which you would then leak to the Agency, and which I would therefore know had come from you when they acted on it. You would have been executed for treason, and I, for having laid such a brilliant trap, would have come out of it secure in the long term. I might even have got the Defence post,' she chuckled.

'Hang on,' said Katie, her eyes scrunched. 'That wouldn't have worked. Because if it was supposed to have been Anson who had blown the operations last year, why would the Agency be abducting her now?'

'Simple: I was going to say that Anson was being run by one of the Agency's black bag outfits, hence the team from the other night had not known she had already been doubled.'

Tempany and Katie laughed. 'Jesus, ma'am,' Tempany shook her head. 'Not even Raphael would have swallowed that! It would never have flown in a million years.'

'I think you overestimate the intelligence of the people I have to convince.'

'Face it, ma'am: your plan was crazy. And, despite the contortions you've had to perform to try to keep it on track, it was predicated upon one thing you had absolutely no control over: you had assumed that I would be turned. Notwithstanding the fact that I'm rather insulted that you thought I would be so weak-willed, what, exactly, was your backup plan had I refused? Which, I must add, had been my intention all along.' This was a lie. Tempany knew that if Irvin McDowell had not said her name and alerted her to the trap, she would have agreed to turn, and would now be in the pocket of the CIA.

Artemis shook her head. 'Believe me, you would have turned. Eventually. And if you somehow managed to hold out? Well,' she shrugged, 'that never occurred to us, but I suppose I would have had to go through the motions of trying to get you back. But in that case you really would have been of no further use to me.'

'Which would have been preferable to ending up in front of a firing squad,' Tempany laughed. 'Now, ma'am,' she said sternly, 'despite the civility we've managed to bring to proceedings, I must say that I am extremely upset with you. Not *entirely* on my account, you understand: had I been in your position, I might very well have done what you've been doing. No. What has got me *really* mad is you sending Spendlove to what you presumed would be her death. Make no mistake about it, ma'am: had she been killed or wounded, I would currently be cutting off your limbs with a blow torch, after having let you watch your husband's throat being cut.'

Artemis swallowed. 'You mentioned assurances,' she said quickly.

Tempany nodded. 'Three things. But first: Spendlove, sweetie – is there anything you would like?'

Katie looked up at her. 'It had occurred to me before we had this little chat that I was going to do something I had never done before: beat somebody with my bare hands.' She looked at Artemis and said, 'Ma'am, I murdered someone the other night, and it's your fault. I'm going to have to live with that for the rest of my life, and I know I'm never going to get over it. I was wanting to beat the hell out of you. I was wanting to permanently disfigure you. But,' she shook her head, 'that was contingent upon you being a coward about all this. As it is, I believe you have answered as honestly as could have been expected, and you have been rather noble in taking responsibility. Regardless of how angry I am, I respect that. So, Edith, I don't want anything else.'

Artemis smiled sadly. 'Thank you, Stephanie. Although I probably did deserve that beating you were planning.'

'You certainly did.'

'What we need, ma'am,' said Tempany, 'is this: letters to both of us, signed by you, the President and the Defence Minister, thanking us for our service, and declaring that our services have been dispensed with for all time, dated yesterday. Secondly, all pay we are due shall be paid into our accounts by midday Tuesday. Thirdly, and I think this goes without saying, we need safe passage out of this country, which we shall be leaving today. I must warn you that, in the event you try to stop us, if we do not contact them at regular intervals today, our several lawyers are instructed to send to the President, the Defence Minister, and everyone in HQ, affidavits from Spendlove and me describing what has happened over the past few days, and attesting to your treason. They will also do so if either of us meets a violent or unexplained death within the next five years. Also, we have emails primed to be sent around HQ and to the Minister and the President at various times today and next week, which will be sent automatically if Spendlove and I do not delete them before the specified times. Do I have your agreement?'

She nodded vigorously.

'Say it!'

'Yes. *Yes.*'

'Thank you,' said Tempany, and got up.

'That's it!?' blurted Artemis.

'Yes. That's it. I'm beyond angry now. I'm just thoroughly disillusioned with you and your goddamned games. You've used me, and it turns out that the cause for which I've been fighting is utterly evil. I'm just kicking myself it needed the madness of the past few days to have seen it. I've been brainwashed. I think,' she mused, 'Spendlove was trying to warn me about all this last year.' Katie nodded. 'She always knew what the real score was, was always sceptical of our motives and our operation, and the results it was having. But I wouldn't listen, being the naïve fool that I am.' She shook her head. 'So I simply don't care. Venezuela and the South can fix their own problems. And you, ma'am, are free to do whatever the hell you like. Besides, I've got more than enough blood on my hands. No more.'

Artemis gave a sigh or relief. 'Thank you.'

'However, we're going to have to restrain you while we get out of here: while we hope you'll honour your word, we can't take the risk you won't. But don't worry. The General and your men will be up soon. You'll be free in no time.'

Artemis nodded, and held up her right hand, which Katie promptly cuffed. 'The keys?' she asked hopefully.

Tempany shook her head.

'Oh, well.'

'Incidentally, you'll have to do some explaining to Raphael. We've told him we were coming here on a mole hunt. We're now going to tell him everything is fixed, and that he doesn't need to know the details. How you deal with him is up to you.'

'You...you haven't hurt him, have you?'

'We've shut him up in his house, that's all. Other than that, he's fine...or, at least, he was when we left him,' she smirked. 'Well, I guess this is it. *Au revoir*, Christina.' Artemis winced at the use of her name. 'It's been...interesting.'

As Tempany opened the door, Artemis said, 'Tempany. Katherine,' with an apologetic smile under sad brown eyes. 'I'm sorry, girls. Truly I am.'

'Apology accepted,' said Tempany.

'Likewise, ma'am,' said Katie.

Tempany looked down at Artemis with a pitying smile. She now knew with certainty that she was making the right decision. Artemis wasn't an evil genius. She was just an ordinary old woman who, like most human beings, was good at some things but incompetent at the rest, and had got hopelessly out of her depth – exactly, Tempany realised, as she, herself, had. The realisation made her melancholy. But it also made her feel sorry for the old bat. 'Thank you for everything, Christina,' she said. 'Goodbye. And, um, if it means anything, I hope you win.'

Artemis's warm smile switched on again. 'It means the world, Tempany. Good luck, girls. I know you'll make me proud.'

They cut the guards' restraints on the way out. The one in the spare room was snoring loudly; the one outside was groaning as if on the verge of consciousness. Tempany patted him on the back and said, 'Jorge, it's Edith Anson. You'll be fine. Someone's hit you with a tranquiliser. Don't worry – I'm on it. The boss is upstairs. Go see to her when you can walk.' She was answered by more groaning.

When they were back over the wall, they changed into their casual clothes, which they had left under the trees, dumped the combat gear, and trotted down the hill and jumped into the waiting taxi. Tempany asked the driver to take them back to Raphael's. She took out her phone and dialled Chloe's number. It took about three minutes to connect, then was answered with, 'Miss Tempany?'

'Hey, Chloe. Any problems?'

'None. Are you okay?'

'Never better, sweetheart.'

'Did we win?'

'We're not quite home and dry yet, but it's looking hopeful. I would suggest you get out of there right now. Maybe don't go home tonight – get a few cabs and go get a room somewhere. I think you should be in the clear, but no need to chance it, eh?'

'Yes, Miss Tempany. I'll leave as soon as I've got my stuff together.'

'Remember – wear your own clothes. And don't bother with any of the makeup. I don't want anyone thinking you're me this time.'

'Yes, Miss Tempany.'

'Good girl. Now, all being well, I'll be in touch in a couple of days for your bank details. And remember: get that passport applied for. You're coming to see us.'

'Yes, Miss Tempany. Thank you. I won't let you down.'

'I know you won't, darling. Goodbye.'

'Bye, Miss Tempany!'

Tempany turned the phone off and threw the battery, the SIM card, and then the phone out the window.

'How's your little helper?' asked Katie.

Tempany grinned. 'Good. She's a wee gem, Spendlove. I just hope the Agency doesn't bust her now.'

'Here's hoping.'

Tempany stared out the window at the buildings passing by. 'Did the recoding work?' she asked distantly.

21. Who Am I?

After a tortuous route, which took them to Port of Spain – the first flight they could jump on – then Toronto then Reykjavik, they landed at Heathrow at eleven the next day. They took the train into Paddington, then a cab to Tempany's flat in Soho. Tempany took some clothes and two pairs of shoes, then they bought some clothes for Katie. They bought a phone and a laptop from Argos, then made their way to Kings Cross, jumping into first class on the 3.00pm for Aberdeen. As they were pulling out of the station, Tempany phoned Chloe for her bank details, wired her the 300,000, and felt pretty good about it. She then drafted an email to Irvin McDowell, and asked Katie to check it before sending. Katie, looking for all the world like a librarian with big, black-rimmed reading glasses, a blue cotton blouse, and her hair scraped back into a bun, quickly read it, then pushed the laptop back across the table, giving her a broad smile and a thumbs up. Tempany gave it a final proof. It read:

Dear Irvin,

I'm terribly sorry that I could not hang around to conclude our contract. You see, I figured out who had given you my name. It was, you may or may not be aware, my boss, the delectable Señora Artemis. This might be news to you, but it turns out she's a mole. For your lot. Who'd have thought it?

So, I decided to pay her a house visit the other night. Don't worry, she's still alive (I think) – yes, I was sorely tempted to kill her, just for the principle of it; and also because it turns out that my six-months' work experience with you was going to end not with me collecting $5 million, but with me being arrested, brutally tortured, and executed for treason.

The reason I decided to keep her alive was that I know that she is one of your principal assets and, as such, there is a value attached to her remaining in situ. I calculate that value to be this: a full pardon for both Miss Kirkwood and me for all alleged and actual illegal activities carried out by either of us in the United States, or against US citizens or property abroad.

I also need a legally binding guarantee from yourselves, in the name of your Director, that you will not put out a contract on either of us or attempt to harm or harass us in any other way. We also wish you to give us an undertaking that you will inform us immediately you have intelligence that anyone else is coming after us.

That is it. I don't need any other protection, and I don't want any money – put it towards your Christmas party or something.

Please email your response within 48 hours of this email.

By the way, if either Miss Kirkwood or I meet with unnatural deaths, or we do not contact them at regular intervals over the next five years, our several solicitors have instructions to release affidavits to the press and to Wikileaks and various other interested parties telling them all about the CIA's infiltration of OCC. Included with these are photos of my injuries from the other night, along with a lurid tale of how the Agency tortured the shit out of me. Oh, before I forget, our solicitors also have Señora Artemis's taped confession.

Should you still choose, in spite of this, to send someone to take care of Miss Kirkwood and me, notwithstanding the fact that I intend to lead a Buddhist-like existence henceforth, please be under no illusion: I shall send them back to you vacuum-packed as fish food.

(Sorry to have to add all this. I know it seems like I am threatening you, and I realise that threatening the Agency is perhaps not the best of tactics for ensuring a long and happy life. But these are high stakes for me, and you will therefore understand that I simply cannot afford to be vague or use euphemisms. I need there to be no room for misunderstanding between us.)

As soon as our contract has been concluded, I will instruct my solicitors to write formally to you confirming that the materials they have will remain under lock and key, and will be destroyed at the end of the five-year period. After that, you will never hear from either of us again. Hopefully.

Incidentally, I did feel kind of bad about taking off before you got back to me. You seem like a decent enough guy, and, believe it or not, I rather like you. But I hope you can understand my reasons.

Best wishes to your friend. I hope her ears are better soon.

Kindest regards,

Edith Anson

She hit 'send', closed the laptop, and reclined back in her seat. 'Edith Anson,' she sighed. Katie looked up at her from *The Times* crossword. 'It's…it's like saying goodbye to a part of me. I mean a *big* part. And, well, what am I without her?' she asked helplessly.

'It's an interesting question,' said Katie, tapping her pen on the newspaper. 'What are either of us now? Are we now going to be the people we were always meant to be? Or, are Edith and Stephanie the people we were supposed to be? Hmm.' She rubbed her chin.

'Will we miss it?'

Katie nodded. 'Perhaps. I won over a million dollars playing cards the other night…'

'*Really?*' said Tempany, agog.

'Yeah,' she giggled. 'But, aside from subtly letting you know how fabulous I am at poker, what I'm trying to say is that I will in all likelihood never do that again. I will never again experience that thrill when I won. And I certainly will never experience the feeling I did a few hours later when I realised you were alive, just when I thought you were as dead as a dodo. But…that's just what memories are made of, I guess – instances when you're involved in extraordinary situations. And had I not been employed where I was, I would have other memories, which, according to my own lights, would have seemed equally as exciting: going on holiday to Spain; my first kiss; getting married. So, instead of regretting turning our backs on all the danger and adventure, we should cherish the memories – the good ones, at least – and thank our lucky stars we got out of it in one piece.'

'Nice way to jinx us!' laughed Tempany.

'Good point,' she grinned, and knocked on the table. 'In any case, what our task now is is to create new memories, and better ones. And we'll do it: remember, we've got seven million pounds to blow, and we won't have the constant threat of danger hanging over us while we're doing it. It'll be amazing, Bells. I promise,' she beamed.

Tempany giggled at the nickname Katie had christened her with. It was the same one she called herself. It was the one Rebecca had called her. For the first time since Bex had been killed she felt a lightness in her chest, as if an invisible weight which had been crushing down on her all these years was suddenly lifted. 'Spen…I mean,' she laughed, 'Kat. I think it's going to be hard. But with you with me, I know I can't fail…I know *we* can't fail.'

'No pressure, then?'

'None,' she shook her head, smiling. Tears rolled down her cheeks.

Katie leaned forward and took her hands and squeezed them tight. 'Tell me more about this place we're going. I can't wait.'

THE END

Printed in Great Britain
by Amazon

40044846R00158